DICKIE'S LIST

By Ann Birstein

STAR OF GLASS
THE TROUBLEMAKER
THE SWEET BIRDS OF GORHAM
SUMMER SITUATIONS
DICKIE'S LIST

DICKIE'S LIST

a novel by
Ann Birstein

Coward, McCann & Geoghegan, Inc.
New York

SBN: 698-10544-3

Library of Congress Catalog Card Number: 73-78739

Printed in the United States of America

Again, to Kate

DICKIE'S LIST

ONE ✦✦✦✦✦✦✦✦✦✦✦✦✦✦✦✦✦✦✦✦✦✦✦✦✦✦✦✦✦

The party today was for Umberto Robertini, though it could have been for almost any author on Dickie's list. It was always the same party, really, a mixed bag of what everybody denied was the New York literary establishment and the *Sunday Times Magazine* section kept running articles about anyway, with hints of feuds and counterfeuds, little black and white photographs the size of postage stamps to liven up the text. Ralph Gorella, Gertrude Dienst, Angelica Ford, Lancelot Hale, William Kohlrobi, Violette de Laniere, Ruby Cohen Mandel, George Auerbach maybe, Vaughn Cranshaw, etc., etc., they would all be there today too, give or take a few of Umberto's friends or enemies, jammed in together on the second floor of Ed's elegant town house, laughing too much, talking too much, drinking too much, absently picking things off the trays being circulated by the hired butlers who had come with the catered hors d'oeuvres.

So then why, Sandra asked herself, since she knew it all so well in advance, realized the utter absurdity of the occasion, was she, also as usual, breaking her neck to get there anyway? Rushing out into the middle of Riverside Drive to whistle herself up a cab, sitting back as they crossed the park with one hand on the scarf hat that had meant something on the ground floor of Bergdorf's but was probably all wrong, not catching her breath until they finally stopped in the middle of Ed's lovely, leafy street in the mid-Sixties. She got out and stood there admiring his black Regency door with the silver chasing, then waved back up to some people who were waving down to her through the billowing white curtains at the French windows on the second floor. French windows, English door, chic friends holding cocktails. It was always at this moment that she remembered herself as a kid in the Bronx following her big sister through some dismal gathering with a plateful of Ritz crackers and pimento cheese. Then she shook it off and thought instead of Clarissa Dalloway awaiting some shivery ecstasy at the top of a velvet stair. Oh, sure, some Mrs. Dalloway, Sandra told herself, descending a few steps and waiting between two yellow plastic sacks of garbage for the maid to open the door. It was a business party for an Italian poet and she didn't even speak Italian. On the other hand, poor Umberto hardly ever spoke Italian anymore, either.

The maid, in a maroon maid's uniform, called her Madame and reached for a nonexistent wrap—Sandra put the uneasy hand back to the scarf hat—then directed her to a stairway brutally awash with the noises of the party, voices spilling down in spiky irregular waves, which, though earsplitting also assured her that the party was at its height, early birds still present and excited, latecomers like herself still arriving. At the landing, she paused in the small remaining breathing space and looked to her right and then her left. Both of the twin drawing rooms were clogged and impenetrable. She could hardly see the billowing white curtains at the French windows on the street side, much less the friends who had waved to her. There was no point even attempting to look for Umberto Robertini, who was hardly the cause of the congestion anyway, only its excuse. Still, this practice of totally ignoring the guest of honor was getting absolutely ridiculous. Like that time, last October, shameful really, when Lancelot Hale was hauled off to Payne Whitney about a half hour before his party began and nobody even noticed the difference until Sandra mentioned it. "Again?" Ralph Gorella had laughed. Or the party before that when Father Grapp finally emerged from his monastery and she had spent that taxi ride over rehearsing a hushed and reverential greeting that wouldn't sound as if she were addressing an interfaith meeting of B'nai B'rith, and then when she arrived there were about twenty identical priests clustered like black crows at the bar, not binding with briars her joys and desires, but drinking martinis. The martini-drinking priests had become a fixture. Ed Gaskell liked the look of them and so did Xavier Cruse, whose idea it had been for Gaskell Press to do Father Grapp's *Confessions* in the first place. A handful of them stood near the threshold, somehow still very Catholic, managing to be of the scene but not quite in it, even though they were being excitedly admired by some chicks in maroon satin pajamas, silver miniskirts, Yves St. Laurent's latest. A benign Xavier Cruse shepherded them all, looking, with that ruddy face and white hair more like a priest himself than one of Gaskell Press's best-selling novelists. Where was Dickie? She told a passing waiter with a round silver tray that she would like a martini and used the few minutes to window-shop before she pushed herself into the fray to find him. In spite of the crush, it seemed to be just the usual last party of the season, the annual June roundup, unless whoever had called "Sasha!" down to her from the French windows actually had been Hershel Meyers, whom she had thought it might be for a moment, and which *could* mean he had come in from Chicago to show Dickie a piece of the new book. Otherwise, as always, there was Ruby Cohen Mandel standing quietly in a corner in her little checked pants suit, examining her clean fingernails, Vaughn Cranshaw, the ultimate black man of distinction resting his elbow on the mantelpiece near where the priests were regaling the chicks, a couple of the younger editors—Aaron Lasch and Penelope Fleece—Erika Hauptmann, the Gaskell Press expert on Auschwitz, laughing hoarsely to Angelica Ford, William Kohlrobi, bending deferentially over a tiny Latin gentleman with a waxed mustache, who was probably that new Chilean critic Dickie was so enthused about, smiling red-haired Freddie Fruchtman, Lancelot Hale, tall, handsome, patrician, sprung from the hatch but still looking mad as a hatter, talking down to a genial Herb and Muriel Fingerwald, who gazed up awestruck, though considering Herb was a psychiatrist, they could have been a little less genial and a lot less awestruck, Seymour Froude, frog-faced and eager, trying to sell Gertrude Dienst on the idea of an original paperback as he had once tried to sell rayon when he was working for his father's business. Gertrude looked about her, bored, trapped between a modern lamp and end table, stroking her young nephew's long lank black hair, which the boy wore in the same style as her own.

At the sight of Gertrude Dienst, Sandra turned around and took her martini off the waiter's tray, suddenly angry and depressed. Maybe she was foolish to draw the line at Gertrude Dienst when it was all such crap really, but she could still too vividly remember Gert's arrival on the scene just a year before, sallow, dark-haired, humble, and so patently on the make it was enough to make you throw up. Except that nobody else seemed to notice it. "Oh, my, such *famous* people," Gert had chittered to Sandra at her first Gaskell Press party, brought by William Kohlrobi, and then to Ralph Gorella who was standing nearby and who she knew damn well was the editor of *Hindsight*, "Oh, I beg your pardon! Are you famous, too?" Okay, so maybe it hadn't been so funny to explain that Ralph, who was as ugly as sin, was actually Rock Hudson and she was Doris Day. God knew, Ralph had been furious with her ever since, and Dickie had just smiled that patient weary smile when she told him about

12

it. But then professional intellectuals had such vested interests in being professional intellectuals, though they claimed to be absolutely dedicated to ideas alone, seeing only what they wanted to see, hearing what they wanted to hear, as easily flattered each of them as Louis Quatorze by his courtiers. So what if Gertrude's success since then *had* been enormous, center spreads in *Vogue* with the usual hand on the nephew's head, name in big black type on the cover of the *New York Review*, a regular quiz kid at the Theater for Ideas? What did it prove, after all, except that she had flattered them all so successfully?

Violette de Laniere detached herself from a group and started toward her. Somehow soothed, Sandra took a sip of her martini, admiring Violette's approach, finding her still as classically beautiful as that first time she had laid eyes on her during her honeymoon in Paris when Dickie had brought her over to Violette's table in that elegant restaurant in the Bois de Boulogne to be presented. She was dining à deux with a gentleman who turned out to be one of the Rothschilds, an amethyst lady in an amethyst gown with a neck like a swan and jewels to match. In fact, people had even spoken of Violette's success that season as they did in Edith Wharton and Henry James. She had been astonished when Violette turned out to be the same age as herself and a Mount Holyoke graduate to boot, and worse than astonished when Violette had suddenly left Paris to return to the United States and devote herself to radical causes. She had one of the latest causes in tow right now, a purplish young man with pimples and a dashiki, Afro hairdo, embroidered yarmulke, and gold-rimmed eyeglasses. Violette introduced them. It was hard to hear above the noise, but she somehow associated the name with Angela Davis. Was she right? Had Dickie asked him to write the biography? Yes? Ah, yes, indeed, she remembered the Xeroxed manuscript very well now. There were references to lampshades.

"And what do you do?" Afro-American said, look-

13

ing her over with bored and sullen disinterest.

"I?"

It was the first word she had spoken at the party, except to ask for the martini, and it stuck in her throat—postnasal drip, not embarrassment. Evidently he had not understood that she was married to Dickie. Should she tell him what she thought of him, social niceties notwithstanding? It was a little crisis of identity, a phrase that Dr. Starkstein ought to have used but never did, and she strangled it with a quick social laugh.

"Do? Well, actually very little these days, I'm afraid," Sandra said, waiting vainly for Violette to contradict her. "A few translations for the Press. From the French. Though there are always these silly questions of nepotism. Also, I've become very much interested in the film lately and I—"

The off-Broadway Julius Lester walked away.

Violette remained behind, smiling her knowing smile, a doting mother at her son's graduation, an Ingres in a crowded Brueghel, her auburn hair sculpted against pale veiny temples, eyes that seemed to be violet, unless the name suggested it in advance, but were actually deep blue, with long black eyelashes dense as fringes.

"Good hat," Violette said.

"Oh, do you really like it? It kind of appealed to me in Bergdorf's, but when I got it home—" She looked toward the African, circulating like a bright thread through the party. Had she told him too much, too little? What about the word "film" when she always said movie?—and then turned back to Violette again. "You really have incredibly long eyelashes," Sandra said admiringly. "They look almost false."

"They are," Violette said.

"Are what?"

"False."

"Don't be *silly!*" Sandra shouted through a sudden upsurge of noise. Where was Dickie, anyway? And where were all the people who had waved to her from the French windows? She felt let down and homeless, deserted by her welcoming com-

14

mittee, ashamed of having been so stupidly proud of having one. Eager Seymour Froude, abandoned by Gertrude Dienst, showed signs of bearing down, and she turned and started to elbow, push, and hello her way through to the drawing room on the right and the bar, surprised and flattered when Lancelot Hale intercepted her.

"Original sin ... Adam's apples ..." Lancelot remarked wittily, or at least she assumed wittily, though it was hard to tell on account of his height and the noise, and the fact of his getting more and more goggle-eyed and weaving as he looked down at her. Even so, he was so extremely Brahmin, she thought for a moment of maybe countering with a phrase or two of what she remembered from the Friday night Kiddush, since nothing ever impressed a Protestant intellectual more than a Jew speaking Hebrew. Then she realized from the eager tautness of her neck muscles that she was smiling up at him like a Fingerwald, and looked away. Besides, Ed Gaskell was getting up from the stairs to the third floor, where he had been sitting on a bottom step between dull Gladys Robertini and the elegant publicity lady from Rizzoli's.

"Sandra!"

"Ed!"

He bent to kiss her hand, upending the palm, then gripped her shoulder and turned her around so that, on account of his Edwardian outfit, beige suit with broad lapels, wide paisley tie, she felt for a moment as if he were Rhett Butler about to whisk her off on a Virginia reel. But the grip tightened and forced her to look at where George Auerbach was sitting alongside the buffet table, back to the wall, morosely staring at his wife's lively flowered rear end.

"Quick, sweetie," Ed whispered urgently, "which one of my stable did George have a piece on in last week's *Book World?*"

"T. S. Eliot."

Ed looked at her blankly. "Oh, yes, that's right," he said with a relieved laugh, as if the joke were on Eliot, or George. "Angelica's biography." The hand patted her shoulder and then let go. "Your friend's in from Chicago, sweetie."

"Hershel? I thought I saw him."

"Why don't you go look for him?" Ed said. "See how he is. Great hat, by the way. I almost didn't recognize you."

"It's more of a scarf," Sandra said, continuing on but stopping deliberately at the buffet table to eat something small and soggy with black caviar on top and tell George Ed's amusing gaffe about Eliot.

"Where's Richard?" George said, looking up at her unamused.

"Haven't you seen him either?" Sandra said, straightening.

Vicky Auerbach spun around, surprised and delighted to find Sandra there behind her. "We flew in with *Hershel* this morning!" she cried, as usual blurting out her special social tidbit a little too soon. "He was absolutely fascinating. Fortunately, we had First Class practically all to ourselves."

"Did he say anything about the new book?"

"Oh, you know Hersh," Vicky said, laughing and tossing her long faculty wife earrings, herself not knowing Hersh. "He probably traveled halfway across the country *not* to say anything about it. As if an artist could produce a *Wait at the Circus* twice on demand."

"He didn't even produce it once on demand," Sandra said. "He was figuring to make a fortune on that play that flopped."

"The play was better," George said.

"I thought so too."

Vicky looked from one to the other of them and then hoisted George up by the elbow, excusing herself gaily to start dragging him through the crowd, laughing each time George frowned. "Well, of course, *artistically* the play was more successful," she heard Vicky say to Seymour Froude at her first way station, and when Seymour answered, "Sure, but from a *material* point of view—" went to look for Dickie in earnest. She found him talking to Ralph Gorella in front of the bar, the two of them obstructing drink traffic, until the bartender tapped Ralph on the shoulder and Dickie apologized for them both and stepped aside. They went on speaking intently, arms wrapped around their chests, as if they were standing waist deep in water at Cape Cod, where she had often seen them in the same earnest conversation. It was a natural enough posture for Ralph, that scarred and grisly veteran of the thirties, but in handsome blond smiling young Dickie unlikely and therefore curiously endearing. He's my *husband,* Sandra thought, remembering what Vicky Auerbach had once said, that every time she saw George up on the platform lecturing, she told herself: "I *sleep* with that man." And for a moment, Dickie was the small shiny golden center of the party, the gold-foil-wrapped chocolate in the middle of all those brown ones. He reached out behind him, knowing she was there without having to look around, and she took his hand, feeling she had just touched home base, looking at Ralph Gorella over his shoulder with a little vindictive gleam of triumph.

"Did Orvietta tell you I called this morning?" Dickie said, turning around.

"Of course not. Was it important?"

"Hershel's in town."

"So the whole world's been telling me," Sandra said. "Except of course our maid. Boy, you should have seen her when I asked her to stay an extra hour until the sitter came. You would have thought—" The inner glow had faded. Also, Dickie wasn't exactly listening. "Is Irma here too?"

"No."

"Well, thank god for that, anyway," Sandra said, almost leaning her head against Dickie's shoulder. Not really. She would never dream of leaning against Dickie in public, though she had seen Vicky Auerbach do it with George. Anyway, it would have unsettled the scarf hat. Dickie hadn't mentioned it, though that didn't mean anything. He hardly ever noticed what she wore and often, when they were getting dressed for a party, told her absently and courteously that she looked lovely when she was still in her slip. She asked Dickie

17

to get her another martini, aware from Ralph's glum silence that she had interrupted what he took to be a serious discussion.

"Sandra," Ralph said, acknowledging her presence with a curt nod and then, when Dickie got the drink from the bartender: "... Listen, I'm only trying to give you a friendly warning. If that manuscript passes through any more hands, you can get it marked down as shopworn. Sophie too, probably."

"Okay." Dickie nodded. "The book's been around, and the author's a bit long in the tooth. I appreciate the tip. But what's the *literary* relevance?"

"The literary relevance is I'm warning you, don't fool with that one, kid. I've known that crazy broad for years. Sophie Katz and I were in the Party together—" His sour face turned more sour. He had just remembered the Party was over. "I'm telling you the woman is a neurasthenic mess. Don't raise false hope in her, Richard. She'll lock herself in your office toilet and take poison. She tried it once at *Hindsight* already, years ago."

"But have *you* read this manuscript?" Dickie persisted.

"No," Ralph said and looked away, snorting, as if he had just been stung by a mosquito he had been kind enough to wave off instead of squashing. He shoved his own glass over to the bartender, saying in his famous gravelly, gangster's voice, "Gimme anodder one," and stuck his hand into his pocket to shake a bent cigarette out of a squashed pack. Where did Dickie find the patience to deal with this type? How could he manage to keep exercising that lovely Harvard restraint of his? True, that nobody had ever accused Ralph of being graceful or charming—even Stella Fruchtman, who was usually blissfully oblivious of basic human traits, called him King Kong, or the Gorilla Man. But today he was even more repulsive than usual, even darker and baggier, especially around the eyes. She would probably never get over the cultural shock of her first sight of him at what was also her first *Hindsight* party

18

years ago. In her innocence, hand in hand with Dickie, clean hair flipping up at the ends, she had imagined that literary men, makers of taste, were effete and beautiful, like Rupert Brooke, the young Stephen Spender. Then there emerged from the bathroom that beefy ape, still zipping his fly as he went past William Kohlrobi, who was gravely awaiting his turn.

"Let me have her send you a piece of it," Dickie said amiably. "Okay? What the hell can you lose?"

"All right, all right," Ralph said, absently looking Sandra up and down, eyes lingering where there would once have been the bulge of a garter—in that sense too he was very much a veteran of the thirties. She shifted her bag on its gold chain from one shoulder to the other, returning Ralph's glum smile with a glum smile of her own, and then, kissing Dickie on the cheek quite deliberately, took her martini to the other drawing room where a sudden burst of noisy laughter extinguished its cool pleasant tinkle in her hand. It was Hershel Meyers, of course, the center of attention as always—but how surprisingly glad she was to see him!—surrounded by the inevitable circle of friends, sycophants, literary admirers: today, the chicks in their silver minis and Jean Harlow red satin pajamas, the martini priests, ruddy Xavier Cruse, smiling Freddie Fruchtman, vaguely smiling Stella Fruchtman looking especially blond and gorgeous, Vicky Auerbach next to Seymour Froude. (George Auerbach seemed to have cleverly vanished.) Sandra waited a little distance away, like an actress on the sidelines, until Hershel turned around and gave her her cue.

"Sasha!" he cried. They hugged and kissed, and Hershel held her off for a moment and gave her a playful right to the jaw. Then, arms around each other's shoulders, they stood together smiling down at the floor, like a dance team, aware that people were watching them, aware that their affection was a matter of public interest and record. "New shoes, sweetheart?" Sandra said, of Hershel's shiny black tasseled

19

loafers. "Corfam," Hershel said, "they wear like iron. Get some for Becky." She turned around to smile again, and then drew back, momentarily unsettled by the closeup of Hershel's face. Why did she still always think of him as that beautiful, long-nosed Jewish boy Dickie had first brought to the house years ago? That passionate young intellectual who looked like an early Leonard Bernstein, played chess and the violin, knew all the Razumovsky quartets by heart, read and reread Turgenev? The new wild hairdo and granny glasses suited him not at all. Irma's influence probably. But why did he need to change with every new wife? Or could it be that she was the one who needed to change? No, look at Jackie Kennedy, once a dignified whispering debutante, now parading around in tiny-titted jerseys, like some barefoot Greek whore. "Oh, baby, am I bushed." Hershel sighed, keeping the encounter ear-to-ear, ostensibly private, but loud enough to be overheard. "Working hard?" "Working hard and taking care of the kid. Every day I have to run back from my studio to show her about formulas and ammonia rash. What does a gorgeous young Wop know from such things?" "I don't know." "But what can I do? I'm an experienced father." "Yes," Sandra said.

"So, Freddie," Hershel said, looking around. "How's the legal business? What are you accomplishing in defense of obscenity?"

"There is no obscenity anymore," Freddie said, grinning too amiably. "Only plagiarism and libel."

"Okay, we'll try for libel."

"I hope you don't mean that."

"But what would be the point aesthetically?" Stella Fruchtman said.

"I don't know, baby. I only write books. I leave it to you chicks to worry about my aesthetics," Hershel said, and turned around, laughing, to the actual chicks, though knowing him he was probably more interested in the priests. Violette de Laniere came gliding into the group, a Mona Lisa in a sea of

20

laughers. It had been a very uneasy moment with those eyelashes. No, it was one thing to pass off a fake as the real thing, but the real thing as a fake? Still beautiful but pained, practically a crushed and bleeding rose, Violette looked away from where Vaughn Cranshaw was now planting his elbow with distinction on his second mantelpiece, while in his turn Vaughn was glaring darkly at Hershel, whose audience now also included Dickie's secretary Norma, to whom Vaughn had just been confiding his "own little vision of reality." It was another hard thing to remember, that Hershel had introduced them to Vaughn in the first place, his pal and sidekick, trumpeter, short-order cook, a literary natural, and that in his enthusiasm Dickie had offered Vaughn a job with the Press, as first Negro senior trade editor, something like that. What a radical idea it had seemed at the time, and what luck that Vaughn had refused, to work on his second novel, now about ten years overdue. He would probably have strangled any original new black talent at birth. No, it had been bad enough when Vaughn accepted all those medals from Johnson, but now he was accepting them from Nixon. She looked down at Hershel's hand, still draped over her shoulder like the little animal head of a furpiece, and then looked around at the party, no longer buying, but selling. In the distance, Felicity Gaskell, a long lean expensive twin to Ed, dressed all in gray and, as always, richly silent, stood against the wall and watched the proceedings in the company of her harlequin Picasso. Ed had probably run upstairs to take a look at his orchids. Then Lancelot Hale wandered by, holding up two drinks, and stopped to make the same witty remark to Hershel about original sin and Adam's apple, except that this time it sounded vaguely anti-Semitic. Hershel laughed anyway. Lance kept going, and in the sudden void made by his absence, there was Umberto Robertini, looking as surprised and bereft as only a guest of honor could at these parties.

"Umberto!" Sandra said. "Congratulations!"

"Grazie."

21

"Well, you certainly—"

Certainly what? Should she lie, even indirectly, by commenting on the quality of the poems in translation? No, it was intellectually too chintzy, too ultra Gertrude Dienst. But why wasn't anybody else talking to the man? She finally gave him a fond, forced smile, like Violette de Laniere beaming on her retreating Soledad protégé. Umberto smiled back with that unexpected European charm of his, his teeth surprisingly white and even in his heavy-jowled face, the face of a stocky, sweetly discouraged Sartre. Suddenly, in the midst of the mindless noise and chatter, she felt an upsurge of love for Umberto, trust, respect for intellectual tradition. But there really wasn't anything to say, and in any case the gap was closing.

"Ciao, Umberto," she said, in that last moment before he drowned in people.

"Ciao. . . ."

She looked around again and this time knew that the party had already swelled and burst, in spite of the continued noisy heated interminglings, in spite of the guests still brushing by each other like butterflies in confusion.

"The star of my stable," Ed Gaskell said, passing through, and putting a manly businesslike arm around Hershel's shoulder. He accidentally included Sandra in the embrace and looked at her with puzzled reproach, trying to decide whether to be proud of this proximity to his author or annoyed by the intrusion. "The star of my stable," Ed repeated anyway. "Whose next book will be an event."

"Where'd you get that word from?" Hershel said. "*Publishers Weekly* or a diaper service magazine?"

"What?" Ed said. "Oh, yes, that's very funny," and with another perturbed look at Sandra, patted Hershel on the back and continued on to the other drawing room.

"Did you try to get me too this afternoon?" Sandra asked Stella Fruchtman as Hersh began to make wisecracks to the chicks.

22

"No, darling, should I have?"

"I just thought you might be worried about Danny."

"Worried?"

"Anyway, he's fine. When I left, he and Becky were eating TV dinners from two different countries."

"Which countries, darling?"

"China and Italy."

"Sweet."

"Your maid said she'd pick him up about seven. I assumed that was okay?"

"This afternoon, I was gorging myself on delicatessen at Gitlitz and reading Anais Nin," Stella said. "I should have been in my studio working."

"Don't worry about it. You will. Is she good, Nin? I've never read her."

"Let's go shopping tomorrow," Stella said.

"I don't know. I don't feel much like clothes, somehow."

"Not clothes, darling," Stella said. "Orientals. Someone told me about this place downtown that has fabulous Orientals."

"Oh?" It was a temptation. She thought of the rug she and Dickie had bought when they were first married and living in the studio apartment in Brooklyn Heights. "Aren't the real ones very expensive?"

"It's an auction," Stella said, getting a cloudy look across the eyes.

"But, I mean, do you have any idea?"

"I didn't ask," Stella said remotely. "If you want to go, call me." She bent to examine a chic little Eskimo sculpture on an end table, and there in space beyond her shoulder—was Adam.

Sandra's eye took him in very calmly as part of the scene. In fact, she congratulated herself on her calm. Adam Brill arriving at the top of a crowded staircase at the tail end of a party. A youngish man in his middle thirties, a bit on the chubby side, with a round face and round English eyeglasses with round black rims. His vest buckled a bit between its buttons, and it was probably streaked with ash from his carelessly held cigarette. Janice was with him, face half-concealed by her straight chin-length blond hair as she rummaged in her purse for a cigarette of her own. Adam lit it for her, and then they started toward the other drawing room and the bar, not looking back at all.

"Where are you going?" Stella said.

"I want another drink."

"Hey, Sasha, don't desert me!" Hershel cried.

She unhooked his arm from her shoulder and went on.

". . . Adam—"

"Oh, hello, Sandra."

"I had no idea you were in the States, Adam. How nice. You're looking very well."

"So are you."

"Am I? Thanks." She started to put her hand up to her scarf hat and then pushed her empty glass across to the bartender.

"Dance hall girls always do that in cowboy movies," Sandra said, laughing. "Push glasses across bars."

Adam smiled.

"It's my third martini—but they've all been on the rocks. I tell myself I'm in safe company anyway."

"Yes?"

"How long have you been over here, Adam?" Adam, Adam, Adam.

"Oh, just a few weeks."

"A few weeks? Really? You ought to have called us."

"I did call Richard."

"Oh? Yes, of course." She looked down into a nonexistent glass. "Will you be staying long? Through the summer?"

"I'm not sure yet."

The bartender handed her the new martini over her shoulder, and Janice Brill turned around and smiled, as if she knew it was a drink Sandra hadn't wanted. Or did she know? Or was she smiling? Damn it, with that face who could tell? It

24

was so young, so pretty, so perfectly normal, until the sudden shock of realizing that the mouth was half-paralyzed, perpetually twisted up to one side, perpetually sardonic and amused, so that Janice looked as if she were always clued in to everybody's dirty little secrets. It was impossible to be smiled at by Janice and not feel outwitted.

"We haven't seen each other for ages," Sandra said.

"September," Janice said. "What a marvelous hat. I always admire people who have the courage to wear them."

"This is more of a scarf," Sandra said.

"I have no flair for clothes at all," Janice said. "Look at this dress. I bought it in Bloomingdale's basement and even have to wear it backwards. It didn't fit otherwise."

Janice pinched a bit of the material between her flattish breasts by way of illustration. Brown banlon jersey, about fifty dollars on the third floor, not the basement, but it looked very Radcliffe, inscrutable.

"Have you had a good year?" Janice said.

"Oh, yes, great. Marvelous. The best."

"You said that last time," Janice said—and smiled?

Oh god, what a capacity this girl had for making a person nervous. Not just her, Sandra, anybody, under any circumstances, she was sure of it. By now the party had turned as thin and watery as this third unwanted martini. All the knowing guests were hurrying off, leaving the dregs behind. It was important at these things to have a terrific sense of timing, to give the urgent impression that you had to be anyplace else but here. Adam so dégagé and bloody English had an absolute gift for communicating this sense of himself, and Janice did too. But she and Dickie seemed more and more inclined to stay until the bitter end, she because she was always sure something exciting could still happen, Dickie because he really didn't have any strong feelings about it one way or the other. Though even Dickie seemed ready to call it quits, and was coming over with Hershel and Ed Gaskell. He put his unfinished drink on the bar.

25

"Why don't you take your friend to dinner, Dick?" Ed said.

"I was just going to suggest it," Dickie said. "Come have dinner with us, Hersh."

"No, I have to work tomorrow," Hersh said, shaking his head, suddenly turning very unpleasant and irritable.

"Go on," Ed said. "He won't keep you up late. He's as anxious for the blessed event as you are."

Hershel laughed and gave in with a shrug, even on that level pleased to be made much of. And so that was it. Dinner with Hershel Meyers. The final toss-up of the evening. What more had she been expecting? Still, this choosing up after a cocktail party was getting to be more and more nerve-wracking, like waiting to be picked for a sorority or a softball team.

"Take him to La Rochefoucauld," Ed said, giving Hersh's shoulder a last paternal squeeze before he went off to speed his other departing guests.

"Is that okay?" Dickie said.

"Sure. It's all the same expense account dreck, anyway."

True. But she was glad Ed hadn't heard him. Poor Ed considered LaRochefoucauld his own personal gourmet discovery, light-years beyond the Italian Pavilion, the Madrigal. Maybe Hershel knew that and was trying to needle him, or maybe it was Dickie he meant to insult. There was nothing in Dickie's easy smile to give her a clue. Still, what was wrong with Hershel today anyway? He had always been a crowd pleaser, never openly nasty like this before.

"How about you, Freddie? Can you and Stella come along?"

"Sure," Freddie said.

"But there's so much food here," Stella said and, with an artist's indifference to how things looked, waved her hand toward the buffet table with its half-empty trays of hors d'oeuvres left lying on grease-stained doilies, dirty plates with cigarette butts squashed in them, abandoned liquor glasses smudged with fingerprints.

"Oh, Stella, for christ's sakes," Freddie said.

26

"Sasha doesn't like this," Hershel said. "Sasha looks depressed."

"Don't be silly," Dickie said. "She's delighted. She loves you. . . . Adam?"

"Yes," Adam said, "thanks."

Sandra took a long last swallow of her drink. Then they were all saying good-bye to Ed and Felicity, who stood at the top of the stairs alongside a lonesome-looking Umberto Robertini and his Gladys—should they ask Umberto along? No, the Gaskells surely had plans for him, and Gladys wouldn't fit in —and said good-bye again to the maid downstairs who now guarded an empty coatrack. As they emerged from the Regency door with its silver chasing, the air was soft and balmy, and a green-gold sun shone like coins through frail black treetops. Sandra linked her arm through Dickie's, aware that behind her Hershel ambled sullenly along with Stella and Freddie Fruchtman, and that behind them Adam walked with his wife. But the evening now reminded her of when she and Dickie were young and in love and working at Gaskell Press together, and all summer days were endless.

Probably Dickie had never mentioned to Ed that they had known La Rochefoucauld years ago, long before Ed had ever heard of it, when it was still only a quiet little Third Avenue bistro with red-checkered tablecloths where refugees would sit for hours over one glass of wine, scribbling away in their graph-paper cahiers and looking up thoughtfully every time the door opened. Actually, the decor had remained substantially the same, French provincial, with red geraniums set in carved wooden scrollwork niches, red-checkered tablecloths with small clean white cloths on top. But everything else about the place had certainly changed and risen in the world, like the dark glass office buildings that surrounded it outside and the skyrocketing prices on the menus within. These days, the clientele at lunchtime consisted mainly of busy young executives like Dickie (though Dickie was Dickie, of course, not a type) and, now in the evening, of the newly prosperous middle-aged tenants from the neighborhood white hi-rise co-ops, some of them no doubt the old refugees come back, like her and Dickie, in new disguise. No, Hershel was absolutely right. In spite of Ed's current infatuation with the place, La Rochefoucauld was just another typically crowded, absurdly posh East Side expense-account restaurant. It was only in the late afternoon at about five that the place had the old empty feel to it, and a pair of lovers could have a quiet drink in the semidarkness of the bar over there.

Adolphe, the maître d', led them past the crush at the door to a choice table in the center, causing several customers to look up angrily from their meals as their party passed, even though they themselves were already safely seated and eating. It was the kind of suspicious resentment that always reminded Sandra of her older sister, Leah, and in fact it was amazing, not to say depressing, how literally many of the customers did resemble Leah and her husband Morty, the specialist, in every other way: the women grim-mouthed and wary, still victims of the Depression in spite of the false gaiety of shiny eyeshadow and blond bubble hairdos, double rows of pearls that met in jeweled clasps at the back of their necks, the men with long sideburns, black silk suits, white on white ties, hats they had checked with the disinterested girl in the booth after an unfunny wisecrack, a fractured word or two of French. Then a few of them recognized Hershel and gave each other smug, knowing smiles, a nudge here and there, and it was even more depressing, even more typical of her sister and brother-in-law, this shtetl humility in the presence of intellectual fame, than when they had been angry about the getting ahead of the line. (She had a quick, unwelcome memory of herself straining upward toward Lancelot Hale.) But was Hershel really so famous, so much of a celebrity in the outside world as he was notorious in their own small circle? She could almost feel him radiating that special warmth, that sense of being sunburned out of season, like a movie star, and let herself bask in his aura, shine in his reflected glory as Hershel guided her by the arm and made a loud public point of sitting next to his Sasha. Then, from across the table, Stella gave her a sweet guileless smile and she was ashamed of herself. Hershel, typically, hadn't said a word to Stella ever since her question about his aesthetics.

"Eh, bien, Monsieur Baxtère," the maître d' said, rubbing his hands over Dickie like a praying mantis. "Ça va?"

"Oui, oui, ça va," Dickie said, looking at Hershel a bit self-consciously as he pulled out his chair beside Janice. Adam. Where was Adam? Adam was at the other end of the red velvet banquette, facing but not looking at her. Sandra rubbed at something that scratched at the back of her neck. It was one of the fake geraniums in the window box.

"Et pour Monsieur, the usual—? Le Beefeater martini, five to one?"

"Oh, christ, I guess so," Dickie said. "But I drank so damn much at the party."

Hershel said no to a drink and took off the wire granny glasses, pinching at the line they had made across the bridge of his nose. "What the hell are we doing here anyway?"

"Oh, come on," Sandra said.

"I think it's amusing," Stella said. During the day, out of indifference to her homelife and respect for her calling as a sculptor, she usually walked around looking like a hippie slob. But tonight she was a gorgeous Stella, with her blond streaky hair falling into her glamorous dark eye makeup, and the pink silk pajamas with the huge jeweled buckle on one side. Maybe it would be her only summer outfit. Stella often bought just one of something and wore it constantly, letting it go at that—though, not to be too Leah, wasn't there a dry cleaning problem? Or else, conversely, she would stock up on lots of the same thing, as housewives bought food for their freezers. One year, long before anybody else had the nerve for them, she had worn pants suits everywhere and exclusively, for cocktails, evening parties, lunch: camel's hair pants suits, black velvet pants suits, tweed ones, all beautifully tailored and extremely expensive. Another year, it was two alternating short Pucci dresses whose geometric prints clung neatly and sexily to her trim, California-style behind.

"In what way amusing?" Hershel said.

"I don't know. Does everything have to have a reason?"

"Stella was reading Anais Nin in the delicatessen all afternoon," Freddie explained.

"Is she okay otherwise?" Hershel said.

"No, but *really*," Sandra said, "why *must* everything have a reason? Why are we always talking about achievement and that sort of crap?"

"Crap?" Hershel said.

"I mean, why can't it be just the texture of our lives that counts, the fabric of them?"

"You sound like a clothing manufacturer, sweetheart," Hershel said, laughing.

She looked over at Adam, cool and British and listening.

"I know what Sandra means, though," Adam said, speaking up unexpectedly.

"Do you?" Sandra said, with a surprised, eager smile.

"That is, surely as a novelist living in a society where large events would constantly seem to outstrip the smaller day-to-day ones, you must often feel—"

Was that what she meant? She doubted it, though it didn't matter anymore. Maybe she had just been trying to defend Stella, who could sometimes be extremely difficult to defend and was at the moment dreamily twisting her wineglass, all sensitive and aesthetic, Birdie to everybody else's little foxes. Never mind. It was enough that Adam, so silent, or seemingly so silent, had spoken up for her, said her name, tried to explain her. It had come as such a beautiful shock.

"Cueillez, cueillez votre jeunesse," Stella said, interrupting to no point. No, really, Stella could be just too impossible.

"Here, honey," Hershel said, laughing again. He pulled a

30

red plastic geranium out of the window box and stuck it into Sandra's hand. "You just gathered your first rosebud of the evening."

She looked down at the thing, appalled. Then a couple of the blond grandmothers at the next table gasped and tittered, and then so did their husbands, and even Adolphe, perspiring and busy as he supervised the distribution of the drinks, eked out a smile. Adam seemed rather amused too. She put the fake flower down beside her plate, finally laughing also, and sipped at her martini, looking at the frosted glass partition near the door. Did Adam remember real roses, red roses, conversations in that semidarkness over there?

"Okay, but just to return to the subject of achievement for a minute—" Dickie began, smiling, when Adolphe flourished a huge red tasseled menu under his nose.

"Des hors d'oeuvres variés pour tout le monde, peut-être? Un peu de pâté, du hareng, des betteraves . . . ?"

"—when *are* we going to see it?"

". . . celeri remoulade . . . des courgettes farcies. . . ."

"Voulez-vous farci avec moi?" Hershel said to Sandra.

"How funny," Stella said seriously, "that's the kind of joke we used to make in high school."

"I wasn't asking you, baby. I was asking Sasha."

". . . des champignons à la grecque. . . ?"

"Greek style yet. Don't bruise me, Sash."

"You know, if you're really serious about that libel," Freddie Fruchtman said, "maybe you ought to let me see the manuscript too, as soon as possible."

"Ah. Now we hear from the literary lawyer."

"I mean it," Freddie said. "The last time with *Wait at the Circus* we had a damn close shave. If Cowley and Lerner—"

"So that damn close shave netted you a profit of close to a half a million bucks. So what do you want me to do? Cry for you?"

Dickie looked up quickly, interrupted by the chef, whom Adolphe had summoned for a consultation about the main

31

dish, a spécialité involving lobster swimming in cream sauce, with just a touch, a mere hint, of brandy, no more than even Monsieur would consider discreet. But wouldn't it all sit heavily on the stomach on a warm summer evening? If so, neither the chef, red-faced and ridiculous in his tall pleated white hat, nor Adolphe, nor Dickie, seemed to worry about it. She looked over at Adam again, who gave her another quiet conspiratorial smile as he sipped his Scotch.

"Where'd you get the pretty hat, Sash?" Hershel said, with a last baleful glance at Freddie.

"Bergdorf's."

"Bergdorf's? Wow."

It was only at the hat bar on the street floor, but there was no special point in explaining.

"How long does it take to pick out a hat like that?"

A strange question, typical of Hershel's novelist's passion for seemingly irrelevant detail. Though, how long *had* it taken? Ten minutes? Twenty? She could only remember that it had gleamed in the case like a blue jewel and turned out to be less expensive than she thought.

"You look like a captive princess in it, sweetheart," Hershel said. "Here, let me deck you out in gold." He slid his big mod wristwatch over her hand and then took off his heavy cuff links and tried to force them into the buttonhole at her throat. The touch of his hand gave her an unexpected shiver of pleasure. Laughing, turning her head aside, Sandra saw the ladies at the next table watching her with excited envy, as if being bedecked with Hershel's finery actually *had* turned her into a captive beauty—what would the real Leah say to see her now?—then whisper among themselves, trying to decide if she were also a celebrity they ought to recognize or, maybe, greater thrill, Hershel's mistress. Even Janice Brill was favoring her with one of those grudging half-paralyzed smiles. Evidently, being singled out by Hershel Meyers had raised her in everyone's estimation. She took an amused sip at still another martini that seemed to have materialized at her place.

32

(But where were the champignons? Had they been taken away or had she eaten them?) Then the silly chef came back, accompanied by the waiter who carried a huge red casserole filled halfway to the brim with the much-discussed chunks of lobster bobbing about in a white sauce with yellow grease stains of butter floating on top. She looked at Dickie so seriously engaged in the ceremony of tasting the inch or two of thin yellow wine at the bottom of his glass and thought how hilarious it would be if Dickie spat it out and sent it back. But when she looked to Adam with another conspiratorial smile, the amused flicker was gone from his eyes. They were just two very distant guests at a party. It had happened many times before, this sudden dying between them, but this time she stared at Adam intently for a moment before she realized that Hershel was reaching for her hat and sticking it on his own head.

"Hershel!"

"I just wanted to know what was going on in that head of yours."

"You look like Mr. Clean," Stella said, thoughtfully.

"Ah, popular culture," Hershel said, shoving the hat practically down to his eyebrows. "The aesthetic lady is clued in to the outside world. . . . Oh, no you don't!" he cried, catching at Sandra's wrist. Then: "Sasha! Sweetheart! Darling! I'm *sorry.*"

He had accidentally hit her in the jaw. It was a hard, sharp blow. The two of them faced each other absurdly, Hershel in the scarf-hat, Sandra with a naked head, hair held up in the back with bobby pins, one of which was sliding slowly and coldly down her neck.

"Sasha, did I hurt you? Did I break anything?"

"No, it's okay. Really. Forget it."

"What the hell do you always have to fool around like that for?" Dickie said.

"It's *okay,*" Sandra said. "Please, let's forget it."

"Sasha, darling, I'm sorry," Hershel said, very gently and

33

contritely, putting the hat back on her head completely askew. He looked at her through his glasses with mournful eyes, and then began to eat, and soon was telling Adam that as a novelist, far from being deterred by those crappy societal considerations, what he was after was, and Adam had taken out a card from his pocket and was making notes. Sandra picked up her fork, aware that her hat was on completely cockeyed and that more bobby pins were sliding out of more skimpy unfurling tendrils of hair in the back, and didn't care. She didn't even care that people were looking at her and that every once in a while Adam stopped nodding and looked up from his notes at her too. After all, damn it, what gave him the right to suddenly darken a corner and just *be* there, with that damn sober face and those damn round black English eyeglasses and the cigarette ash that. . . . Suddenly the lobster went white and swimmy. She hurriedly put down her fork and slid out from her place on the banquette. It was a jagged walk to the safety of the ladies' room. She looked into the mirror over the sink and stared at a parody of herself, her face white, her eyes red-rimmed and too distinct, like the eyes in a child's drawing. Keeping a hand on the lopsided hat, she went into one of the toilet stalls, lifted the seat and tried to throw up. It was no use, and the dry retching made her feel sicker than before. How strange. She tried to concentrate on the floor tiles, which made opposing designs, black against white, white against black. How very strange. She hadn't been this drunk since college—you see, Adam, you make me young again—when she used to think it was the height of sophistication to go staggering out of the White Horse Tavern arm in arm with some boy she never meant to sleep with anyway. And what would they think of her now, those alrightniks, those older sisters and brothers-in-law, who had mistaken her for a celebrity, and whose tables she had bumped up against trying to make it to the toilet? It was going to be a difficult and dismal trip back. She went back over to the sink, took off the scarf hat and put it on a dusty vanity table, wiped away the

34

black smears of mascara from under her eyes, pinned up her hair again, and firmly re-tied the scarf hat. She looked into her pocketbook—a dollar and a nickel, not enough to slip off by herself and take a cab home. Then she stepped out the door, wincing as it banged shut behind her and, with head held high and taking deep breaths all along, managed to thread her way back to where Adam sat at the end of the red velvet banquette calmly eating his dinner.

She bent down quickly to whisper in his ear. "Adam, could you possibly lend me two dollars for a cab? I've got to get home and—"

A little act of complicity, more domestic than clandestine, but the sight of Adam reaching into his wallet without any questions, without even nodding, made a little spurt of yearning well up in her heart. Dickie always asked questions, Dickie always needed everything spelled out for him, as now, for instance, when he swiveled around to ask what was the matter.

"Nothing, darling, nothing's the matter," Sandra said. "I was just feeling rocky and I thought I'd borrow some taxi money from Adam and—"

"You don't need to borrow money from Adam." Dickie laughed, surprised. "I'll take you home if you don't feel well."

"No, darling, don't be silly," Sandra said. "I don't want to interrupt your dinner. Just go ahead, and I'll—"

"What's up?" Freddie said.

"Nothing. I just—oh, Richard."

"Come on," Dickie said, slipping out and grabbing her by the elbow. He asked her why she hadn't told him she felt so lousy and, as they headed for the door, motioned to Adolphe to take care of the account. Adolphe in turn motioned to the waiter, who shifted his napkin and nodded.

"Hey, Sandra!" Hershel cried. "Sasha!"

They both turned around.

"Sweetheart, aren't you even going to kiss me good-bye?"

* * *

35

"Okay," Dickie said, "so you got tanked. So what?"

"No, you don't understand," Sandra said. "I feel terrible. I haven't been that stupidly drunk since I was in college." She rubbed her jaw. "Also it was that sock. I don't think I've ever been physically assaulted before. Have you? Oh, yes, the Army."

"Does it hurt?" Dickie said.

"No, as a matter of fact," Sandra said, "it doesn't," and was embarrassed to find herself thinking of that absurdly sentimental scene in *Liliom* when he comes back to earth and slaps his daughter who miraculously feels no pain at all. Dickie was sitting on the edge of the bed taking off his shoes, and she was slumped in the armchair by the window watching him, no longer caring that her clothes, her floppy pants and her blouse, were riding up and wrinkled, that the hat of which she had expected so much that afternoon lay carelessly flung on the foyer table tangled with the gold chain of her party pocketbook. Why were men's shoes so touching? When her father died, the sight of those creased black oxfords in the hospital suitcase had been almost the worst part of all. Not that Dickie's shoes were anything like her father's. Dickie's were English-made, brown, buckled, expensive. Her father's were always black and blunt-toed, worn with white cotton socks as a precaution against athlete's foot, which he didn't have. Still, just the thought of those shoes, of loss and death, made her get up and go to check on Becky again, in spite of having checked on her several times already.

Becky was sleeping soundly in the darkness, her sweaty face pressed against her Raggedy Ann. Her special worn, nubby, once-pink blanket had fallen to the floor along with her copy of *Mad*. Sandra picked them both up, placed them at the foot of the bed, and kissed Becky on the moist and glinting young hair at her temples. The golden thread of my life, Sandra thought, though there wasn't quite enough light coming from the half-open door of the bathroom for Becky to shine by.

Tiptoeing out, Sandra tripped over one of Becky's rubber snow boots, wondered what it was doing out of the closet at this time of year, thought about doing *something* about Becky's room, and as usual was exhausted by the idea as soon as it came to her. Why was she tiptoeing anyway? Behind her she could hear Becky's steady light snore, like the buzz of a summer fly. The minutiae of real life seemed to be popping up everywhere: on the dinette table, a note in Orvietta's third-grade handwriting that Sandra's mother had called, in the kitchen sink two tinny crusty TV dinner trays deposited by the Barnard baby-sitter. Though what made all this more "real" life than the Gaskell Press party? She was halfway down the hall to the bedroom before she realized she was clutching Adam's dollar bill inside her pocket, and stopped and smoothed it out, holding it against her cheek for a moment, like a sweet souvenir—of what? Back in the bedroom, she stuck it under her jewelry box.

"Did Hershel bring anything for you to look at?" she asked Dickie, who was taking off his trousers.

"He says he doesn't have anything yet."

"Then why the trip to New York?"

"He says to find a summer place out on Long Island for Irma and the baby."

"Baloney. He just wants to be wooed."

"All authors want to be wooed," Dickie said.

"Yes, I know. But this is *Hershel* for god's sake. What's come over him anyway? It's getting almost impossible to remember what good friends we all once were. My god, when I think of how the three of us—"

She turned to Dickie with a rueful reminiscent smile, but he was busy undoing a pair of freshly laundered blue pajamas, and so she remembered by herself those days when she and Dickie were first married and living in Brooklyn Heights and working at Gaskell Press together, and how on Sundays Hershel would come over for a late brunch, and then they would take a walk along the esplanade, looking across the water at the imminent dream of Manhattan, all three in sweaters and slacks, like something out of a college novel. *The Folded Leaf.* But in that hadn't one of the friends been queer? Never mind. The point was where had it gone, when was it ended? When Hershel married that fat cow Winifred? When he divorced Winifred to marry stupid, boring Dottie with her hair rollers and real estate? When he almost killed that ugly savage Irma at that famous party? Ironic that that party should have made Hershel's fortune, the basis for *Wait at the Circus,* which so many idiotic women had wept over, including her own sister Leah, and that in the end Hershel had married Irma too. But it had been a terrifying and ugly experience in real life. She would never forget being down at the police station with Dickie, and the *Daily News* photographer snapping away. She rubbed her jaw again. To be connected in this way with *Irma!*

"Did I tell you Violette said her eyelashes were false?" Sandra said, starting to unzip herself in the back and opening the door of her overcrowded closet. Funny, but when she was young and still living in the Bronx, she had imagined that the future and marriage would bring her endless closet space and neat drawers, whereas, oddly, living in one of these much-vaunted "spacious" West Side apartments, she seemed to have less room than before.

"Of course her eyelashes are false," Dickie said. "Everything about that woman is false."

"Oh, Dickie, that's not fair. Men just never appreciate Violette, that's all. No, that's not true either really. I mean, I always imagine her with a great *history* of passionate love affairs behind her, don't you? Le Comte de Quelquechose, Rubirosa, Richelieu. . . ."

"She's just an elegant toothpick," Dickie said, touching Sandra's back.

Sandra turned around.

". . . Who's Sarah Katz?"

"Who?" Dickie dropped his hand. "Oh, you mean Sophie. Sophie Katz. She's a novelist."

"Is she any good?"

"To my mind," Dickie said, "she's written what could be a truly successful book. Why?"

"Does Ed think so too?"

"I don't know. He hasn't seen it yet. I was trying to get Ralph Gorella to take a piece of it for *Hindsight*. . . . You ought to go to bed. You look bushed."

"Gorella, the ape man," Sandra said. "King Kong. Stella thinks so too and Stella can't even tell one person from another."

"Oh, Sandy, for god's sakes."

"—the ultimate in cold war warriors. Dostoyevsky si, Tolstoy no. Whenever somebody's sent to Siberia he practically gives a party. Except now the Party's over."

"Sandy, we know that joke," Dickie said. "Also maybe you and your aesthetic friend Stella could try to remember that though he may not be pretty, he's got a damn fine magazine there."

"Oh, sure, *Hindsight,* which gave us Gertrude Dienst, whose editor thinks nothing good's been written for the last forty years. Why won't you ever admit that he's just a lecherous old garter popper?"

"Has he ever tried to pop your garter?" Dickie said, laughing.

"On occasion. But that's not the issue." She hoped that Dickie wouldn't point out, still laughing, that, apelike or not, Ralph happened to be enormously attractive to an awful lot of women, which unfortunately was true. Gertrude Dienst had certainly had an affair with him her first season out, soon after that Gaskell Press party. But then there was a type of female who was always madly attracted to famous intellectuals, no matter who, no matter what, viz.: the chicks, secretaries, assistant publicity girls, buzzing like honeybees around Hershel and the priests. In fact, the intellectuals didn't even have to be so famous, just in a position of power. For example, in her own day at Barnard there had been that repulsive professor of philosophy, Arnold Belinsky, who had come to class in the same grease-stained gray pinstriped suit every day, each of its three pieces—vest, coat, baggy trousers—a different, unmatching pinstripe. Yet many girls, including her best friend at the time, Connie, had vied for the honor of sleeping with him, boasting about it afterward. One would think even a lowly undergraduate would have more pride.

"Dickie," Sandra said, "this Katz person isn't one of your weak sisters, is she?"

"I've never even laid eyes on the woman." Dickie said, and did laugh again. "How come you're taking such a dim view of everything tonight?"

"I'm not taking a dim view. It's one thing to question life and another to complain about it."

"Oh? Whose life are you questioning?"

"Nobody's," Sandra said, after a moment.

With a friendly shrug, Dickie went off to the bathroom, and after he had come back Sandra allowed a moment or two for the gurgle and general wetness to subside and then took her turn. On her way back, she tripped over the furled edge of the Oriental rug that Stella had reminded her of and that used to be first in the living room and after that, in the dining room while it was still good enough, and thought of Stella's invitation to go shopping tomorrow. Where was it, in *Of Human Bondage,* that the hero found the meaning of life in a Persian carpet? She could still remember her thrill as an adolescent when she understood that this meant the design. Could this also hold true if the rug came from Abraham & Straus?

"Oh, Dickie, I feel so lousy. I made such an ass of myself. I—"

But he was already in bed, reaching to turn off the light. It didn't matter. He would only tell her to see Dr. Starkstein if it bothered her that much. Still, in that brief illuminated glimpse

40

of his face under the outstretched arms, how young Dickie had looked with his small nose and bright sandy hair. She climbed in next to him, telling herself in the dark how intelligent Dickie also was, and how charming. Then why, more and more lately, was sleeping with Dickie like sleeping with a brother, a confrere, rather than a husband? Which oddly hadn't been at all true in the old days when they worked at Gaskell Press together and really had been equals. She put her arms around him. Who are you, she wondered, looking out at the river and the twinkling lights of New Jersey, who are you, dear boy in your clean pressed pajamas whom I am holding so tenderly but without hope of gain?

TWO ✦✦✦✦✦✦✦✦✦✦✦✦✦✦✦✦✦✦✦✦✦✦✦✦✦✦✦

The offices of Gaskell Press were not exactly modern, especially compared to the ones at Harcourt, Brace or Random House, or even, for that matter, Ed Gaskell's summer place out at Greenwich. But of course that was part of its charm and character: the small, quality publishing house, occupying not some new architect's dark glass tower but just a suite of elderly offices in a building not far from the Forty-second Street Library. Which also had trouble keeping its doors open these days, Dickie realized, looking down at the notation on his calendar of a ten o'clock appointment with Sophie Katz. Norma, his secretary, had just reminded him of it again, which wasn't necessary—Norma was just a great reminder-of—and also brought in the folder that now lay open on his desk on a great messy heap of other papers. He picked up the carbon copy of the letter on top: "To my mind, Miss Katz is very close to writing a truly successful book. If she would care to come in and discuss the matter, I would be delighted to talk to her in greater detail. . . ." He glanced at the blank space where his signature had been on the original and then looked out the window, consoling himself with the view. It was high and misty, a crisscrossing of gray stone rooftops along Fifth Avenue, and a lot better than what those young editors on Third Avenue were looking at, what with the low fluorescent ceilings and corrugated partitions and blank walls. Maybe in trying to replace Aaron Lasch, whom Ed Gaskell just hadn't been able to stand, they should advertise "windowed offices," like the "windowed kitchens" in the apartment ads in the *Times*.

The telephone on his desk began to ring, and after stalling a moment, he told Norma to have Miss Katz take a seat and he would be right out. He had always made a point of being courteous to his authors, present and prospective, and he certainly had no desire to keep Sophie Katz waiting just to impress her with his own importance. Nevertheless, as he started down the hall, having taken one more look out the window, it seemed to Dickie that it was getting more and more difficult to deal with writers lately, novelists especially (in spite of Lancelot Hale's oft-repeated thesis on the necessary madness of poets). Look at Hershel Meyers, once the sweetest nicest guy in the world, now an impossible egomaniac. That sock in the jaw, accidental or not, hadn't been funny, though Sandra kept insisting it never hurt at all. Physically. Spiritually, almost a week later she was still rubbing her jaw and talking about the actual experience of violence. Where the hell did she think she lived anyway? A look at the news from Vietnam, a walk to the IRT, though she refused to take the subway anymore, would have told her more about violence than she needed to know. Should he have socked Hershel back? That didn't seem right either. No, it was a lot easier on the nerves and frankly more civilized to deal with academicians, even the poets, even such surly types as George Auerbach, who fancied himself a literary lion at dinner parties but was an absolute lamb when it came to questions of contracts. Though even here you could never tell in advance. For

46

example, a year ago, when they had accepted that first novel by Gertrude Dienst, then unknown, except that she had just been divorced from a famous husband whose pseudo-Freudian interpretation of history she was reputed to have written, they had all feared the worst. A terrifying young woman, tall, dark, oily-skinned, with a very strong dyke potential. But in no time at all, Gert had graduated from intense first novelist to all-around femme de lettres, and now there wasn't a party you could go to where Gertrude wasn't always accompanied by that very Jewish-looking nephew with the dark olive complexion, even darker and more olive than his aunt's, and the long sideburns that could have passed for forelocks. Practically a living illustration for Eli Mandel's new coffee table (he had almost thought Christmas) book, *Jew of the Old Country*.

"Miss Katz?" Dickie said, pausing in the doorway of the reception room and addressing his question toward the woman who was nervously investigating the glass case of new books.

There was a loud clearing of throat and a squeak that could possibly be interpreted to mean, "Mr. Baxter." Dickie smiled and, with a courteous wave, indicated that perhaps Miss Katz would be good enough to precede him back down the hall. He went behind with a sinking heart. This was no good old Gert Dienst. Whatever Sophie Katz was, she would remain permanently, which happened to be, as that one quick glance at her had revealed, wet-eyed, eager, middle-aged, probably glandular, and, as this longer view of her back confirmed, endowed with long lank graying blond hair whose stray locks snaked their way into the collar of her navy blue raincoat.

"Sorry—this way," Dickie murmured as they collided at the corner of the corridor. He opened the door to his office and then the two of them regarded each other dubiously.

"Won't you sit down?" Dickie said.

"I'd *love* to. Where?"

"Where?" Dickie repeated and then, adding "Oh, here,"

indicated a small couch in the cluttered corner by his own bookshelves. He watched her sink down with her collar crowding her ears, returned to his desk, realized that she was sitting too far away, beckoned her to the chair facing him, and finally helped her off with her coat. It did not surprise him that neither of them knew where to put it and, also, that a slightly rancid odor hovered about the person of Miss Katz, as of old perfume impregnated at the dry cleaners or, actually, almost an animal smell of acute nervousness. Suddenly Dickie pitied the woman, always a bad policy, and hoped more than ever that the interview could be accomplished quickly.

"Miss Katz—" he began, resuming his seat and leaning forward on his elbows.

"Yes?"

Dear god, why did the woman have to speak in italics?

"We feel, *I* feel—" now he was doing it "—that you are very close to writing a—"

"Truly successful book," Sophie Katz finished for him.

Dickie surreptitiously glanced under his arm. Had she been reading the carbon copy of his letter upside down?

"A truly successful book," Dickie agreed. "However . . . it's awfully good of you to come in, by the way. I'm glad you were willing to discuss it."

Sophie Katz nodded, impatient of the ceremony, and fixed him intently with her large, protuberant, red-rimmed eyes. "Where do you think it goes sour, Mr. Baxter?"

"Sour?" Dickie said. "Well, that's the thing. What I mean is that, well, look, I think what you have here is a first-rate tragedy of innocence for about one-third through of this novel. The influence of *Joseph Andrews* is great, by the way. I recognize your use of it and think it's terrific."

"I've never read *Joseph Andrews.*"

"Haven't you?" Dickie said, with a surprised, interested inclination of his head. "Maybe you should. It's damn good. Very reminiscent of your work. Or should I say, vice-versa—?"

He laughed, waiting vainly for Miss Katz to join him, then cleared his throat. "Fielding."

"I know. I'm crazy about *Tom Jones*," Miss Katz volunteered.

"Are you really?"

"Oh, yes."

"Well, then I think you'd like *Joseph Andrews* too."

"Oh, I'm sure."

"Yes," Dickie said.

Miss Katz fixed him again with her bulgy, anxious eyes. "You say one-third. Why do you stop just at that point?"

Dickie took a deep breath. "Because, well, you see, I think her fall comes too early on. Before we're sufficiently clued in on the topography of this book. The reader's confused. He's not sufficiently clued in to the background. Now, if there were some way you could postpone her commitment, tantalize the reader a bit. . . . Otherwise, you see, she trips but—"

"Doesn't fall."

"—stoops, but—"

"Doesn't conquer," Sophie Katz finished for him. He didn't bother to lift his arm again. She knew the letter by heart.

"Yes, exactly," Dickie said.

"But how would you change it?"

There was a silence that Dickie let prolong itself. He looked down at his entwined fingers, then out the window in the general direction of the Forty-second Street Library—turnstiles for the general public?—then back at Miss Katz, who had kept staring at him with those tremulously eager, protruding eyes. She was even older than he had first thought. Her skin, a chalky white, sagged on either side of her chin, reflecting the yellow of a double string of amber beads. Little planes of gray showed under the straight blond hair at her temples.

"Shift the seduction scene," Dickie said.

Miss Katz blinked and gulped hard, as if she had just swallowed a marble.

"*Shift* it?"

"That's right," Dickie said.

"But that's a major change."

"That's right," Dickie said.

"But where would I shift it *to?*"

"Well, I don't have the text right at hand," Dickie said, and continued quickly before Miss Katz had time to finish rummaging through what looked like a child's plaid schoolbag. "But, just roughly, mind you, I'd say certainly west of page of page 150."

"But that means—"

"Figuring out what to do with the reader until the two of them climb into bed together. Right—" Dickie smiled. "But I think, in fact I'm sure, that much of the material that you now have coming in afterward can be interwoven with the stuff that comes before. This way, you see, you'll be able to carry the reader's interest right along through all the complicated exposition—much of which can be cut, by the way—instead of losing it two-thirds of the way through."

The telephone rang.

"It would require eliminating an awful lot of Lester," Miss Katz said dubiously.

"Well, yes, maybe—" Dickie said and told Norma not to put through any calls for about ten more minutes.

"On the other hand, of course," Miss Katz said, screwing up her face in overagonized concentration, "it might *just* give the love affair itself a deeper meaning."

"It might," Dickie said, excusing himself. Chicago? Well, in that case, could Norma please find out who was calling?

"I mean, *per esempio,* coming at the end, the seduction scene might come as a less dramatic but more natural climax, couldn't it? Forgive the pun. I mean, giving Nolan's refusal to marry her a double edge to the affair. Mightn't it?"

"Well, that hadn't occurred to me, but yes, I suppose so," Dickie said. cupping his hand over the receiver for a moment.

George Auerbach? Then would Norma please explain he was in conference and would call back later?

"Sorry," Dickie said.

". . . And then, when the brother's letter arrives, the fact that she literally can't read it, wouldn't invite any top-heavy symbolism. We could skip right over to the wife's bedroom."

"Terrific," Dickie said, more disappointed about the call than he should have been. "Marvelous idea."

"And then, when Mona—" Miss Katz's eager chin sagged down again into the region of the amber beads. "No," she said, sighing, "it won't work."

"Oh? Why not?"

"Because the brother isn't there anymore."

"How about using Stephanie to get him back?"

"Stephanie? Because she's seen him at the party? You mean, she could ask him to take her home, something like that?"

"Well, unless," Dickie said, "you'd prefer not to—"

"Oh, no! You're absolutely *right!*" Miss Katz said excitedly. "God, yes, it's *perfect!* I mean, you've suggested all kinds of possibilities to me. My mind's agog with them, absolutely *awhirl.*"

"I'm glad," Dickie said.

"Well, I'm not sure *I* am," Miss Katz said, with a laugh that reminded Dickie of a line from Fitzgerald, ". . . *the stiff, tinny drip of a banjo. . . .*" She cocked her head coquettishly. "It would be an enormous job, you know. Like breaking a bone and setting it again."

"I guess it would," Dickie said.

"Could you help me with it? Could you give me advice as we go along?"

"I don't see why not," Dickie said. "Look, let me read it again. Let me go over it very carefully."

"Oh, good! I will too. I have my own Xerox."

51

"I won't make any marks," Dickie said. "What I do is put in these little slips of paper."

"How long will it take you?" Miss Katz said.

"Well, actually, I'm a little pressed right now," Dickie said, "but give me a week, a solid week, and I'll call you. Okay?"

He stood up, as did Miss Katz, rising from the wreckage of her raincoat, a middle-aged parody of a shipwrecked Venus.

"I can't tell you how *happy* I am about all this," Miss Katz said. "How terribly excited. I'm terribly, terribly grateful to you for all your suggestions."

"Well, it would be a fun book to publish," Dickie said, holding out her coat at arm's length. It turned out to be a cape. How did you help a woman on with one of those things anyway? "A lot of books you do are drags. But this would definitely be a fun book."

The faint warm nervous aroma suffused the atmosphere between them again. Miss Katz swiveled her head and gave him a frightened look, like a rabbit about to be trapped in its own bag.

"Look, Mr. Baxter," she said, before Dickie could quite complete the anxious business of draping the heavy navy felt over her shoulders, "I'd better explain that much as I want to work with you, and happy a connection as I feel it would be, I'm afraid I simply couldn't embark on such a venture, that is, I literally couldn't afford to commit myself to a major revision of this kind—"

"Without a similar commitment from us," Dickie said. "Sure, that makes sense."

"Can you give me one?"

"Not right now," Dickie said, after a slight hesitation. "But let me read it again. And if my opinion of it holds, which I'm pretty sure it will, by the way, then there'll be plenty of time to discuss—"

"But is your opinion enough?"

"I could hardly function as an editor if it weren't," Dickie said, smiling.

52

"Yes, I understand that," Miss Katz said worriedly. "But I've had some experience . . . I know of firms where—"

"Right," Dickie agreed, hoping that if he put her at her ease, he could end the interview that much sooner. "Technically, what you're suggesting is absolutely justified. I have a boss and my boss has a veto I can't override. That's technically." He smiled. "Untechnically, Ed Gaskell hasn't used his veto in the twelve years I've been here. Okay?"

"I only meant—"

"No, please don't apologize," Dickie said, ushering her down the hall again and out past the switchboard to the bank of elevators. "You've got an absolutely legitimate concern there, and if I were in your place I'd ask the same questions. In fact, I'm glad I've had this chance to—ah, here's one going down."

"You'll call me?" Miss Katz said, halfway into the elevator.

"Absolutely."

"Then I'll be waiting!" Miss Katz cried, right before the door slid to and swallowed her up. "Oh—and *thank* you!"

"Thank *you,*" Dickie said, waiting there civilly for a moment. He turned and started back to the office. In her glass cubicle, Norma rolled her eyes in exaggerated sympathy, and he shrugged and smiled. In fact, the interview had not only taken less time than he had feared, he was more excited by the book than he had let the author know. He would mention it again to Ralph Gorella when they had a drink later—why did Sandra dislike the man so much—since if *Hindsight* took a piece, however small, it would grease the wheels all around. The thought of drinks made him mentally run down the rest of the day before then. Lunch with Carol Curtis at La Rochefoucauld, an interview with a prospective young editor at three, and then, well, what about Hershel? Ed had said something about wanting to see him. He started toward Ed's office and changed his mind, not particularly anxious to hover over Ed's desk just then, sharing honors with the silver-framed photograph of Felicity and the unused onyx ashtrays. Maybe he'd give Sandra a call, tell her he had just seen Sophie Katz and that she had absolutely nothing to worry about. But when, laughing, he dialed his home number, the desultory voice of the maid answered instead. Or should one call Orvietta a maid? The term "cleaning lady" seemed to be in better order these days, also "housekeeper." "Mother's helper" in this case was out of the question on account of the helper being about twice as old and fat as the mother. Funny that there really always was some slight nagging anxiety about the subject, though, in fact, Orvietta herself called herself the maid. Anyway, whatever she was, she told him Mrs. Baxter was out and hung up. Which was just as well, because now that Dickie thought about it, it hadn't been such a hot joke about Sophie after all.

The overfriendly doorman asked Sandra how she was feeling, and she answered too brightly "fine," introducing the first tiny note of constraint since she had left Dr. Starkstein's office. She shook it off, like a fly in the ear, and walked over to Madison Avenue, consciously savoring the sweet balmy air, always sweeter and balmier on the East Side than the West—though why didn't either Dickie or Stella care about which side of town they lived on?—trying to hold on to the wonderful sense of purposeless liberation that these sessions always left her with, the sense that life was flowing all around her and that if she wanted, she could pinpoint herself exactly in time and space, take a little snapshot of herself to pull out and mull over, maybe even show Becky in later years. Sandra Wolfe Baxter, a woman in her prime—thirty-six, about the same age as Christ when he died, did that matter?—just released from the analyst to live life to the fullest, half in love, no, more than half, standing at a sunny, busy corner in one of the most expensive sections of town. Of course, Morty Schwartz's office was also in the general neighborhood, which tarnished the image a bit. But never mind. She was still full of the radiant morning, though as she walked along she was less and less sure what to do with it, except to repeat to herself what a radiant morning it was.

Actually, to be perfectly honest, it hadn't been such a hot session with Starkstein. For one thing, the fact of his abysmal furniture had been even more distracting than usual, a dreadful mélange of heavy mahogany (maybe brought over from the old homestead in Austria), curlicued wrought iron, green- and gold-flecked upholstery, whose flecks she kept picking at, the catercornered desk, where after she left he would answer the calls from the telephone service and send out bills, his chairside lamp table trailing its wire a great tangled distance from its plug in the baseboard. There was even, believe it or not, a window-box arrangement of green plastic fern and purple orchids, which today had kept reminding her of the fake geraniums in La Rochefoucauld and herself sitting with bowed and naked head, like a freshly exposed French collaborationist. It was funny, but when she first went to see Starkstein a few years ago at Herb Finger-wald's recommendation, and imagining that great revelations lay before her, she had been positive that his awful taste in furniture, or worse, his wife's awful taste, would be an insurmountable obstacle between them—which wasn't even to mention his loud sport jackets and flowered ties—since what did this make of his presumed omniscience? But by now, of course, she understood that omniscience wasn't even desirable or necessary. Questions of philosophy, the meaning of life, shrinks were no good at. Period. Where Starkstein helped was with specifics, rage about maids, this new phobia about flying, waking up in the morning with a sudden dread of being invited to a party by Violette de Laniere and having nothing to wear. Though what specific had made her go to him today remained uncertain. Not the business with Hersh, though it had left a funny taste in her mouth. Not this recurrent obsession with Adam, which anyway they'd gone over so many times already to no avail. Because after all, in the end what

55

was there to say about a lover (?) who could leave the country without even saying good-bye or, even worse, have his wife say it for him? A man she could go without thinking about for months, and who then had only to pop up at a party to suffuse her whole atmosphere? It was also rather embarrassing to be the only person who really liked Adam. Hershel thought he was an English prig and a bore, an intellectual middleman, Stella kept asking why he was married to a woman with a twisted face, Dickie just about tolerated him, which was no news since Dickie just about tolerated everybody. She thought of Starkstein's unwelcome suggestion that maybe Adam reminded her not of her father but of her mother. She had looked up from picking at the gold flecks in her chair to see if he was joking. But he had covered his face with a tent of fingers in that irritating way of his, and almost in retaliation she had switched the subject back to Hershel, who when last heard from was back in Chicago giving interviews on the death of fiction. A bad sign—even Dickie was worried, though naturally he didn't admit it—since only blocked novelists gave interviews on the death of fiction, unless they tried to start magazines. Ralph Gorella had laughed himself sick over Angelica Ford's poor attempt a few years ago, and laughed even harder when she failed and had to give back all that money to the safflower-oil millionaire who turned out to be funded by the CIA anyhow. And then, as Dr. Starkstein leaned forward, eyes furtive with interest, she had deliberately fed him a few more tidbits, that William Kohlrobi, believe it or not, thought the Our Gang comedies were literary masterpieces, that Angelica Ford, who knew nothing about math had been asked by *Commentary* to review Ruby Cohen Mandel's *Devastated Decimal,* that George Auerbach, the original male chauvinist pig, was embarked on a new translation of Sappho, with illustrations so pornographic that even in this day and age Freddie Fruchtman was worried sick, and, of course, repeated Ed Gaskell's gaffe about T. S. Eliot being in his stable. Starkstein had leaned back again, solemn and proud. But what if in

56

the end it was Dickie's list he absorbed and digested, not her own life?

"Listen," she had said suddenly, "when you think of me, do you call me Sandra or Mrs. Baxter in your mind?"

". . . Sandra," he had said, after a pause.

"I call you Starkstein."

Something very sexy and reassuring pervaded the atmosphere.

"Okay," Dr. Starkstein said, which did not mean agreement, but only that the hour was up.

The landscape had changed. She hurried past the windows of Schrafft's where a series of prosperous-looking yentas sat lunching, framed like passengers in a train, glum, imprisoned in their latest platinum-blond bubble cuts and gypsy jewelry, and whatever else *Vogue* had decreed, having made the transition from West Side to East without any improvement at all, without for one minute leaving behind the impression that they should all be back in babushkas peddling fish. She walked farther east, then east again, finally leaving the residential apartment buildings with their white-dickeyed doormen, the discreet branches of Gristede's, and found herself flanked by new modern office buildings soaring so high and glasslike from their plazas and arcades that they seemed about to converge overhead. In between it was elegant New York, side streets lined with boutiques, safari shops, metal sculpture, whirlpool baths, Italian men's shops, French silk scarves and suede coats, antique buttons, custom shirts, needlework, plaques saying *"honi soit qui mal y pense"* and, some twenty years out of date, "by appointment to His Majesty." Lunchtime crowds were issuing from lobbies, overfed young men with slim attaché cases, skinny young girls straight out of the latest avant-garde films, with knobby legs, rouged cheeks, eyes blackened round with mascara, headscarves tied low on the forehead, fashions so close to the fashions of her childhood that it was like wandering in a foreign country. Though why was she thinking of herself in the past when she had just decided she was in her prime? Anyway, it was all undeniably stimulating, all very much more a scene to arrive at than good old Fifth Avenue and the Plaza, for example, which she dearly loved and would always love—except that the other day a Jewish flag with the Star of David had been disconcertingly affixed to the pole below the green mansard roof, Golda in town probably—or St. Patrick's with its *papier-mâché* flying buttresses and the out-of-town Catholic high school girls sidestepping pigeons on its steps, holding lace handkerchiefs to their heads. On still another side street—she had lost track of which one—Sandra stopped in front of the window of an antique jewelry store, admiring a filigreed diamond pin, which was very much like the one her father, mistakenly taking her advice, had once given her mother as an anniversary present. A terrible occasion. Opening the blue velvet box and seeing a pin so old-fashioned inside, Lena Wolfe had burst into hurt tears. The next year the anniversary present came out of her father's own stock, a shiny gold disc on a chain with a cut-out חי. Leah's taste this time, which it ought to have been in the first place. Oh, well, as Leah would have been the first to say, why fight City Hall? She lifted her head, tuning in again to the great city din, the brutal clang of metal, iron against steel, buildings wrecked, others rising, the rumble of wooden sidewalks, and thought of Pip just arrived in London with his great expectations. At the corner, she paused, anticipating the changing traffic light, and there, in front of her but impervious to her, was Felicity Gaskell, also waiting to cross the street, dressed all in gray as usual (in her case, grey?), light-gray fur, gray dress, gray stockings, gray suede pumps, gray borzoi. How magnificently rich to have a dog to match oneself! Even in the movies she had yearned through as a child in the Bronx, such magnificence and riches had only been hinted at. The traffic light changed to WALK and Felicity glided on, enveloped in her silent atmosphere of utter luxury.

Sandra stayed behind, watching her. Not so long ago, just

about the time of the diamond pin fiasco actually, she had imagined that one day she also would be like that, not so much rich, as one whom the ordinary events of life would never seriously touch: marriage, childbirth, death. Yet each of them had taken its toll of her in turn, each incredible at the time. When her father died, she hadn't been able to believe it. Five years later, she still couldn't believe that such a thing had happened to him, *or* to her. "You ought to ask Herb Finger-wald to send you to somebody," Dickie had said, around the third year, "you're taking it much too hard." Which, though it signaled the advent of Starkstein, was a perfect example of sensible advice that wasn't really all that sensible. Like the time they had made that astronaut—Edward White? Was that his name? The first man out in space?—reel in the tether at whose end he was floating around ecstatically, even joking with the ground communications' crew in Houston about severing his lifeline completely. And then about a year later, having obediently returned, he had burned to death inside a mock-up capsule that couldn't even go anyplace.

La Rochefoucauld, a change of subject, appeared just ahead, pretty and pink-stoned, soon to be crowded inside with the young executives having lunch but, outside, a souvenir of dinner last week with Adam. And what if Adam should come walking along right now killing time before *his* lunch, maybe with a new batch of paperbacks from Brentano's under his arm? He wouldn't see her at first, of course, and that would be good because it would give her a little time to watch him unobserved: head down, serious, intent. And then, at the last moment, she would call out to him, and he would look up and smile, smile in that heart-stopping way of serious young men, and she would ask him where he was going, and he would tell her, and ask her to come along, and wherever it was, she would say yes, and after that, they would. . . . She closed her eyes and shivered, overcome by her physical ache for the man, then looked around, hot-cheeked and embarrassed as if she had just been caught walking around naked in a well-dressed crowd on a busy street. Not, god knew, also Starkstein (bad joke), that it had ever been much of an affair with Adam, she really mustn't pretend that it had. A couple of afternoons one summer at Cape Cod when everybody was particularly depressed about Vietnam and didn't know where it would all lead them. She had always been kind of disappointed about the afternoon part and that it was on a scrubby beach, not at night and romantic. Even the Staten Island ferry and having her ear blown into would have made a difference. Was this why there was always such yearning, so many unresolved chords when she thought of Adam? And that whenever it was a lovely day, rain *or* shine, she dreamed of passing La Rochefoucauld and meeting Adam? It was late, time to move on, but for Adam she would gladly have abandoned the whole rest of the day. Oh, what wouldn't she have abandoned if Adam asked her?

Across the street, the crosstown bus lurched to a stop, and her heart lurched with it as an extremely familiar man got off. But it was an extremely dark man, Vaughn Cranshaw, who gave a quick look around as if to make sure no one had caught him alighting from a public conveyance, preened himself, and hurried on into La Rochefoucauld, very much the homme de lettres. Once she had met him in front of Doubleday's when she was taking Becky shopping, and she had been glad for both their sakes that she was heading for Bonwit Teller's rather than Alexander's. Anyway, there they had stood on Fifth Avenue, liking each other over Becky's head, everything bustling and bien élevé. Vaughn was on his way to the Monday party at the PEN Club, which when he talked about it sounded like the Century, and he had on a porkpie hat and his sideburns were a bit too frizzy and there was, alas, something not quite first rate about him, one iota not top drawer. She had suddenly felt very sorry for Vaughn. It must be terrible and hard to be distinguished in a porkpie hat. She continued on past La Rochefoucauld, leaving it firmly behind her, though it was getting harder and harder to make a souvenir of the day in spite of all the other places she kept pinpointing to herself: the elegant jewelry shop where Dickie had once bought her a garnet ring for her birthday ("Just like that? *Retail?*" Leah had said), the unfamiliar bar next door where they had impulsively gone to celebrate afterward, intimidated by the striking sudden blackness and the fairies, though Dickie had laughingly denied being intimidated by any of it, the upstairs gallery where Stella had taken her one Saturday afternoon to see an exhibit of balloons blown into distorted shapes and encased permanently in white plaster, the bookstore full of precious and rare leather bindings, the Danish delicatessen, and then—nothing. She stared at the gaping hole on the block, feeling for it with her mind like a tongue a missing tooth. But there was only a crude and temporary wooden fence plastered with handbills within which a skinny orange crane poked itself into empty space and sky. Incredible. If anybody had told her she would be standing on a street two blocks away from La Rochefoucauld and not remember what used to be there, she would never have believed it.

"Hi, darling."

"Stella! What are you doing here?"

"Well, on the East Side it's always an exhibit or the shrink, isn't it?" Stella laughed, without telling which.

She stepped off the sidewalk to hail a cab, a far cry from the Stella in the pink silk pajamas. This time her bleached hair was dark-rooted and streaky, and she was wearing a pair of tight faded jeans, a baggy T-shirt, desert boots, and, in spite of the warm weather, an old brown suede jacket. It was the sculptor Stella, the one who drove Freddie crazy.

"Are you going home now?" Sandra said.

"Home?" Stella said. "No, I think I may just drop in at the Nordness. Want to come along?"

"I can't. I have to go see my mother. She's at this awful hotel in New Jersey."

"Oh, poor *thing,*" Stella said with tremendous sympathy, though the object of it was a little obscure. "Must you go this very minute?"

"Well, my brother-in-law the specialist is giving me a lift out," Sandra explained, hoping Stella would try to talk her out of it anyway. But Stella shook her head even more sympathetically and flailed away at a passing cab.

"Aren't you marvelous," she sighed as the thing screeched to a stop. "I wish I could be *half* as responsible as you are." She reached for the door-handle and turned to Sandra with a smile that was dazzling in its sudden radiance.

"Darling, listen—I went to this party last night. I haven't been so turned on in years."

"Oh? Who was he?"

"A German," Stella said, curving her lips with a sly and secret amusement. "I think maybe even a Nazi."

"A *Nazi?*"

But Stella had already climbed into the cab, waved goodbye through the window and, still smiling that curvy smile, leaned back, lost in darkness, speeding off to god-knew-where.

A block more, and there was Morty's office. Once a town house, something in the style of Ed's, now a nest of Jewish doctors. Sighing, she rang the doorbell: Morton Schwartz, MD. Morty's black Lincoln Continental with its privileged, matching MD plates sat low slung and illegal at the curb. The only reason for the lift, not often proffered by a man so self-importantly busy and car-proud as Morty was that he was taking the afternoon off anyway to play golf. Perhaps, anxious not to waste time, he would emerge already clad in his golf outfit: stout-waisted red plaid Bermuda shorts, a white polo shirt with a golf ball and tee embroidered over a bulging breast pocket. Ironically, Leah had originally picked him up on a golf course, though neither of them were golf players yet at the time. He, only a young medical student sauntering across the putting green at Camp Lochdrake, where she, a girl

62

in a red bathing suit, had gone to catch a husband, already afraid at twenty-three that it was too late. Autres temps, autres moeurs. (There was almost fifteen years' difference between her and Leah, and two celebrated miscarriages in between.) Or perhaps, though even to put the question in such a way made her feel uncomfortably snobbish, poor young girls still saved up all year to go husband hunting in the summer. The door yielded with an impersonal clicking of the latch. With a last thought of that damn Stella leaning back and smiling in her dark taxicab, Sandra pushed her way inside.

"So take the diamond pin."

"I told you. I don't want it. I have no use for it."

"So what use do I have? Papa's dead."

"I know Papa's dead," Leah said with a short impatient laugh, turning to Sandra.

Sandra hesitated. "Maybe you ought to take it, Leah. Lee. It's actually something of a jeweler's piece." Mrs. Wolfe nodded, temporarily triumphant, and sat back in her folding chair, hands clasped on the mound of her stomach, short square feet in their black canvas sandals, crossed at the ankles several inches above the grass.

"—in fact, I was looking at one very much like it this morning in the window of, Gumbiner's, was it? No, you know, that other one—" Leah had begun to look grim, neither knowing about the other one, nor caring. "Anyhow, all I mean is that that sort of diamond filigree work was actually a kind of high point in Victorian design. My friend, Stella Fruchtman, who happens to work in welded sculpture but knows a lot about jewelry, says that plastically—"

"Baby, I'm afraid old-fashioned things hold no fascination for me whatever," Leah said, smiling so tensely that two veined sinews stood out on either side of her neck. ("Leah's prison bars," Dickie called them, laughing.) Her head suddenly caught the New Jersey country sunlight, and as always it was a shock to realize that Leah, who had started out life as a homely Jewish girl with black kinky hair, then after marriage to Morty acquired red highlights, had now become a total blond, exactly like the dinnertime ladies in La Rochefoucauld, the lunching ladies at Schrafft's. "I'm afraid I've never been able to get sentimental about my past, *or* the Depression years."

Depression years? Leah's past? How the hell had they blundered into that subject, though, of course, like Rome, Leah's deprived childhood could be reached by almost any road. Leah was simply unable to get over the bitter historical accident that made the Wolfes poor when she was a kid and fairly prosperous when Sandra was growing up. In fact, of course, it was World War II that had come between, not any special favoritism, but there was no point trying to convince Leah of this.

"Just give me something modern and easy to clean," Leah said, smiling tightly, prison bars straining. "I have a six-room home with two-and-a-half baths to worry about, which is enough of a headache I assure you, not to mention a husband and two large children, plus a class of forty third-graders, without knocking myself out polishing diamonds also."

Mrs. Wolfe shrugged, leaving the two of them to fight it out, though in fact they never fought. There was too much of an age gap between them, too many generational differences. Leah had just been arguing with herself, of course, fate, the world in general. But it was the kind of mean, maddening legend their mother loved to perpetuate, the quarrelsome sisters, the cold, cruel husband, weaving an endless elaborate background tapestry for the golden thread of her martyrdom. Satisfied with her work, she squinted at each of them in turn, recrossed the little stout feet in the air, and cracked a couple of beringed knuckles on her stomach. Mother in exile. A Jewish Duchess of Windsor. Only once, one time in her life when she was pregnant, had Sandra understood the discomfort of such a stomach, the need for straight-backed chairs, and sympathized. But after nine months, even that little bit of sympathy was finished and done with. By now, she could hardly see any connection between herself and this endlessly complaining old lady—I'm too young to have such a mother, Sandra thought—this puppet whom Leah had stuffed like a pillow into Gertz's latest finery, a blue print silk summer dress, the rubber-soled black canvas sandals, adding as jewelry a couple of gold and ruby cocktail rings from twenty years ago, and the gold disc with the letters חי . It was impossible to believe that this woman was the same mother in the wraparound housedress and carpet slippers who had bustled and scolded and nagged her way through Sandra's childhood. Where had the other mother gone to? What had become of her? All that was left were the red-veined Russian country girl cheeks, another source of bitterness because when she was sick she still looked so healthy nobody believed her, and the habit of biting her lips before she blew her nose, which was often. She blew again, put the shredded Kleenex back in her pocketbook, a lacquered straw basket with a lidful of cherries that had been a Mother's Day present from Leah and that was almost empty except for a pair of reading glasses that she kept for close perusal of the *Forward,* a dainty unused handkerchief, another wad of Kleenex, and a tan powder puff from the Five and Ten. She snapped the thing shut, and leaned over with some difficulty to lay it on the grass alongside her dangling feet.

"What's she crying about?" Sandra said. "Why are you crying?"

"Crying? Ma's not crying, are you, Ma?" Leah said in a bright chirrupy voice and, without waiting for an answer, continued: "Did I tell you Itsy got herself a part-time job after school? Isn't that good? That's why she couldn't come today. She sends regards."

More tears, nose blowing, a bitter biting of the lips, silence.

"Bitsy sends regards too. He's studying for his finals."

Mrs. Wolfe nodded curtly. An empress receiving boring tribute.

"And Becky? She also remembers her grandmother some-time?"

"Oh, for god's sakes, Mama," Sandra began, before Leah laid a restraining hand on her arm.

"Now, Rebeccah is a very lovely little girl who loves you very much, Ma. You know that."

Shrugging and sighing more deeply, Mrs. Wolfe produced a shredded Kleenex from her pocket this time, pointedly ignoring the Mother's Day present. Poor Leah. She looked so especially old and tired today. It was really no joke. Life *had* been rough on her, starting with that famous Depression and somehow knocking her for a loop every time she tried to raise herself up. And now, here she was, in addition to all her other responsibilities, which were heavy enough, assuming most of the burden of their mother, visiting her at the hotel, taking her out every other weekend like a model prisoner, bringing her to a beauty parlor in Great Neck from which she emerged with a head of tight little blue curls dispersed at random over an innocent blue scalp. (I ought to do more, Sandra thought, pitch in—but how?) And then, there was also the class of third-graders, who had turned black under Leah's very eyes. She had never quite understood why Leah, who had bitterly resented having to work for a dentist all day while she went to Hunter College at night, seven long years, pure *Rocket to the Moon* stuff, and who had then bitterly resented having to care for her own two children when they were little, should have suddenly decided to become a schoolteacher as soon as they were old enough to go to school themselves. Obviously, it was no longer a question of needing the money. Probably the idea was that it would challenge Leah, get her out of the house. But again poor Leah, who never sounded challenged, only out of the house. Still, it was interesting that of the two of them, Leah had the career while Sandra stayed home. Or was "interest-

66

ing" the word, Sandra suddenly wondered, squirming around in her own canvas folding chair, as if it had become decidedly uncomfortable to sit in the sparkling sunshine of a sweet grassy June day.

The elderly clientele sat scattered like buckshot across the lawn. Among them, a bony lady with wrinkled lips who stared at her and Leah reproachfully. She had been introduced as a Mrs. Zimmerman, and it had been clear from the first that she had heard the story many times of the ungrateful daughters, the thorns of aggravation in Mrs. Wolfe's side. The poor old creature still didn't realize yet that the intimacy would last only up to the moment when she tried to get in a few tales of aggravation of her own. Still, Sandra thought, biting into the Oh Henry bar her mother had pressed on her from the vending canteen at the poolside and sipping at a Coke through a wilted straw, it really hadn't been such a painful visit, only, as usual, boring. Why did she always remember the pain and forget the boredom? The Schwartzes had transported her out like a hot potato in a relay race, Morty as far as the house, then Leah, after coffee in the breakfast nook, and a look at the new genuine Cézanne watercolor over the credenza in the living room, up to the gates of the hotel. "Why are we stopping here? It's not Saturday. It's only Thursday." *"Shevuoth,"* Leah said. Their mother, crying out of joy presumably that time, had led them into the hotel dining room for the big hotel lunch, a Proustian experience that was still repeating itself, unfortunately. Roast chicken, roast potatoes, carrot tsimmes. ("Oh, darling!" she could imagine Stella laughing, when she said, well, what the hell, Proust was Jewish too.) Afterwards they had changed into their bathing suits for a swim in the pool that the hotel color-brochure called "Olympic size" and looked even vaster, then, for health reasons, raced back to their mother's room to get out of their wet suits. Now, as the afternoon waned, the pool lay almost empty behind its fence of chicken wire, rippling and turquoise, its sole inhabitants a few teen-agers horsing around at the diving board, their voices thin hollow sprays in the late sunshine, a few mothers with bulging armpits and silver curlers chatting at the shallow end. Only the kiddie pool was still excited and alive, a paradise of little visiting grandchildren, who splashed and sat and carried their sandpails up and down slippery wet green steps. Why was it so hard to picture Becky among them, though she often had been, running up and down in the polka dot sunsuit tied at the shoulders, a present from Grandma? Why was it, oddly, much easier to imagine Dickie coming back from a long late lunch at La Rochefoucauld? What if he *had* been having lunch with Adam?

"So he's all right your husband?" Mrs. Wolfe said, ending her sighing silence with still another sigh.

"Dickie?" Sandra said, coming back, not to herself, she had just been with herself. "Oh, yes, he's fine."

"And the mother too?"

"*Mama*—" Sandra said ominously.

"She lives and laughs," Mrs. Wolfe said, herself laughing bitterly.

"Now, listen," Sandra began, "just because a woman's a widow doesn't mean—" and caught herself this time without Leah's intervention. "Actually, she's in Israel at the moment."

"Israel?" Mrs. Wolfe said, cocking her head to one side and, in spite of herself, impressed.

Again without Leah's help, Sandra shut up in time. She was only committing a lie of omission, and Starkstein had certainly made the point often enough that there was no need to be the last of the just. Still, the fact was that Wilma's stay in Israel was just a stopover in a long luxury cruise of the Mediterranean. A fast look at the Wailing Wall, an overnight stay in a kibbutz, a tiny tree planted in a clay pot in a desert forest, and off she would be to Greece. To Leah, Sandra couldn't help saying in an aside: *"She sent us a picture of herself riding a camel." ". . . That's funny, a mother riding a camel,"* Leah said thoughtfully. *". . . I know it."*

After another moment's reflection, Leah shook the thought

loose and stood up, tying a black net hood over her new blond hair to protect it from car breezes.

"So, be well, Ma."

"What kind of be well? Where are you rushing?"

"We're not rushing anyplace, Mama, we've been here all afternoon," Sandra said, needing to establish the truth even more for herself than for her mother, who was ignoring Sandra in her panic anyway.

"Swim a little more," Mrs. Wolfe pleaded with Leah, reluctantly getting up too, so incredibly short, not much taller than Becky, and waddling behind her past the main building of the Hotel Waldbaum to its pink stucco annex.

"We swam already."

"Swim a little more."

"Now, Ma," Leah stopped and turned to say severely, not caring for the water anyway. It was part of her bitterness at never having been sent to camp. "You know we don't come for the pool, we come to see you."

Where had Leah acquired this gift for making the truth sound so false? Leah held out her hand firmly, and with a dull stymied look, a third-grader for whom there would be no redress, Mrs. Wolfe fished her key from the cherry basket. Leah opened the door to the small dark room, about half the size of the one their mother and father had stayed in together the last summer he was alive. It seemed to be furnished with leftovers from before the hotel was remodeled, a single bed covered with a pink chenille spread, a scarred Swedish modern bureau, a dirty blond wooden armchair to match stuck in the corner by a bridge lamp. Under the window, a pair of pink rayon underdrawers lay drying on a towel spread across the radiator cover. The boxes with the ritual presents for the grandchildren were still open on the bed, where they had already been exclaimed over: a red plaid sport shirt for Leah's Barry, alias Bitsy, a white cardigan with a sequined poodle for Janice, alias Itsy, and for Becky, an album of Pete Seeger folk songs. "Gee, Ma, it's awfully thoughtful of you,"

Leah said brightly, and as if she hadn't gone out to buy them all in the first place. Sandra went into the bathroom to fetch her wet bathing suit, trying to ignore the inevitable enema bag hanging on the hook behind the door. Like the other room, the bathroom was also small and makeshift, with a thin green marbleized plastic toilet seat, thin green marbleized tiles in the combination bathtub-shower. It was hard to imagine her mother standing up naked in the shower.

"When Papa was living we were in the Main House," Mrs. Wolfe was saying to Leah as Sandra came out again.

"I know, Ma, see you on Wednesday."

"Have some tea first, at least."

"Ma, we'd love to, but we can't," Leah said, ushering her out and closing the door firmly behind them. She handed back the key.

"A little fruit," Mrs. Wolfe said urgently, following them on her short legs across the lawn and out the Hotel Waldbaum gates. "A cookie."

"Mama, we *can't* stay any longer. We have to be home. Our husbands need us."

And who had mentioned the word "husbands"? Me, Sandra thought glumly. Who else would make such a tactical error? Not Leah. The tears that had been seeping from their mother's eyes on and off all afternoon, suddenly gushed forth in a bitter torrent. She put her hands to her face and rocked back and forth, moaning and keening, the way when Sandra was little she would bless the Friday night candles, hiding a mystery of suffering.

"Mama—" Sandra said.

"Look, Mama, listen," she tried again, bending down to touch the convulsed shoulders as she might have touched Becky. She smiled. "People do need people, you know. There's no sin in it. I mean, for example, believe it or not, I need you now, and—"

She felt Leah's cautionary touch on her arm. Mrs. Wolfe stopped crying and emerged from behind her hands. Her

70

pale-green eyes, dulled by suspicion and fear, were small and hard.

"What are you talking?" Mrs. Wolfe said.

"Nothing, Ma, she was only kidding," Leah said.

But the afternoon was ruined, and Sandra, naturally, had ruined it. Out on the country road, the three of them drifted around in a sea of misery by Leah's light-blue fender until it was unquestionably time to go. Goddamn it, Sandra thought, getting into the Ford convertible with its closed top and watching Leah release the emergency brake, if I don't come I neglect her, if I do it's on purpose to torture her. What was it Lyndon Johnson had once said about the guests at his Arts Festival? Some of them are insulting me by coming and some of them are insulting me by staying away? . . . No, she won't be happy till we're both widows too, Sandra thought. So how could one even be human with that woman, how could one be *nice?*

They were arriving by stages back into the world. Fewer and fewer billboards for Kosher-style hotels lined the roads, fewer and fewer bungalow colonies, though occasional guests of both wandered out from weedy side paths, a pair of fat, hennaed ladies strolling along arm in arm, slacks bulging. An old bearded Jew in a frock coat and shtreimel hat, serious, distracted, as if he were still in search of a homeland. What an anti-Semitic thought, though. Lancelot Hale would have converted it into one of his wittier metaphors. Why shouldn't orthodox Jews live in the country?

"No, but I still admire your patience," Sandra said. "I really mean that. I don't see how you can stand it. The woman has cost me a fortune already in analyst's fees."

"She's just an old lady," Leah said, and gave Sandra a quick look to see if it was true about the analyst.

Funny, but for some reason which Sandra herself didn't understand, she had never told Leah about Starkstein, though

Leah had told her endlessly and in great detail about her sessions with her own analyst, a clinical psychologist—for obvious reasons Leah was wary of confiding in MD's—and Sandra had listened endlessly to the details, with the kind of interested condescension that Leah expected of her in these matters.

"What do you mean old lady?" Sandra said. "We don't even know when her birthday is."

"Listen, pussy," Leah said, "birthday, shmirthday. I'm so relieved they're keeping her at that hotel I don't care if she's passing for twenty. The manager's getting fed up. She's driving all the other guests nuts. He told me she never stops complaining about that room day and night."

"Sixty-five, maybe," Sandra said. "That's the real irony of it."

"Ma?" Leah said. "Oh, no, she's older, she has to be older."

"What I don't understand is how Daddy even managed to put up with her all those years. My god, even when that man was lying in the hospital turning brown from all those tubes—" She stopped, remembering suddenly a day near the end, when she had walked in on him as he lay dying and dozing, hooked to his bottles on the chromium stand. The sheet had fallen away, and the bottom half of him was naked in his hospital gown. She had pulled up the sheet quickly, with her face averted. It was the only time she had seen him down below. He looked like Dickie.

"I mean even when Daddy was dying," Sandra said with a short laugh, "even *then* our dear mother tried to get the interns to take *her* blood pressure first."

Leah laughed too, but the neck veins stood out tensely again beneath the ribbon tie of her black mesh car hood. She had probably shocked her with that seemingly offhand allusion to their father's death. One had to be so careful about words where Leah was concerned, who was always much more sensitive to how things were put than what was actually said. But Leah was so sensitive in so many places, it was hard to say

72

exactly what the trouble spot right now really was. Maybe even some slight vagary of her car, for example, which Leah, who had learned to drive late and in spite of Morty's hoots of derision, tended to invest with an overly nervous importance. No stranger looking at her in the sleeveless yellow polyester dress with those arms of a skinny stevedore would ever dream that Leah was so touchy. Physically she was still as strong and wiry as the young woman Sandra used to watch with admiration in the Bronx apartment, leaping around the big dining room table in an Isadora Duncan tunic and chamois slippers, tense calves bulging, "expressing" herself. (There was also a Betty Boop imitation that maybe it was better not to think about.) But if you did know where to look there were a million little vulnerable places that gave the game away: the thin lines like skin cuts at the corners of Leah's eyes, the downturn of the mouth, the whiteness of the slightly arthritic knuckles as she gripped the steering wheel. And in fact, maybe the reference Leah was reacting to had nothing to do with their mother or their father or the car. Maybe she had been hurt on an altogether other level. Sandra looked at her sideways, wondering where she might have said the wrong thing, failed to say the right one. For example, had she been sufficiently enthusiastic and congratulatory about the new genuine Cézanne watercolor? But it had looked like a Museum of Modern Art reproduction, a cousin to all the Van Gogh sunflowers that once hung on their walls along with ornamental china plates, before the Schwartzes had worked their way up in the world. "Doesn't it look a little bit lopsided to you," Sandra had asked very tentatively, "crooked?" "Cézanne doesn't paint crooked pictures," Leah had said, laughing, though a furtive glance through the dealer's catalogue on top of the antique credenza had shown very clearly a tear on the side that must have been matted over. Or maybe she should have remembered to bring some sort of present, "a hostess gift," as Leah and her friends did whenever they came together. (She tried to imagine Felicity Gaskell's closets suddenly overflowing with ceramic cheese servers, cork coaster sets, apothecary jars filled with tiny pieces of soap the size and shape of strawberries, barbecue aprons with cute sayings.) Maybe she ought to have been more enthusiastic about Itsy's enterprise at getting an after-school job, Bitsy's brilliant record at Amherst, though even their names stuck in her craw. Leah suffered from the same problem. *"Becky"* she had cried, bringing flowers to the hospital. "You're going to waste a name like Baxter?" Was it ironic, or just sad, that here were two sisters unable to call each other's children by name?

A main stretch of highway suddenly asserted itself ahead of them. Billboards sprang up on either side to advertise furniture stores, motor oil, a Howard Johnson's 300 feet ahead. There was a sudden resurgence of diners, drive-in barbecues, service stations, a custard stand shaped like a custard cone, a huge hot dog selling hot dogs, many other cars, Chevrolet ads, a pink and green Starlite Motel. Leah was beginning to look more at home with herself, though still nervous and preoccupied. At the first big intersection, Sandra looked around at her warily. One sign pointed them back to their mother's hotel, another to Paramus and the cemetery where their father was buried. Was there no third alternative?

"Leah, isn't this where we always get lost?"

"Oh, pussy," Leah said, with a driver's annoyance.

Nevertheless, which way *was* New York? Did life consist entirely of New Jersey? We'll never get home, Sandra thought, panicked by an on-coming futuristic vision of a shopping center. By mistake, Leah drove them straight into it, circling repeatedly around Alexander's, J. J. Newberry's, a brand-new bowling alley, until, with a determined swing of the wheel, she maneuvered them out onto the highway again. The cutoff to the cemetery was now safely behind them. But instead of being relieved, Sandra was seized with a longing to go back, an ache like homesickness. She could barely understand it herself, this desire to see her father's grave, his tombstone in the family plot, his chiseled name, a set of dates, a Hebrew inscription, anything that was tangible proof he had once been alive. For that matter, how could she even explain the strange pleasure it had given her before to say, "When Daddy was dying," as if the very act had brought him back to life again? Daddy. Leah called him Papa. Generation gap again. The whole thing was already embarrassing. Bit by bit, the idea of the cemetery relinquished itself until it went out with a tiny *ping* like a bubble in a highball glass.

A new white-on-green sign indicated the George Washington Bridge, and Leah leaned back in her seat, the worst part of her mission accomplished.

"She's in love with a schvartzer," Leah said so casually it took Sandra a moment or two to grasp what she had heard.

"Who is?"

Silence. Cigarettes reached for on top of the dashboard, the lighter punched in.

"*Itsy?*"

"You won't laugh when your daughter brings one home to you," Leah said, "I assure you."

"I wasn't laughing."

"Yes, you were."

"Okay," Sandra said, though in fact she hadn't been laughing, only smiling to mask a sudden, senseless disappointment that Leah's problem had nothing to do with her after all. "But how seriously do we have to take it? The girl's only sixteen."

"And the boy is twenty, that marvelous bargain, that beautiful cultural drop-out that she met on that glorious job. Daytop."

"Daytop?"

"Something like that. Some marvelous haven for drug addicts." Leah lit her cigarette and jammed the lighter back. "So, okay. I didn't say a word when she brought him home. After all, you know me. I don't have to justify myself to anybody. I teach them, I welcome the chance to reach out. But let me tell you, that day I came home and caught him with his hand in

75

her pocketbook and he tells me he's looking for a comb—disgusting in itself—and the next day she asks me could I let her have an advance on her allowance, let me tell you that day—"

"Tell me what?" Sandra said. "What happened? What did you do?"

"Do?" Leah said, smiling bitterly ahead at the sideswiping traffic. "What could I do? I told Morty to slip him a few bucks and be done with it. Though, my god, if Morty knew the real reason . . . I tell you, San, it's a friendship we can ill afford."

"Then you shouldn't try to buy him off, Leah. Lee," Sandra said.

"Buy him off?" Leah said, caught by the phrase. "Is that what I was trying to do subconsciously, do you think? Actually, what I thought I had in mind was that if he maybe had some small sense of financial security. . . ." She looked around for a moment and then shook her head, fixing her eyes on the road again. "No. No, I'm sure I didn't mean afford in the literal sense. Though maybe you can tell me why it's okay in our modern society for a man like Morty to work himself into a coronary supporting a wife and two kids during the best years of his life, and then along comes this young piece of dreck and thinks just because he's black—"

Leah caught herself and looked puzzled, as if she had just opened the wrong faucet and let out a gush of rusty water. "But it's not the money. I don't *care* about the money," she said. "It's just that—well, you can hate me for saying it if you want to, but it happens to make me physically sick to see the two of them together. It's the truth. I mean it. Physically, literally sick. Nauseous. Like morning sickness. Daytop. Treetop is more like it. When I see that hand on her neck, and she smiles, I tell you it's all I can do not to run to the toilet and puke."

The roast chicken and carrot tsimmes rose up again like brown bile. Unfortunately, Leah had always had a terrible talent for disseminating digestive disorders all around her. "Wake up! Wake up! Leah's baby has diarrhea!" their mother

76

used to cry that first summer Sandra was home from college. Still, granted Leah's obvious prejudices, how could anything your own child did revolt you so? Could Becky ever revolt her? Never.

"It's making me hate them," Leah said. "That's the worst of it. I don't want to hate them. I'm a good teacher. I don't want to come home and cry every day. . . . '*Shee-it, Miz Schwartz, fuck you.*'. . . They bring them in on the bus. They shit in the hall, god forbid you should mention it. You call up a parent to complain, you figure you'll be knifed to death before you get home. And did anybody help us, tell us how to deal with the situation? Never. And *still* I try. I bring in study aids, Cuisenaire rods, tinker toys, I stay up till midnight making lesson plans, games, and at the end of three hours, a hand shoots up and says, '*Miz Schwartz, what do dat* x *mean?*' You could die. . . . Then you and your friends run to Ocean Hill."

"*I* didn't run to Ocean Hill," Sandra said, and Leah said, okay, she was sorry. Still, it was awful and ironic that the child who was truly repulsive, her skinny, pimpled and perpetual Bar Mitzvah boy, Barry, was the child Leah adored. "C'mere, genius," she would say, laughing, and up to the age of eleven at least, Barry would obediently climb up on her lap and lavish her with hugs and kisses so that even good old Grandma Wolfe, who practically wept if you even said "mother of pearl," would turn to Sandra and say, "He's meshugah, or what?" Whereas poor overweight Janice had never had a chance with Leah, who blamed her for everything, from the endless postpartum depression to her domestic servitude to Morty, sent her to Hunter High School, where she didn't want to go, rummaged through her mail, listened in on her phone calls, peered at her good-night kisses through the peephole in the front door, questioned her innocently bloodstained underpants. "Mommy, it's my *period*." How could Leah be so fascinated with psychology and fail to see the stuff operating right under her nose? And of course, poor Janice, who had been a charming little girl, had become as awful as Leah thought she was from the beginning, maybe worse. A silly obnoxious show-off, overweight, clumsy, with dirty blond hair, shiny green mascara anointing the bulging lids under her myopic eyeglasses, a long suspicious white nose. It was rather moving that the poor child had volunteered her services at Daytop, or wherever it was, or for that matter found any admirer at all.

"Look, Leah," Sandra said, "don't think I'm trying to minimize your feelings, because I'm not. But in these things it's terribly important to distinguish between what's real and what you've brought to the situation."

"You think I made it all up?"

"No, of course I don't. I only said that you have to be very careful to distinguish between—"

"I understand," Leah said, patting Sandra's hand consolingly. "I'm sorry I spoiled it for you, baby. I know how fond you are of her. I won't do it anymore."

Spoiled what? Wouldn't do what anymore? What was Leah talking about? And how had Sandra suddenly become to her the kid sister again, who needed to be coddled, shielded from life? The transition was not only too swift, it was bewildering. Also, damn it, suddenly she wanted to hear much more about her overweight niece and the black boyfriend; and also just as suddenly knew that Leah would never tell her, not even if she asked, particularly if she asked. Leah glanced up at the rearview mirror and then out over her shoulder through the window. They went skimming off the great white bridge over blue water, and then slowed down, passing a series of dreary tan avenue blocks, looking for a subway station where Sandra could be let off. How strange. How somehow unfair that their time together, seemingly limitless when Morty dropped her off at the house that morning had suddenly come to such an abrupt end. No, there ought surely to have been some little warning signal, a coda, some little sign of tapering off. Otherwise, really, parting was what the French said it was, a little

78

death, which came upon you in the middle of a story, in the midst of some trivial preoccupation that you had been meaning at any minute to put aside. Or, if the metaphor of death were exaggerated, and perhaps she had been overimpressed by its being a translation from the French, then what it really reminded her of was one of Ed Gaskell's parties. Because there you would be, with the person you most wanted to see safely in view, and hours and hours ahead of you to spend like money in the bank, maybe even to squander, time to talk, time to grow weary of talking, time for long good-byes. And then suddenly it was all over, and you were caught in the streams and eddies of people leaving, and you would never have gotten around to it, whatever it was.

Leah had already pulled up to the curb, and reached across Sandra to press down on the inner door handle—she's trying to get rid of me! Sandra thought—though they continued to sit there for a few more minutes and promise to call each other soon. Actually, in the time this took, Leah could almost have managed to give Sandra a lift all the rest of the way home. It was dreadfully hot and sticky in the city, and the buildings looked beige and broken in the still broad daylight. Halfway down the block, some Puerto Rican children had opened a fire hydrant and were stomping about in the gushing water in their unlaced sneakers, barefeet, slickly clinging pants, crying "Mira! Mira!" at each other's wetness. Really, it wouldn't exactly have killed Leah to. . . . But no, it was almost the rush hour. Why should poor Leah buck traffic, arrive home nervous and sweaty-fingered to a husband who would be furiously awaiting his late dinner? Squat Morty was awful in his rage, no longer the golfer but a handball player. And all for the sake of what? A sister. Of course, if it were *my* car, Sandra thought, and got out.

An old IRT station rattled and vibrated below to the rush of some mysterious incoming or outgoing train. There was no cab in sight. Which meant that she would not only have to take the dreaded subway home, but sit there carrying a plastic bag with a wet bathing suit wrapped in a purloined hotel towel. Was it so easy for old lives to claim you?

"Listen, you'll never guess what happened to me the other day." Sandra laughed, turning back. "Hershel Meyers—the one who wrote *Wait at the Circus?*—socked me in a restaurant."

"Oh, my god," Leah said, usually fascinated by tales of Sandra's literary friends, grateful for any tidbit—like Starkstein, Sandra thought unwillingly—but today a bit too dutifully shocked, more concerned with the dangling traffic signal that was about to change.

"Actually, it was an accident," Sandra said. "To tell you the truth, it's his wife who really scares me. The new one. Part Indian, Hershel claims, American Indian. But, anyway, a raging dyke."

"The people you know," Leah said, laughing and shuddering dutifully, and also swiveling her head around to oncoming traffic.

"Listen," Sandra said, "I'll probably have to be having a few people in soon. Not a real party. Just a few people. Would you and Morty like to come?"

"Us? Oh, sure, we'd love to." The blue convertible with the closed top began to inch away from the curb.

"Hey, Leah," Sandra called out. "I love you!"

Leah looked back at her out of the window. "Why, I love you too, pussycat," Leah said.

It was strange that there were no messages. She had been so certain it would be a day for them. But if there were, Orvietta had not deigned to take any, and was, as usual, in a very bad mood. "No, there wasn't none, Mrs. Uh—" After two years she still had trouble remembering the name. She was working by the sink, fat, black and imperious, with a wigful of blond dynel curls that stayed stiff and motionless even when Orvietta took

80

a sponge and cleanser and rubbed furiously at a brown stain in the porcelain that had been there for months but that she was now determined to wipe out. Little chunks of plaster had fallen onto the burners of the stove from a cracked patch of kitchen ceiling, but these she ignored.

"You're positive about the messages?" Sandra said in an absurdly plaintive voice, and when Orvietta gave her a dull look of smoldering discontent, walked off to a rattle of pots and pans, the fearful sound of a violated washing machine chugging its heart out. It was really funny now to remember that when she first hired Orvietta she had assumed with a delicious little thrill of guilt that she was getting a real Southern Mammy. She could still see Orvietta at the interview, holding the card from the agency, plump, kindly, capable, with a nice respectable pot of a hat on her head, the broad rest of her perched on the edge of the sofa where Sandra had democratically urged her to sit down. That was on a Friday. On Monday the hat came off and the blond dynel wig appeared, plus a set of scratchy silver bangle bracelets that Orvietta insisted on wearing at all times, with particular relish when she was rubbing and polishing the rosewood table in the dining room. Obviously it had been an impossible dream to begin with. (She tried not even to think of Vaughn Cranshaw.) And not that Dickie had ever even remotely understood the problem. How could he? Wilma in her Central Park West eyrie with the little matching wooden salad bowls and the grand piano in the living room had always simply had a maid. Dickie didn't know about schvartzehs and following them around the house in carpet slippers and cleaning up before and after. Maybe she was still too much under the spell of Leah. Nevertheless, it was upsetting that all that remained of that first interview was a nagging sense that Orvietta was concealing something: a note, a telephone call, a love letter from the world.

Dickie wasn't home yet, which meant he was probably having a drink with an author. The apartment looked too big, too white, too sparsely furnished without him, the bamboo tree in its tub by the window dry and untended. Actually, she suspected Orvietta of emptying slops into it, but every once in a while Dickie sweetly and carefully plucked off a leaf or two, watered the thing, and it perked up. It was a curious switch of perspective. When she was little and came back to the Bronx after a couple of weeks' vacation in the Catskills, she had always burst into tears the minute she stepped foot in the apartment, it all looked so cramped and cluttered up with furniture and knickknacks. The pouffed-up green satin sofa and the tasseled portieres, and the snake plants on the windowsills, and the china domino ashtrays from the Five and Ten, and the upright piano her father had gotten at an unrefusable bargain price from one of his many business connections and which poor Leah had to take lessons on, though she really wanted to play the violin. Now it was the space, the whiteness and emptiness that depressed her, the fireplace whose natural brick she had restored but which was functionally still a fake. "Sasha looks sad," Hershel had said that night at the party and Dickie had said no without even bothering to look around. She went on into the bathroom, hung her wet bathing suit on the towel rack, debated with herself a moment, hung the purloined Hotel Waldbaum towel next to it, tried not to think about enemas, and went to look for Becky. She was in her room playing with Daniel Fruchtman, who was staying to dinner again, a fact which she oughtn't to have resented but did, vaguely, especially since she knew Stella could have Becky to dinner five nights in a row and not even know the difference. The children were wet and busy at Becky's bathroom sink, filling a plastic Baggie with water.

"You ought to put that goldfish back in its tank," Sandra said.

"It's an experiment," Daniel explained, frail and blond, about a head shorter than Becky. It was always a bit startling to see them together. She had so vividly imagined when she

82

was pregnant that she would have a little Oliver Twist, a skinny delicate dreamer, who had to wear eyeglasses early, and would play chess and the violin. But that was Daniel; of all people Stella had had him. Beside him, Becky stood peasantlike and stolid with a head of thick reddish-gold hair, like Aunt Rose's before she had yielded to a complete henna job.

"Look what Grandma sent you, sweetheart," Sandra said, holding out the Pete Seeger record, which suddenly looked very dated, very Popular Front. "Oh, boy," Becky said, tearing it from its wrappings and kissing it passionately before she put it down on the toilet seat. She was wearing her navy-blue middy blouse dress with the sailor collar, which ought to have been straight out of *Gigi* except that the front was dark wet and shiny where it bulged over the curve of Becky's stomach and that as usual her hair was caught in the hook at the back of her collar. Oh, well, Tante Leah wouldn't have been able to teach her how to eat an ortolan in any case.

"Listen, Mama," Becky said excitedly, "did you know that in laboratory experiments it was proved that the rat is the most cooperative of all rodents?"

"Really? . . . Orvietta wants to know if you want mustard."

"A little bit," Becky said. "Not too much."

"You too, Danny?"

Danny said yes, thank you, interestedly trying out a fish puddle with his toe. The information about the rats had no doubt come from him, as had Becky's Table of Elements hanging on the wall. No, Stella had really had very little to do with him, even genetically. It was all Freddie. Though why she should feel sorry for him when he didn't feel sorry for himself, she didn't know. There was just something about him that gripped her heart. Like that time last Halloween when Stella had sent him down on the Broadway bus alone to go trick-or-treating in the building with Becky and there he had stood with his head wrapped in a towel, a long terry-cloth bathrobe with a chain belt around his middle and a silver kid gardenia in his lapel. "What are you, Daniel?" "A sheik." Oddly, Becky had gone as a nurse and carried her doctor's kit.

"Daniel wants to go to the pet shop," Becky said.

"No, darling, it's too late."

"I'll take her," Daniel said.

"Don't be silly."

"Daniel feels you treat me like an infant," Becky said, pulling at the crotch of her black tights, which had a hole the size of a silver dollar on the inside seam.

"Maybe he'll do better with his own children."

"That's not the point, Sandra," Daniel said patiently, turning off the faucets and carefully drying his hands on Becky's washcloth. "But you have to go everywhere with her, and my mother lets me go everywhere alone."

"Let's just say you're separate but equal," Sandra said.

"I don't get you."

"She's a girl and you're a boy."

"I don't consider her a girl," Daniel said.

Becky, who for a moment had looked excited and proud, caught Sandra's eye, and changed the subject. "I once had a splinter in my big toe for three days," Becky said.

"Okay," Danny said, "why do you think children have more splinters than grownups?"

"They walk around in their bare feet more," Becky said.

Daniel shook his head. "Wrong. They have thinner skin."

"I don't agree," Becky said.

"Well, then, why do they vaccinate babies? They vaccinated our baby."

"I don't care," Becky said.

"Do you realize," Daniel said to Sandra, "that one in ten thousand vaccinations fails to take?"

"So what?" Becky said, laughing wildly. "Life's a matter of taking chances." She marched out of the room, and Daniel followed her, tripping on the red checkered cuff of his jeans. At the door, he turned to Sandra with a sheepish smile and a

84

shrug. They had left the goldfish in the sink, frantic in the plastic bag bursting with water. Sandra poured it back into the tank on the windowsill to swim above a cloudy layer of colored pebbles. She was no good at goldfish, maybe having flushed too many down the toilet bowl when she was young, nor canaries, nor really pets of any kind, another heritage of a strictly Jewish past, though neither, for all her talk of rodents and science, was Becky much good either. "My science table," the sign on her windowsill said, again inspired by Danny, "please do not displace or remove any of these objects." Next to it, Becky had put an abalone shell and a colored picture of Dorothy Crowfoot Hodgkin. Also a lined index card on which she had carefully printed out the rules for a new club she and Daniel seemed to have formed that afternoon. "Becky Baxter is here to help *you*. She is to take special care in the things that cover the fields of science and literature. She is to be a good citizen. She will try hard in her schoolwork and in extra work. She will be kind to animals. She will try very hard to be a thinking citizen.

(please turn over)
Special rules
1. To warship God
2 To obey the Ten Commantments
3. To practice a musical instrument
4 Not to lie or break promices
5 To learn another langage
6 To try to get a penpal or other perso to write to
7 To think before saying
8 To be interested in *other subjects other* than club ones
    To be a good American"

On top of Becky's toy chest the latest issue of *Hindsight* lay half-buried by last year's Peanuts calendar and a box of flashcards for multiplication. There was a list of articles and contributors on the yellow cover . . . "New Currents in British Fiction—Adam Brill." Sandra picked it up, almost pressed it against her chest, shook her head, and carried it off to the

85

magazine rack in the living room. Leah would be terribly impressed with the child's intellectuality in having such a thing in her room in the first place, Stella would laugh and think she was square for taking it away. But it didn't matter. "Mama . . . Mama. . . ." Why was the word so sweet on Becky's lips and so bitter on her own? She suddenly saw herself as a little girl having a long heart-to-heart talk with her mother across a white kitchen table, just the two of them seated across from each other, the mother in a flowered apron cutting a black, pumpernickel bread across her chest and rubbing a slice with garlic before handing it over. But was it real, this dim and faded memory, or a scene from some Italian movie?

When the doorbell rang, she called out to Orvietta not to bother to answer, not that Orvietta would have dreamed of answering, and went to get it herself.

"Oh, hi, Norma," Sandra said. "What brings you here?"

"Richard asked me to leave this off in case he gets a chance to look it over in Washington. He tried to get you several times, but you weren't in."

"Washington?" Sandra said, taking the big manila envelope. "What's in Washington?"

"I don't know," Norma said, looking as if she did.

"Well, come in and sit down," Sandra said, "I'll get you a drink," and wondered why she was suddenly so downcast. After all, Dickie was away a great deal.

Norma entered cautiously, sniffing around on the threshold, a perfect model of Hunter College deportment, kinky pony-tail, overdeveloped calves, navy blue dress, meticulous enunciation and all, practically Leah in the depths of the Depression, except that Norma had gone to Smith, and not even on a scholarship. She had been working for Dickie for almost a year now, and Dickie had certainly been glad to get her, notwithstanding her dour homeliness, since all the other

86

secretaries had been gigglingly eager, first for the chance to break into publishing and then for the chance to break out of it and get married. Repeating that "Richard" had hoped to look over the manuscript, as usual calling Dickie by his full name and Sandra nothing at all, Norma perched on the edge of the sofa, like Orvietta at her interview, in a posture so insistently self-effacing that the long cushion rose up on either side of her dent.

"This is a very lovely apartment," Norma said, as she did every time.

"Well, of course most of the furniture's catch-as-catch-can," Sandra said, also as usual, and laughed. "But then, of course, one can't be in thrall to Bloomingdale's for every aspect of life, can one?" Norma nodded gravely, and Sandra's little social laugh died.

"That's a particularly lovely walnut dining table," Norma said, looking through the archway.

"Rosewood," Sandra said. "We bought it from Arthur Handel when he went to teach at Oxford."

"Arthur Handel?"

"The art historian. As you can see, he had excellent taste," Sandra said, and remembered that the last time they had discussed the furniture and the amusing second-handedness of it, using such phrases as "objets trouvés," with little side cracks about Bloomingdale's thrown in between, Norma from her depression in the sofa had suddenly begun to talk about her sex life. Not only talk but talk with amazing intimacy. Had Dickie ever been a part of it? Would he do Norma that favor, even as a one-shot affair, just to keep her? A mean idea maybe, but in so many ways dark, bony, unlovely Norma was more Dickie's type than herself, exactly the kind of woman Dickie had a weakness for, thought he owed something to, maybe because widow Wilma ostensibly demanded so little. Sandra looked down at the fat manila envelope with a certain thrill of possessive pride at the words "Katz ms" in Dickie's neat editor's handwriting, and offered Norma a drink.

"Rosewood," Norma said. "Yes, I'm sorry. My brother had a very similar table—before his wife broke it on the move to Connecticut."

"Yes, I think I remember your mentioning that," Sandra said, excusing herself to get them both a drink and ignoring the smoldering looks of Orvietta as she dished out hot dogs and carrot sticks in the dinette. What was she smoldering about this time? That she had forgotten to give her Dickie's message? That Dickie had tried to leave one in the first place? Becky, chewing on a roll, contentedly dropped crumbs on her front while Daniel craned his neck sedately to see the portable TV better. The galloping and thunder of cowboys followed Sandra back into the living room.

"We used to go over almost every day, my mother and I," Norma said, sipping a very strong Scotch and water. "Now we're lucky if we can get out there every other weekend."

"Out where?" Sandra said, wincing at a sudden crash of pot against pan in the kitchen.

"To Connecticut."

"Oh, yes, that's right. I forgot. To see your brother."

"Well, hardly my brother," Norma said, smiling. Would Dickie really have permitted himself—? "In fact, we always urge him and his wife to go on about their business when we come. We're really only interested in the child—children." She patted the dark kinky ridges on either side of her center part and smiled again. "I can tell from the sound that your daughter is allowed to watch television. So are my nephews. Constantly."

"Oh, well," Sandra said.

"It doesn't bother me so much about the younger child. But the older boy, Billy, does have intellectual capabilities that could be stunted by that sort of exposure. Not that my sister-in-law cares. She's never been able to cope with him in the first place. Quite frankly without my mother I doubt that she could ever have brought him up at all. Not to mention the baby."

88

"And your sister agrees with that?"

"Sister-in-law," Norma corrected her, taking another strong sip. "I suppose so. Though quite frankly she has very few ideas of her own, one way or the other. Nothing ever seems to seriously concern her. I mean, for example, this third so-called accidental pregnancy. You can imagine how shocked and horrified we were to hear of it. In fact, we told my brother so quite plainly. But would you believe it, my sister-in-law just never got around to an abortion? Can you imagine that? Through sheer inertia and carelessness, she's willing to deprive the second child of its childhood."

"I'm sorry, I seem to have missed something," Sandra said. "How will the second child be deprived of its childhood?"

"Well, for one thing," Norma said, "he won't be able to be aired twice a day any longer—this is already happening. And if he doesn't get out, how is he supposed to establish appropriate relationships with his little peers? Also, there'll be less than two years between him and the next one, which is certainly the minimally necessary interval between siblings."

The sun was going down behind the couch, leaving a darker, bonier, kinkier Norma in the shadows.

"And yet, with all of it," Norma said with another sip and a smile and a sigh, "it's not the second one I feel most sorry for. Isn't that funny? Billy's my boy. He always has been. I remember shortly after he was born, there was talk of my brother getting a divorce and coming to live with me, but I wouldn't hear of it. Because it would mean giving up custody of the baby. I remember—I had a lover at the time, the one I told you about?—I remember I used to look down into Billy's crib and think, if I had to be deprived of my lover or this baby, I would rather be deprived of my lover."

The thought that she had been deprived of them both crossed their minds and they were silent. Then the key turned in the lock and in a shaft of light from the hall, Dickie was home. Norma bounded to her feet, gave him a few messages about messages, and refused to have another drink.

"Let me know if there's anything I can do for you while Richard's away," Norma said to Sandra before she left.

"Oh, *Dickie*," Sandra said, kissing him as he casually shuffled through his mail on the hall table. He looked around, vaguely surprised by the kiss. She didn't blame him. It had been right out of suburbia, straight from the *Donna Reed Show,* whose re-runs Daniel and Becky watched avidly, imagining life outside of New York was like that. "What's up? I mean what's in Washington these days?"

"There's a big peace meeting."·

"Oh, christ, not more Publishers *for,*" Sandra said, watching Dickie push aside his mail, mostly unopened. Nothing interesting ever came for him at home anyway. Just pleas from the Save the Children Federation, the Wilderness Society, invitations from the Istituto Italiano di Cultura, whose list they had been put on years ago by Umberto Robertini and stayed on·though they never went to anything. It was always so disheartening to open the door and find it all lying there, left on the welcome mat by whichever Puerto Rican elevator man happened to be on duty. It was like picking up the phone on a dark rainy morning when Becky was at school and Dickie at work and hearing one of the mothers say hello at the other end.

"Do you really think it will do any good?" Sandra said.

"Well, it won't do any harm," Dickie said, laughing.

"Will Hershel be there?"

"Maybe." He headed on into the living room.

Yes, of course, she might have known. First the interviews on the death of fiction, then the talk of a magazine, which would never get off the ground, and now the great writer as political activist. Really, what had come over Hershel anyway? Didn't he realize it had all been done before, the speeches, the march on the Pentagon, the whole works? And

90

here was Dickie chasing after him, though of course Dickie would have denied it, explained that in an election year . . . that even after Vietnam, there was always Laos and Cambodia. . . .

"Hi, Papa!" Becky cried, running in from the dinette to wrap her arms around Dickie's waist. Daniel followed suit, and then stepped back, picking up his metal cowboy lunchbox and plaid briefcase and explaining to no one in particular that he would probably have to be going home now. She walked him to the elevator, waiting until he was safely on his way down. When she came back, the scene in the living room was vaguely irritating, Becky on Dickie's lap, Dickie ruffling Becky's hair, fondling her in the few minutes before he got up, had a quick dinner, then threw a few things into his attaché case so he could fly off to pursue that fool. All in the name of peace. In fact, if it came right down to it, she didn't like Becky calling Dickie "Papa" either. The name didn't suit. He was too young, too blond, too American-looking. Becky had just picked it up from a precocious reading of *Little Women.*

In the kitchen, where she went to get herself some ice for another drink—Dickie hardly ever drank at home anymore on account of all those lunches—she found Orvietta glowering even more fiercely than usual as she scraped the hot dog plates. She spoke so rarely that when, as now, she did, there was a hysterical break to her voice.

"Why did you ask me to keep an eye on them that time?" she demanded. "Did you have something special in mind?"

"Who?" Sandra said, though her heart beat a bit faster. "What?"

"Them children. The night you went to that party and the sitter was late."

"Oh, that," Sandra said. "No, they were only whispering so hard I thought maybe they were up to something."

"They was."

"What do you mean?"

"I never seen anything like it," Orvietta muttered angrily,

twisting her soapy sponge. "I taken care of many children in my life, but I never seen anything like *that*."

"What are you talking about?" Sandra said.

"I didn't know if I ought to tell you. I was up all night, figuring should I or shouldn't I."

"Now look, Orvietta," Sandra said, "if there's anything wrong, it's my business to know about it."

Orvietta turned off the water and looked around suspiciously, hot tears in her eyes. "It wasn't *my* fault," she said.

"What wasn't?"

"I was in the bedroom doing my job. I was dusting up."

"Orvietta, I understand that."

". . . then all of a sudden I notice they been quiet a long time. Too quiet. So I goes into the living room, and then I looks through into the dining room and at first I don't see anything at all. I gits scared. Then I looks under the rosy wood table, and oh lawd, underneath it—"

"Go on, Orvietta."

She was laughing hysterically, holding on to the edge of the sink as the tears splashed and wriggled down her cheeks. It was easy to believe that Orvietta had not slept all night for thinking about whatever it was.

"—and I looks underneath the table, and there she is with her legs up, and she yelling, 'Come on, Danny, *git* on top a me! Git on top a me like I showed you!' . . . Oh, god, I been taking care of children before, but I never seen a chile like that, I never seen a little chile that young who—"

"Okay, Orvietta," Sandra said. "That's enough."

"I didn't know should I tell you," Orvietta said, looking fearful and ashamed. She took up the sponge, automatically sprinkling it with cleanser, and started to rub away again at the rust stain in the sink.

"All right. Now forget about it," Sandra said to Orvietta's agitated fat blue back. Orvietta nodded sullenly, still working away, though it was past the time to go home.

There was a peculiar sweet taste in Sandra's mouth, that she

92

knew no amount of brushing her teeth or spitting would make go away. It was like the time Hershel socked her. She tried to tell herself all the things that she would have told Leah. That the woman was a total hysteric. That children often imitated innocently what they had seen not so innocently. But none of it worked. Dickie was in the dining room bent over the rosewood table, hands in back pockets, studying the Katz ms. She had expected it to be a great untidy mess, pages spilling out of a crushed typing-paper box, but in fact they were all neatly held together in a shiny new black binder, nicely double-spaced with big wide margins, and the look of having been typed by a professional. Dickie made as if to release the text, changed his mind, and frowning thoughtfully, penciled in a line alongside a bottom paragraph and lightly scribbled a comment next to it.

"Are you going to buy it?" Sandra said.

"What? Yes, I guess so."

"You guess? Should you write in it if it's not all settled yet?"

"What's wrong with you tonight, Sandy?" Dickie said.

". . . Nothing . . . I went out to the hotel to see my mother."

"Oh, poor girl," Dickie said, and scribbled another quick comment on the next page.

She ought to have been grateful for his sympathy. But after all, what was so marvelous about Wilma?

"Itsy's in love with a schvartzer," Sandra said, not surprised when Dickie shook his head and laughed. Out of some weird obscure sense of loyalty, she decided not to mention the lop-sided Cezanne.

Becky was in her room, lying on her back on her red shag rug, holding up a tracing of Pegasus that the Barnard sitter, a classics major, had once done for her.

"She's nice, but awfully arty," Becky said. "Mama, can I have a date with Daniel tomorrow?"

"No."

"Why not?"

"You had one today."

"So what?"

"Becky, please don't argue with me."

"What are you sore about?" Becky said.

"I'm not sore," Sandra said. "I just think perhaps you've been—naughty."

"Naughty?" Becky said, laying aside the tracing, then suddenly scrambling to her feet. "Oh, I *told* him! I *told* him if we ate cookies in the dining room we'd get crumbs on the rug, but he refused to believe me. He said *his* mother wouldn't care and—"

Without Daniel's little face for contrast, Becky's, upturned, was smaller, sweeter, more innocent, but somehow not small and innocent enough. The sweet sick taste remained. "Mama, you *know* how boys are about cookies," Becky began earnestly as the telephone rang. Sandra went to answer it, but Dickie had already picked it up on the bedroom extension and was looking thoughtfully out the window, nodding, and saying "uh, uh" from time to time.

"Yes, well I'm damn sorry too. But when I spoke to Janice she said. . . ."

"For me?" Sandra said.

"What?" Dickie said, putting his hand over the mouthpiece. "No, it's Adam. I was supposed to have lunch with him tomorrow."

"Tell him to take me instead."

Dickie laughed. ". . . Sandy says to take her instead. . . . What? Yes, of course she means it. . . . Don't you?"

"Of course."

On the bed, Dickie's attaché case was already open, with a couple of English shirts, a few pairs of English lisle socks lying beside it. Were even Adam's clothes so English? She envied Dickie his capacity for traveling light. With all the trips to the Cape, to Europe, and the patina of sophistication, she still seemed to go everywhere steerage, acquiring bundles and bags, dropping packages all over the place.

94

"Okay," Dickie said. "One o'clock at La Rochefoucauld. I'll tell her. And get in touch when you come back."

He put down the phone, still laughing to himself a little.

"Don't go," Sandra said.

"What are you talking about?" Dickie said with vaguely amused irritation.

"I mean it's all such crap politically. We've been there before. You could even get arrested."

"I won't get arrested."

"Then don't fly. It's dangerous to fly in this weather."

"It's summer," Dickie said.

THREE............

It was so typical of Stella to live on the Upper West Side when she and Freddie could easily have afforded Sutton Place, the UN Plaza, the East Sixties. But no, Stella said, the East Side made her feel ten years older, as had Washington, D.C., when Freddie was a young lawyer working for the Justice Department, an experience which had also completely turned her off the Kennedys. And then, of course, nothing could compare with the suburbs of San Francisco where Stella had spent a great bohemian youth and embarked on her career as a sculptor, abandoning it all to marry Freddie Fruchtman from Brooklyn. So there they were, in a crumbling Gothic co-op on Riverside Drive with a doorman who sat outside on a car fender in his uniform cap and flowered sport shirt, chewing on a matchstick. "Come on, Becky," Sandra said, pulling her along by a sweaty hand. The day was already a shambles. She had forgotten that after this morning's assembly, school would be finished for the year and that Becky would have to be deposited some place at lunchtime. (It was out of the question to leave her with Orvietta. Should she tell Dickie about Orvietta? Should she tell Starkstein? Neither of them would understand why she hadn't already fired her.) With the prices they paid, it probably would have been cheaper to put the kids up at a Miami Beach hotel. Also, to make matters worse, the temperature had suddenly shot up to the nineties, wiping out all tender springtime possibilities with one hot sickening breath. It was hard to believe that only the other day between Starkstein and Morty Schwartz, she had subtly savored the joys of a civilized society across the park, observed well-groomed pedestrians, hotel cafés, frail green trees and poodles. Here on Broadway the freaks were out again, emerged from god knew what dank holes they had hidden in during the wintertime, winos, junkies male and female, some of indeterminate sex, all with scabby skin and drooping socks, dozing and reeling on subway islands, Puerto Rican whores resting their elbows on pillowed windowsills and shouting down into the streets, black homosexuals with peroxided hair in curlers sashaying arm in arm past the green-frosted Bar Mitzvah cakes in Cake Masters, dykes in slacks and boyish bobs strolling two by two like nuns, hysterical outdoor fruitmen, pregnant young women in flowered shifts and bare legs wheeling earlier children in strollers, a Greek pizzeria ("No, Becky, you're having lunch at Stella's"), Loews 83rd, still closed but smelling medicinal and air-conditioned. It was worse than Hong Kong. On Stella's corner, the residents of the Hotel Granada sat outside on green benches on the sidewalk, old, gnarled, with veiny legs spread apart, waiting, not even for death, just waiting. She thought of her mother on the lawn outside the Hotel Waldbaum in Spring Valley and tried not to think of her again.

Stella's lobby was the perfect set for *Don Giovanni*, with a stippled beige balcony and several medieval tapestries hanging from the walls. She gripped Becky's soft bare shoulders as the elevator began its shaky metallic ascent, shielding her in case of danger, as if they were on the way to the doctor, and

100

then hurried her down the hall when at last they had lurched to a stop. A Haitian maid, carrying the Fruchtman baby, answered the door, turning several complicated locks, and pointed down the long hallway toward the dining room where Stella sat alone in a negligee of Alençon lace, eating a late breakfast of coffee and a bagel.

"Darling!" Stella said, looking up with an air of delighted surprise, as if she had never said it was all right to come over in the first place. She was gorgeous and disheveled and it was hard to tell whether she had just had a fight with Freddie or slept with him.

"Are we too early?" Sandra said.

"Too early for what, darling?"

"I don't really know," Sandra said, shaking her head and laughing. "I just totally forgot school would be over today. Though my god, for the prices we pay, we could put these kids up at a Miami Beach hotel." Stella kept smiling expectantly, as if the joke hadn't yet occurred.

"Where's Danny?" Sandra said.

"Danny? In the park, I think. Would Becky like to go find him?"

"No."

"Darling, don't look so worried," Stella said, laughing. "Nothing will happen to her."

"I'm not worried," Sandra said.

Becky looked around reproachfully. So she would have to play with the baby, what was so terrible about that? Would she have liked staying with Orvietta better? The thought of that mean sullen face made her sick to her stomach all over again, and she knew that Dickie or no Dickie, Starkstein or no Starkstein, she would have to fire the woman one of these days. Oh, damn it. Why did everything get so fucked up whenever you asked Stella a favor? What was the big deal, anyway, in asking a friend to take care of your child for an hour or two? The joke was that if you *didn't* ask her, Stella could be incredibly generous on her own. Like the night last spring when both the husbands were away and Stella had treated her to dinner at La Rochefoucauld just for the hell of it, spending her last penny, literally—she had shaken out her change purse and along with the change two silver blazer buttons had fallen out onto the checkered tablecloth. But if you tried to arrange something on purpose, the whole thing fell apart, dissolved like a spun-sugar confection, and Stella just kept smiling and went completely non compos mentis. It was no wonder Freddie was always so exasperated.

As if on cue, the baby crawled into the room, diaper askew, followed, as Stella bent to frisk with it, by Freddie, who stood in the doorway scratching first his balding red head, then his chest in between the folds of an Indian blanket bathrobe.

"Freddie, what are you doing home?" Sandra said.

"I have a cold," Freddie said, taking a bite of Stella's bagel, then with a shake of his head, putting it back. "What do I want, Stella? Tea with lemon or milk?"

"How would I know?" Stella laughed, turning to Sandra. "Darling, how's the weather?"

"Awful. A scorcher. All the freaks are out."

"In Sausalito, it was always lovely. Always spring," Stella said, sighing and smiling. "I suppose we'll have to be making plans for the summer soon."

"They've already made plans," Freddie said. "Am I right?"

"Have you, darling?"

"Well, it's just a matter of a few weeks at the Cape," Sandra said, hating herself for sounding apologetic.

"I think I'd prefer Portugal actually," Stella said.

"You have to plan for that too," Freddie said. He watched Stella bend over the baby with the piece of bitten bagel. "What's Sandra having, coffee or tea?"

"I don't know. What would you like, darling?"

"Nothing," Sandra said. "Really. I have to be going soon." She looked at the Louis Quatorze ormolu clock on the mantelpiece, under the poster of Humphrey Bogart pointing a gun

102

at her. It was still early. She didn't want to be early. "Okay, coffee then."

"Get her some coffee, darling," Stella said.

"You get it for her," Freddie said. "I'm sick."

"Oh, darling, you're up."

"Not anymore, I'm not," Freddie said, quickly falling back on a large antique Spanish settee across the room covered in carved rust-colored velvet. It was another of Stella's many false stops and starts at decorating, like the Victorian plant stand with the potted palm and the lucite framed photograph of Stella with one breast exposed, and its opulence diminished him, made him look really sick, pale and doughy, too freshly made, a very far cry from the Fred Fruchtman who advised Gaskell Press on legal matters. It was all so silly. He and Stella had just married too young, that was all, and stayed the same age with each other as at their wedding. Nevertheless, suppose he were contagious? Suppose poor Becky—?

"Well, go ahead, Stella, get her the coffee."

"I don't want any," Sandra said.

"Oh, my, what a silly fuss," Stella said, getting up and trailing her lace negligee behind.

Freddie and Sandra smiled at each other uneasily, a little daunted at being left alone with each other, like a pair of in-laws required to make sexy small talk.

"Where's Dickie?" Freddie said.

"In Washington. Arts and Letters are protesting again. He'll be back tomorrow afternoon."

"I was in Denver at an international legal conference," Freddie said. "I just came back last night. I was exhausted. That's how I got this cold."

"I'm sorry," Sandra said.

"You're looking good, though. That's a nice dress."

"Is it?" Sandra looked down at herself quickly and guiltily, like a man suddenly asked the color of his necktie. "Actually, I'm just having lunch with one of Dickie's authors."

Freddie nodded and then the two of them fell silent until Stella came drifting back in with a small carafe of boiled water and a jar of Nescafé on a tray. Becky, who had been squatting on the floor in her pinafore, rolling a ball back and forth to the baby, looked up at Sandra wide-eyed. Even at her age Becky got the point. The whole argument had been about *instant* coffee. What was wrong with Stella, anyhow? Did being an artist preclude hospitality? My god, when Stella came to *her* house she always went straight to the refrigerator and took out anything she wanted, a piece of salami for herself, cheese and fruit for Daniel and the baby, who went around rubbing it all into the carpet anyway. And even then, she was always being asked to sit down, take it easy, have a napkin, handed spoons for the one the baby had just chewed on and thrown away. She realized now that she really ought to have let poor Becky have the pizza because the chances were that if Daniel ever did come back from the park and if Stella ever did remember about lunch, she would probably just airily tell the maid to fix them something amusing, a piece of pâté from yesterday's drinks, some Boursin aux fines herbes on stale melba toast. And of course the maid, whichever maid it was—Stella's turn-over was fantastic—would obediently make something amusing and then retreat back into the shadows, sometimes permanently.

"I guess I'd better be going," Sandra said, looking guiltily at Becky.

"No, wait a minute, darling," Stella said. "I want to show you this new piece I've been working on."

"Yeah," Freddie said, getting up and scratching his chest again. "Well, take it easy, kid."

"Thanks, Freddie, I will."

A hugged and reproachful Becky followed him down the hall a moment later, on her way to Danny's room with the baby trailing behind.

". . . I always think today will be different," Stella said.

"We all do."

104

Stella laughed. "Yes, but he was away for a week."

"I know, in Denver. He told me. You should have called and come over."

"I couldn't, darling. I was working on this huge new piece. Come. I'll show you." As they left the dining room there was a sudden great shattering and tinkle of glass from outside in the street and then a woman's voice screaming in Spanish, but Stella unperturbedly walked past the window without even stopping to look out. The studio was actually a back bedroom, dark and curiously out of place in the apartment. There was a great big hacked-up worktable in the middle of it, burners for melting wax, and blackened pots and tools on ledges and on the stained and littered floor. In the midst of it all, leaning against the wall under a dirty window, was a piece of black metal abstract sculpture which the two of them stared at blankly, Sandra because she wasn't sure what to say and Stella because she wasn't waiting for an answer anyway.

"I suppose now that I'm working bigger I'll have to get a studio outside somewhere," Stella said, absently fondling a headless female figure from an earlier period, stroking its buttocks, thumbing and tweaking a breast and nipple. "Though, of course, I *could* work in Danny's room if Freddie would let him move in with the baby. Or else the dining room would be perfect if Freddie didn't have such ridiculous feelings about eating in the kitchen. It's a marvelous kitchen actually. There are marvelous things you could do with it. Uncover the wooden beams in the ceiling. . . ." Stella cupped her hands outward. "Install a great black Franklin stove in the middle and bake great loaves of bread on top."

"There's no flue," Sandra said.

"What? Yes, that's true," Stella said, arresting her hands in midflight and then sighing and scraping a callus on the inside of one of her palms.

"Anyway, Scarlett, you'd probably do better with a studio outside. Those are not the hands of a lady."

"What, darling?"

105

"It's just a line from *Gone with the Wind* when she goes to borrow money from Rhett in jail."

"Yes?" Stella said, smiling blankly. Though she read a great deal, sometimes far into the night when Freddie was mean, it was impossible to think of Stella actually being influenced by a book. "Freddie used to love my calluses. Now I think he hates them."

From down the hall came the blue and white sound of TV, though it was hard to tell whether it was from Freddie's room or the maid's.

"Did he tell you why he was angry?" Stella said.

"No."

"He brought me this mink stole from Denver and I laughed and threw it at him."

"Why'd you throw it at him?"

"Can you imagine me in one?"

"No."

"The box was marvelous, actually. A great lavender thing, absolutely fin de siècle Paris."

"Can I see it?"

"What, the box? I don't know where it is. I hardly know where anything is anymore," Stella said, and quickly led the way back to the dining room as if she were afraid they would find it. The baby crawled out from under the Spanish settee, and laughing with delight, Stella lay down on the floor with it and began to teach it yoga. "Come, darling, let's salute the sun." Her lace negligee fell away. She was wearing sheer panty hose and a sanitary napkin which, though vaguely shocking, was a kind of contradiction in terms.

"Look, Stella, I'd really better—"

"He kept telling me how expensive it was," Stella said, turning her head sideways. "He was furious because I didn't care what it cost."

"How much does one cost?" Sandra said, surprised to be asking Stella instead of Leah.

"How would I know?" Stella said. "My god, when we were

106

first married we didn't even have a sou, and I couldn't have cared less. Just so long as the work went well and Freddie had time for his novel."

"But Freddie doesn't want to write a novel anymore."

"Invitations to lecture, teach, he throws them all away. I take them out of the wastepaper basket and cry."

"Stella, have you ever thought seriously of getting a divorce?"

Freddie poked his head through the doorway. "Listen, I'm taking a nap now. If the office calls, would you take a message and say I'll call back? . . . What's the matter, am I asking too much?"

"Of course not," Stella said. "But I won't be here much longer. I'm going to see *Persona* at the New Yorker with Gertrude Dienst."

Persona? The New Yorker? Gertrude Dienst? But what about Becky? Hadn't she promised to take care of Becky for a few hours? Where was Becky anyway?

"Is something the matter?" Stella asked the two of them, smiling from one to the other.

"No," Sandra said, and Freddie said, "Forget it."

"All right."

"One of the servants will take care of it," Freddie said.

"What servants?" Stella laughed. "We only have Hattie. And George, I suppose, but he's only here for dinner parties."

"It felt like more. Listen, why don't you give Hattie that mink thing? As a reward for freeing you from drudgery or something."

"Maybe I will."

"I mean, what the hell. You don't intend to wear the damn thing, do you?"

"Can you imagine me in one?" Stella said.

"I mean, what the hell difference does it make what it cost?"

"Money, money, *money*," Stella said, inhaling deeply with a hand on her diaphragm, and then slithering into the cobra position. The maid came in for the carafe of plain boiled water, which nobody had seemed to want in the first place.

After the yellow heat of the streets, La Rochefoucauld was almost Caribbean, dark and slatted, a perfect setting for Tennessee Williams or Somerset Maugham, the potted flowers blood red in their niches, the lowered blinds throwing latticework shadows across the tablecloths, the interior all cool and deep, with the customers talking quietly, and even a hint of a mosquito-netted bedroom somewhere in the back with a slowly revolving ceiling fan. She had rushed out of Stella's place into a taxi, afraid she would be late, panicked in a traffic jam on Second Avenue, got out and walked fast, then slowed down for fear of being too early. But suppose Adam hadn't even come? Suppose he just thought Dickie was joking? Her eye sought and finally found him in an all-too-obvious place, Dickie's regular table in the far corner. He was standing up, plump and patient in his round black eyeglasses, publicly awaiting her approach. No, there, how lovely, Sandra thought, threading her way to him, he publicly and patiently awaits my approach, and then said, *"Adam—"* holding out both hands and waiting just a moment too long after Adam had shaken one of them and released it before she sat down.

"Have I kept you waiting?"

"No, not at all," Adam said.

"I'm sorry. I had to leave Becky at Stella Fruchtman's. I didn't remember that school would be out so soon and—though, for the money we pay per diem—"

Adam was smiling too politely. She caught herself in time.

"I hope I haven't forced you into this," Sandra said, which was exactly what she had promised herself all the way down not to say.

"Of course not," Adam said.

The waiter came by and asked if they wanted a drink and the two of them said yes, and then smiled at each other, and picked up and studied the menu, Adam in profile, silhouetted against the window, which meant that all during lunch half of him would be lost to her. Oh, god, I do love him, Sandra thought, loving him too actively and too pointlessly for the occasion, not quite knowing what to do with the fact of him in the flesh. It was like all those times she told Stanley Starkstein about, when she forgot about him for weeks and months on end, and then suddenly there he would be at one of Ed Gaskell's parties, talking to somebody in a crowded corner, or maybe fingering the book by the guest of honor, or looking quietly out the French window, and her eye would very calmly, oh so calmly, take him in as part of the scene, and she would congratulate herself on her calm, and then suddenly her heart would cry out, "Oh, Adam! Adam!"

"Oh, Adam," Adam mimicked her.

"Sorry," Sandra said, "I seem to be talking to myself like the rest of the nuts in my neighborhood." She took a sip of the sweet Cinzano that the waiter had just brought her, fighting the temptation to change it for a martini and get plastered like the last time. "Well, now that I've got you here, what's up, what's new?"

"New?" Adam said, looking aside from the menu.

She reminded herself that from the tax point of view Adam was just another author on Dickie's list and that, judging from the painful evidence of the table, Gaskell Press was probably picking up the tab for this particular pique-nique à deux too. It wasn't even that unusual. As Mrs. Baxter she had often lunched in this same corner with Dickie's authors over the years, Hershel, Vaughn Cranshaw, Ruby Cohen Mandel, to name just a few. Except that, just as at the parties when she had finished warning herself not to go near him, forget he was there, not to blow the accumulated cool of a whole autumn or spring, and inevitably ended by strolling with a falsely casual air straight to where he was, all her resolution dissolved now too. She wanted to show Adam off to everyone, even Adolphe who was flicking at a nearby empty table with a napkin. You see, you phony French maitre d'? You see, all of you? It's

Adam, he's with me. He's actually here. Adolphe twitched the tablecloth, shifted a glass and went off.

". . . I meant, how's the new book coming along?"

"Which new book?" Adam said, smiling.

"The one you were working on last time you were here."

"The Press is doing it in September," Adam said, registering real emotion for the first time. "Didn't Richard tell you?"

"Oh, yes, that's right. Of course he did. He's crazy about it. They all are." It was a lie, a Dickie-type lie. But dear god, even though Gaskell Press was paying, did Dickie's ghost have to lurk so forcibly between them? She wished now that she had read the section of Adam's book that had been printed in that issue of *Hindsight*. But she had put it aside in the middle, having lost track of at least three new currents in British fiction. Could you be in love with a man whose work bored you stiff? Evidently.

"Is that why you're here, to puff it?"

"My new book?" Adam said, laughing and pleased. "No, love, I'm much too small potatoes. I'm just traveling a bit, doing a piece for the *New Statesman.*"

"Take me with you," Sandra said.

"Where?"

"Wherever you're going."

Adam laughed again and lit a cigarette, forgetting the one that already smoldered in the ashtray. At Adolphe's suggestion, they ordered, she deliberately not answering in French, thinking how endearing it had once been, Adam's untidy chain-smoking, the ashes on the vest of his dark conservative English suits. She really ought to try to remember how conservative Adam actually was, how straitlaced and British, not only in dress and the round black medical service eyeglasses, and the straight black hair that kept falling over one ear, but also in manner, the pudgy drumming fingers, the tendency to be not so much expressionless as stare straight ahead. Actually, of course, feature by feature, Dickie was much more handsome, and much more charming too. Then why did

Adam magnetize her? Because Dickie was always Dickie, and Adam remote and inaccessible? Were remote people more to be valued than accessible ones? Oh, what did it matter? At the moment, there was only Adam beside her, roundish, infinitely dear with that sober face and those round sober black-rimmed eyeglasses.

"Adam, I really meant it before, you know," Sandra said. "This time I would go."

"No, you wouldn't."

"Take me with you and I'll prove it. We'll go to Chicago by train. There'll be lots of writers to interview in Chicago. Hershel. George Auerbach. We'll make love all night on the train."

"They've discontinued the run, love," Adam said.

"Only the name, not the run."

"Sandra," Adam said, turning to her, sober and miserable. "You know you don't mean any of this."

"But I *do*. I *do.*"

Okay, so maybe he was right. Maybe, to be realistic about it—but why?—an overnight trip to Chicago was a little out of the question. "But we could manage a day, Adam. A day in the country. I saw this marvelous ad in *The New Yorker* for an inn in Connecticut. And I know Stella would cover for us. She's such an idiot about these things she wouldn't even ask why. She didn't even ask why today. . . . Or maybe even just an afternoon. An afternoon at the Plaza. We could rent a suite. Wouldn't that be beautiful?"

Adam reached for another cigarette. She stubbed out the smoldering other two.

"Listen. It would be raining, and we'd look out at Bergdorf's and the fountain from our window, and it would be all glistening and gray. And we'd have roses on a marble coffee table and a gilded bed. Wouldn't that be beautiful? . . . Oh, Adam, darling, please, I'm not kidding. If you only knew how I dream about a few such hours. How it keeps me going."

"We can't," Adam said.

"Why not?"

Adam sipped his Scotch and looked around the room. And, in fact, what could he have said? Honor prevents? My wife's a cripple? . . . Or: Well, of course not exactly a cripple, just a little bit paralyzed on one side. . . . Or: Now, love, your husband's a brick, how can we betray him? . . . Great. Perfect. Only it hadn't prevented them the last time. And what had she been asking for after all? The moon? Only a few stolen hours, not even strictly stolen, for a purpose which—oh, how it hurt to remember—had been Adam's urgent idea once upon a time. He was now looking worriedly over at the row of attaché-case carrying young men in the banquettes across the way, one of them Aaron Lasch, and then at the next table which was now occupied by Carol Curtis and a client, then over at Adolphe at his station in front of the frosted glass partition that separated them from the bar. No, but surely she was misjudging him. Even Adam couldn't be that frightened of what people saw or thought they saw. She tried to remember what it had been like when the shoe was on the other foot and Adam was entreating her. No, not really entreating, one had to be fair—why? It was hardly Adam's style to do more than lightly suggest. But the train to Chicago, that had been Adam's idea. The Twentieth Century Limited. He had associated it with Dreiser, and on his first trip to the States, had wanted to take it. And the roses, the dark red roses. The dozen American Beauty roses he had once sent her from the florist shop at the Plaza, with thanks, after a dinner party. Dickie had laughed and explained it was an English habit this profusion of flowers for the hostess, and maybe it was.

"Actually, besides the fact of it not costing anything," Sandra said, looking around too, "I suppose La Rochefoucauld is the safest place for us also, isn't it? . . . I mean, we're practically two purloined letters hiding out in the open."

"Oh, Sandra," Adam said.

"Are you very sorry it had to be here? Were you secretly dying to take me some place wildly extravagant? Le Pavillon, the Colony, if they were still open?" Mean joke. All visiting Englishmen, not only dear Adam, were incredible spongers.

"Why do such things as restaurants *matter* to you so much?" Adam said bitterly.

"Because I'm *lonely* all day."

It was the first intimate thing she had said to him and she regretted it immediately. She felt that she had lost face, and that Adam was no longer interested. The joke was that she was no longer interested either. They were just two more quasi-intimate strangers having their lunch at La Rochefoucauld. She picked at the shrimp she had ordered at Adolphe's suggestion. "Shrimp scampi," whatever that redundancy meant, aside from the fact of five or six shellfish, rubbery and cold on a metal baking dish, saturated in oil and garlic, and with no vegetable or potato on the side, the small salad a dollar extra. It depressed and surprised her to be thinking about food prices with Adam sitting there beside her. She stole another look at him, eating his liver heartily, and already felt herself losing her calm detachment of the moment before.

"Look, Adam, I'm sorry. It's wrong of me to pretend that it was ever much of an affair. I know perfectly well one swallow doesn't make a summer."

"Three swallows," Adam said, trying a smile.

"Three swallows." She nodded. ". . . three swallows on three afternoons two years ago. Even the time of day is ambiguous."

"Ah, well," Adam said, eating again, talking in between bites, "that's always the enemy, isn't it? Ambiguity."

"Then you're *my* enemy," Sandra said. "You're all my enemies put together. I never know how I stand with you. I never know who you are. Who *are* you, Adam? Where *are* you, Adam? Adam, do you *love* me at all?"

Adam kept smiling and shoveling food from knife to fork to

mouth, but the smile was now as forced and constrained as when his little boy Morgan was playing the fool in front of company.

"Why did you even come today?" Sandra said. "I mean aside from the fact of Dickie making you? Really, I can assure you your pub date would have been safe and sound anyway. Or is your interest in Dickie perhaps other?"

More smiling silence, but a distinct flicker of pain. And, in fact, what could poor Adam do but suffer her pinpricks? It was the price of coming on as an English gentleman.

"Okay, Adam. That was lousy. I'm sorry."

"Look, love," Adam said, finally putting down his fork and turning to her perhaps more gently than she deserved. "Truly, you really would only back out again at the last minute."

"No, not this time. Oh, Adam, I'm thirty-six! The same age as Christ when he died."

"Thirty-three." Adam sighed, reaching for her hand under the table. She lowered her head. The waiter came back and forth, brushing crumbs, clearing away, bringing coffee. Between times they remained holding hands in silence on the velvet banquette, hidden from view by the stiff white under-tablecloth. From a cake stand of petits fours, Adam took a sugary pink heart and put it on her plate. She left it there because, of course, it was impossible to eat it up. Adam's hand in hers was getting sweaty. He bit his fingernails. He's so young, she thought, in a sudden access of pity, what do I want from him? And then, since Adam had already explained that he had a three thirty appointment at Gaskell Press, having to do with quotes from his book jacket, it was time to go.

Outside, astonishingly, there was no bright Caribbean sun. It was a typically gray, humid, New York day. They walked across Forty-eighth Street in the general direction of Gaskell Press, side by side, bumping into and hindering each other. A light rain began to spatter the sidewalk. Unexpectedly, Adam wrapped his mackintosh around both of them, and they were enclosed in a dark cavey warmth while the rest of the city rose

114

like wet slate above them. She wanted to wrap her arms around Adam's waist and did not dare. She wanted to cling to his jacket, look up at his face, and did not dare that either. But he was there. Umberto Robertini, walking toward them, did a little bit of a double take, and smiled. Adam stiffened, but she could sense that he was smiling back. Please, let us be suspended this way forever, the two of us, wrapped together, lightly touching. But the Gaskell Press building was just up ahead. Adam undraped his raincoat, kissed her, and was gone.

It was a kiss that any of Dickie's authors might have given her. But I'll see him again, Sandra thought. I'll be walking along the street, and I'll look around, and he'll *be* there.

FOUR ••••••••••••••••••••••••••

The small ballroom of the Adams Plaza was littered and noisy. On the blackboard behind Herb Fingerwald, who was up at the mike asking those who wished to get arrested to please sign the list that was being passed around, there was a big blown-up floor plan of the Capitol, with the Rotunda circled in red. Other large blowups, photographs, posters, were tacked on the brocaded walls, some with slogans, some with pictures of maimed and screaming Vietnamese mothers carrying burned children, though when the pacifist lady with the gray braids wanted to show slides of even gorier atrocities, she had been voted down. "My god," Angelica Ford cried, "would we *be* here if we didn't already know that?" To which the hippie type on the floor had strummed an assenting chord on his guitar. It had been like that all day yesterday, all this morning. He hadn't expected that in the end so many would be so anxious to get arrested, or that of all people Herb Fingerwald and his simpering Muriel with the blond bangs and pageboy would be the ringleaders of the group, prac-

119

tically panting into the mike in their own eagerness to go to jail, referring to themselves (humorously) as a pair of virgins ready to get laid at last. Okay, so Sandra had been right. Nevertheless, he still wasn't sorry he had come. People had to do what they could, damn it, even if they failed, even if they made themselves ridiculous.

Sighing, anyway, and also rubbing his shoulder, Dickie got up to help himself to some coffee and Danish over at the sideboard, dropping a quarter into the slotted cardboard container for voluntary contributions. Room service had never answered his call for breakfast—there seemed to be several other conventions going on at the same time—in addition to which he had awakened with this painful stiffness on the left side. (Bursitis? He had never before thought of himself in connection with a disease of middle age.) And before that, there had been the business of being stranded last night at dinnertime with the young guitar strummer in his denim shirt and beads and ponytail, who had turned out to be an associate professor at Yale, and tried for two hours to interest him in a revealing new interpretation of the actual relationship between Thoreau and Ralph Waldo Emerson.

"Ah, good morning," George Auerbach said, waiting his turn at the coffee urn.

"George!" Dickie said, not particularly surprised when his belated attempt at enthusiasm fell flat. He ought to have called after him last night in the lobby. He had realized at the time that George must have seen him. But the man was so dreadfully surly, and he had been exhausted from the dinner and dying to get to bed.

"I didn't realize this sort of thing was your style," Dickie said.

"It isn't. I came in for the coffee. I'm in an ALA symposium on the Poet as Profit across the hall."

"Well, I'm glad to hear that." Dickie laughed. "I mean, just in terms of college sales alone. . . . Oh." George nodded wryly and started out again with his steaming styrofoam cup. "Listen, let's get together on those graffiti soon, shall we?" Dickie called after him and, receiving no answer, went to take another hard red and gilt folding chair amid a growing audience whom red and gilt did not exactly suit: more and more protesters filing in, some to sit, some to stand against the wall, more folk singers, Quakers, Methodist churchmen, the wife of William Kohlrobi, all spruced up in gray-streaked hair, printed silk and pearls, who kept exclaiming: "But I thought the whole *idea* was to be well-groomed!" There was even short Bruce Bamberg, smug and smiling, who after years arguing Marxism in the City College cafeteria, had gone to England where he worked for a CIA-sponsored magazine for six months and returned with an Oxford accent and conversation in which words like "flat" and "lorry" abounded. ("Here," Sandra always said, holding out the telephone, "it's either Bruce Bamberg or the Duke of Edinburgh.") And in fact, what was Bruce, now with some third-rate book club, doing here? Surely not spying for the government again? There was also Percy Ridge, breathing fire in his dashiki, who had already called them all motherfuckers ten times around, to great applause from some corners, and several young editors like their own Penelope Fleece, who at Gaskell Press meetings kept leaping up to suggest that they get Hershel Meyers to write a book about it—whatever it was, moonshot, political convention, death of the Pope, anything. No, it was not exactly a distinguished group. And where was Hershel? He had been featured in all the announcements, but there was still no sign of him, though it was almost twelve and the final decision of the meeting was to march on the Rotunda (*not* the Pentagon) at three. Even Talbot Weaver didn't seem to know where Hershel was, and Talbot had evidently followed him all the way in from Chicago on the off-chance that they might spend a night in jail together. Talbot, had just seized the mike for the third or fourth time, exhorting them to get with it, quoting long passages from his novel *Wait at the Hippodrome*. (Unpublished novel. Gaskell Press alone had turned it down

121

at least three times, though Hershel kept recommending it.) "My god, how could even Hershel not puke at being followed around by that untalented sycophant?" Sandra said. But she had become so embittered lately, so passionately disillusioned with everything she would once have been enchanted by, that there was no point even trying to discuss some things with her. Like her hatred of Gertrude Dienst or of Erika Hauptmann, and of course of Ralph Gorella who, true, was getting more and more repulsive, especially now that the whole intellectual mystique of the thirties was vanishing, but who was still no ape, for god's sake. Looking around, Dickie rubbed his shoulder again, wondering if he ought to run in and take a quick look at George Auerbach's panel and decided it wasn't worth it. In fact, he wasn't even sure at this point whether he wanted to stay for the march on the Rotunda at all. Maybe it would just make more sense to make a break for it at lunchtime and catch an early shuttle. Meanwhile, as Talbot droned on, he opened his New York *Times* discreetly and turned to the book page, folding it lengthwise as he did on his way downtown in the subway each morning. The ad for Ruby Cohen Mandel's *The Devastated Decimal and Other Modern Dilemmas* looked very good, small but distinguished, with an ultra-distinguished quote from William Kohlrobi, though privately William had laughed and boasted to him and Ed that he had failed math at Columbia, as if it were still another intellectual feather in his cap, made him comparable to Einstein. Still, Dickie had known the time was ripe for Ruby, that after the pitch and fever of ecology and sex manuals, people want to rest their brains with the cool abstract puzzles of math. Maybe if Angelica Ford did review it for *Commentary*, they'd get the Jewish vote. He turned over to the amusement page where there was an extremely favorable review of Gert Dienst's two new experimental films, now showing at the Bleecker Street. ". . . *Siegfried and Sassoon,* though oft and brilliantly unintelligible on account of having been made and dubbed in northern Denmark. . . . " He looked up for a

122

moment. Talbot Weaver had been shoved aside by Herb Fingerwald, who wanted to emphasize again that being arrested was a matter if individual conscience and that those who didn't want to be arrested when they got to the Capitol, should, however, please sign the petition in support of those who did, and then the lady with the gray braids announced once more that she would be distributing free dimes in the chartered buses and that women should please not wear jewelry and to please put their money in their shoes. In the row behind him, Bruce Bamberg was explaining to somebody that hell, there was nothing new about any of this, that it was all in Scott Nearing, always had been, and up front Percy Ridge had grabbed the mike again and was exhorting them all about Standard Oil, the Third World, Zionist Lackeys. (Aaron Lasch applauded lustily, while several of the churchmen shook their heads and slipped out.) Then Hershel Meyers came in. In fact, he came in so quietly and shyly that hardly anybody even noticed him at first, and like the least likely candidate in a hotly contested election, smiled and took a seat a little behind and to the side of Herb's blackboard. Dickie put down his newspaper. It was that shyness he always forgot, what used to make Ralph laugh and call Hersh a hayseed, but was actually just a childlike, almost terrible eagerness to please. And in the old days, of course, Kohlrobi, Gorella, any heavyweight intellectual, had only to breathe on Hershel to make him fall down. But even now, with all the toughness and swagger, the fake machismo, there was still something very vulnerable and appealing in that figure sitting there in his clean white T-shirt and jeans, hands patient on his knees, yachting cap pushed back off his unruly hair, something that though Hersh had stolen books to pay his way through the University of Chicago (and even then never managed to scrape up enough money to graduate) reminded Dickie of his own days at Harvard, made him want to relive them again in a crazy way, like those kids in the yard at Adam's house that May when he had gone up to try to get the Leverett kid's

123

memoirs, and seen them hanging out the windows, playing rock loud enough to shatter eardrums, zapping each other with frisbees. Angelica Ford had leaped to her feet for some angry irrelevant rebuttal just as the paper for those who did want to get arrested reached the end of Dickie's row. He watched it being passed from hand to hand and then looked up again at Hershel.

"Oh, here's Hersh," Herb Fingerwald said, glancing over his shoulder and managing to get Angelica to sit down and contain herself. "We're about to break for lunch. Anything you want to say?"

Hershel got up slowly and gripped the mike, staring out at them benignly but dangerously, bulking his lips over his teeth like a fighter manipulating a mouthpiece just before the bell. Dickie took and held onto the list of potential arrestees.

"Sure," Hersh said, laughing, "let's all take a leak."

Afterwards people clustered around him, as they always did, minor editors, Talbut Weaver ardently working all sides, a couple of remaining churchmen, the Quakers, the lady with the gray braids, who diffidently held out a paperback edition of *Wait at the Circus* for him to sign, Bruce Bamberg smiling with his usual air of pleased superiority, even Percy Ridge, though he stood a bit apart, forlorn and angry, until Hershel chummily draped an arm over his shoulder. Percy suffered it stiffly, clearly unable to understand this whitey's camaraderie when he had included them all among the motherfuckers.

"Oh, hi, there, Ricardo," Hershel said. "I understand you were trying to reach me last night."

"And the night before. But that's okay," Dickie said. "I've reached you now."

"Yeah. Maybe tonight they'll even put us in the same cell."

"I'm afraid I can't go to jail."

"No? Why not?"

124

"Well, somebody has to mind the store," Dickie said, laughing. "Listen, how about lunch?"

"There's no time for lunch," Hershel said, greeting the young guitar player with a friendly sock in the solar plexus.

"We'll have a quick one."

Hershel sighed and looked around, then removed his arm from around poor Percy, who looked even more surprised by his rejection than his acceptance. Was there another Vaughn Cranshaw in the making? "Okay," Hershel said, "come on upstairs. We'll have something sent up."

"I can take you to a restaurant."

"No, there's no time for that. Anyway, you have to see the kid."

"The kid?"

"Sure. Irma's here with the baby," Hershel said, pushing his yachting cap even farther back on his wild curls, then slinging his jacket over his shoulder and hanging onto it with one thumb. But to a captain is he a captain? Sandra would have said. Though why, Dickie wondered, had he been thinking all day about what Sandra would have thought? They rode up in the elevator in silence, in itself uneasy-making and unusual. Hershel, who all these years had had a thousand brilliant erratic theories about everything, stories, anecdotes, quotations, jokes he laughed at so hard that by the time he got to the end nobody could hear the punch line, Hershel had suddenly become as taciturn as Gregory Hennessy, his own hero in *Wait at the Circus,* that silent leader of safaris, reader of Conrad in deep jungle. Except of course that in the book Hennessy was tall, athletic, and Gentile, whereas in real life Hershel remained short, unathletic, and Jewish. They walked down the long carpeted hotel corridor. "Hello, hello?" Hershel called as they entered the living room of the suite, and stopped to order steak tartare from room service before he led Dickie into the dustless, newly bought sunshine of the bedroom, where Irma was bending over a rented crib, a cap-

125

tured savage in brown shorts that were badly creased in the
crotch, crying, "Fuckit, fuckit! This goddamn little cunt won't
stay still!"

"What's the matter, honey?" Hershel said soothingly. He
reminded her that she knew Dickie.

"She's rubbing shit all over the place!" Irma said, not caring
whether she knew Dickie or not.

"I told you we should have brought along Bessie."

"Screw Bessie."

"She's a registered practical nurse, honey."

"I don't care what she is. If I see your mother's fat knees
anywhere near me again, I'll puke."

"Okay, sweetheart, calm down," Hershel said, replacing her
at the cribside. Irma stepped back, breathing hard in the
creased shorts and nippled red jersey, as if she had just won a
drag race along the Potomac. Did she realize how dangerous
those words about Bessie had been or didn't she care? Not that
it really made any difference. No matter how Irma provoked
him, or failed to, Hershel would remain kind and tender up
until the moment he threw her out of the house. It was that
way with all his wives, and in a way it made sense, Dickie
supposed. (Not the violence, of course. Was it against Dottie's
chest Hershel had crushed out his cigarette butt on that last
night—or had he already stopped smoking?) Only that none of
the wives really existed until Hershel made them up and then
fell in love with his own creation, as usual. The hard part was
being one of his friends through it all, having to agree that, yes
indeed, the fat cow Winifred was the ultimate in earth
mothers, that poor rich moronic Dottie with the dark lipstick
and perpetual hair rollers was the quintessence of classical
beauty, and that now this dirty roughneck whore was a wild
untamed sex goddess. Doubly hard, because if you didn't see
it his way, Hershel looked at you with pained reproach, a Mafia
godfather about to give you the kiss of death, and you were
through. Only somebody like Talbot Weaver could stick with
Hershel for more than a year or two on a strictly nonprofes-

126

sional basis, and even he had been reduced to laying Dottie on the side, or was it Winifred?

"So what brings you here?" Irma said, across Hershel's bent back.

"Indochina."

"I meant up here."

"I wanted to see your baby."

"Sure," Irma said. "No two babies look alike." She retired to a chintzy maple chair in the corner and inspected a pimple on the inside of her thigh.

"Where's the bottle, honey?" Hershel asked, whipping off a diaper with a fast malodorous flourish and keeping his hand extended. Dickie took a step backward.

"What bottle?"

"*What* bottle?" Hershel laughed, finally straightening up with a fresh and neatly diapered baby in his arms. "How do you like that?" Hershel said, twisting his head and laughing some more as the baby started to pull the yachting cap down over his forehead. "Some mother. . . . No, no, honey, don't get sore. It's only natural in the beginning. . . ." Hershel rolled his eyes to indicate what else was only natural in the beginning. "Believe me," he said to Dickie, looking Irma over appraisingly, as he always did his wives, like a horse dealer, "this girl's other instincts are in great shape. Anyway, who says mothers are born? They're *made!*" Hershel laughed, again heartily, though in her corner Irma continued to ignore him and sulk over her pimple. Actually, Dickie felt sorry for her. She had so obviously never wanted a baby in the first place. The babies were always Hershel's idea, the little souvenirs of each marriage that he deposited with the world, leaving the world—and Bessie—to take care of them. In fact, it was even Bessie who had invited him and Sandra to the famous, infamous party, that famous, infamous night. "Hello?" she had said. "This is Mrs. Meyers, Hershel's mother."

"So now you know everything," Hershel said, looking at Irma in her corner and then unexpectedly handing the baby over to Dickie, who took it with surprise, returning its dubious one-eyed stare with one of his own.

"Know what?" Dickie said, laughing too, though the baby was breathing hot and moist down his neck. "You haven't even said a word about the new book yet."

"What word? What does the word mean with the world the way it is?" Hershel said, shoving his hand into the back of Irma's blouse and massaging her up and down. "Besides, I'm teaching a course in social thought two mornings a week at the university, did I tell you? And then I have to run back to take care of the kid—honey, don't get sore—and then Irma and I maybe drop a little acid. . . . Hey, watch it there, pal, I said acid, not the bambino."

Dickie took a tighter grip, though what he wanted to do was throw the damn kid back in Hershel's face. He was suddenly so damn tired, tired of playing nursemaid, literally, tired of all the sick and wretched megalomaniac authors, tired of all the years and years of literary and emotional blackmail, tired of swallowing so much goddamn shit. Suddenly and coincidentally, a warm, heavy bulge deposited itself in Dickie's hand where it supported the rubber pants. Yet, far from being repelled, he was strangely moved. Moved by the memory of Becky when she too was a little baby, warm and squirming in her blanket, and the incredibly delicate awkwardness of holding her, and the fear that he might forget himself and hold too tight. Funny that it should have escaped his mind until now, but the night Becky was born it was Hershel he had called first from the hospital telephone booth, called even before any of the parents, especially before the parents. And, yes, on the day Sandra's father died the first message that came was a telegram from Hershel—THINKING OF YOU WITH LOVE—HERSH AND DOTTIE—though even in her grief Sandra had been furious that Dottie's name was included. Dickie handed the baby over to Irma, who seemed surprised to get it, and followed Hershel into the hotel living room. There was a knock on the door, and the waiter wheeled in the room service

128

wagon, with the ingredients on it for the steak tartare.

"At home I do the cooking too." Hershel laughed, taking an egg from the saucer and holding it up to the light, like a toy he was particularly intrigued by. "My specialty's pasta."

"I know."

"That's right."

Dickie laughed. "Do you remember when you stayed with us on the Cape while you were finishing *Wait at the Circus?* I must have gained fifteen pounds those few weeks."

"Yes? I don't remember your exact weight," Hershel said, breaking the raw egg into a plateful of raw ground beef. He picked up the little dish of chopped onion and inhaled deeply, then dumped that in with the rest too, grinding up pepper, pausing occasionally to rub his nose with the back of his hand. The familiar gesture, the onion, the pepper grinder, the eager reach for the fork to mash it with, all suddenly reminded Dickie of the little kitchen in Cape Cod, and Hershel the guest, running around the wooden cottage with a rusty can of Ajax, wanting to do everything, cook, clean, scour. Once he had even ironed five of Dickie's long-sleeved shirts that Sandra had just brought back from the laundromat, pressing them beautifully, sleeves and cuffs first, collars held taut as Bessie had shown him when he was little, until Sandra finally got angry and told him to stop. But what had annoyed her so much? "It's so hard to remember what good friends we once were," Sandra was fond of saying now. But actually it was easy. Too easy. Hershel just didn't want it to be over, that was all, he couldn't bear for all the bets to be in. That was the reason for the silly wives, the megalomania. The reason that each time life knocked him down, he wouldn't go to his corner, but struggled up again, mitts out, asking for more.

"Hey, it's *me,*" Dickie said, smiling, "*Ricardo,*" using Hershel's name for him long before there ever was an Irma Balducci. "Tell me about the new book. Really."

"When is a book not a book?" Hershel said. ". . . When it's a mezzo?"

This time neither of them laughed.

"I saw *Wait at the Circus* when it was only half-finished too," Dickie said.

"Did you?"

"And it was in pretty lousy shape too."

"Was it?"

Dickie took a breath, wincing at the smell of the freshly cut onion. "So what I mean is, I could give you a pretty fair reading on this one too."

"Could you?"

"I think so."

"I don't," Hershel said. "But take it with you if you want to."

"You have it here?"

"Sure," Hershel said, cocking his head at a big manila envelope on the sofa. He pushed back the yachting cap and finished mixing the steak tartare, laughing when he saw Dickie's face and offering to order him a cheese sandwich. Dickie said it was okay, that he'd pick up something at the airport, and then they went in to say good-bye to Irma who was sulking over the crib where, miraculously, the baby had gone to sleep. Irma said she wanted to get arrested too, but Hershel chucked her gently under the chin and said no, but he'd be up for a minute before. Then he accompanied Dickie down in the elevator all the way to the lobby, where he handed him the manuscript at the last minute, just as Dickie was giving the bellman a quarter for the cab. There were a couple of chartered buses marked SIGHTSEEING parked down the block, and several of the group, foremost among them Talbot Weaver, were already climbing in.

As the SEAT BELT sign went off, Dickie reached under his seat for his attaché case and then changed his mind, opening the complimentary copy of the Washington *Post* and putting that aside also as the stewardess came down the aisle with her wagon, making change, giving and receiving credit cards and tickets. For some reason he kept thinking of the last few minutes before departure, the unceremonious scramble for the plane across a field full of gasoline pipes and hoses, service crews in coveralls and green plastic helmets listening to the underbellies of planes with stethoscopes, realizing as the wind flattened his trousers against his knees that he was not the only one making a run for it, and that behind him there were also Penelope Fleece and Bruce Bamberg, and the hippie, guitar-playing Yale professor. It was not at all like the convivial flight coming out. This time they all avoided one another and took separate seats. Except that as the plane took off he had imagined he heard a voice crying, "Yoo hoo, Richard Baxter!" In fact he thought he heard the voice again and, frowning, turned around to see a woman coming down the aisle who looked like Sophie Katz, and then turned out to be Sophie Katz.

"But what a marvelous surprise!" she said, laughing breathlessly as he quickly removed the Washington *Post* from the empty seat beside him. "Imagine finding *you* here of all people. Just the person I think about constantly."

"Do you really, Miss Katz?"

"Sophie. Oh, yes."

"I think I'm too dangerously flattered to ask why."

"But you must *know* why," Sophie said, cocking her head at him and looking, if possible, even more ridiculous than at their last meeting, the bangs longer and grayer, the nose more eagerly protruding. Also, she was dressed for full summer now, in a kind of dark shapeless tent bordered at the hem and sleeves with a vaguely Navajo design. There was a huge silver eagle hanging on her breast from a leather string tied in a crooked bow at the back of her neck. Her thin white legs were bare—why was he so sure that in winter she wore black or purple tights?—and her feet were planted flat in their large brown thong sandals. Yes, absolutely ridiculous, and, even more ridiculous, he was very glad to see her.

131

"It was that fantastic conversation in your office," Sophie said. "I'm still afire with it. I'm aflame."

"I wish I inspired all my authors like that," Dickie said.

"I'm sure you do."

"I'm afraid the inspiration has to come from the text," Dickie said, forcing a polite smile as he realized he had just completely confused the metaphor.

"And Mr. Gaskell?" Sophie giggled, too excited to notice. "Is he inspired by the text too? I've been waiting for you to call me."

"Ed?" Dickie said. "Well, no, that's the thing. He hasn't actually seen it yet." He smiled again, this time reassuringly. "Look, there's absolutely no need to worry. Do you have an extra copy, by the way? I'd like to shoot one off to Ralph Gorella. It won't hurt if *Hindsight* takes a piece of it."

"I'll see that my agent sends it to him first thing in the morning," Sophie said. "No, I'll take it myself. . . . Ralph Gorella. My god, how is he? I haven't seen him for eons."

"You know Ralph," Dickie said.

"Yes," Sophie said, "I know Ralph," and glanced past him out the window, quickly and apologetically murmuring something about "the poetry of flight." A dull gray cloud scudded by and she stared down at the complimentary copy of the Washington *Post*, which had somehow found its way into her lap.

"Were you in Washington on business or pleasure?" Dickie asked.

"Oh, pleasure!" Sophie said, eyes bulging gratefully. "Pure and absolute pleasure. I have a married daughter in Chevy Chase. . . . Though I must warn you I told her all about us."

"A married daughter," Dickie marveled politely.

She giggled again, one of those thin nervous dripping laughs like the tinny banjos in *The Great Gatsby*, and opened the newspaper at random. ". . . Just look at these baseball headlines. Aren't they positively *Martian?* Minnesota Twins, Houston Astros. . . . And to think there was once a time when

132

I could have named you every single player for the 1936 Giants. Let's see. Bill Terry, manager. Mel Ott, pawing up right field. Frankie Crosetti, shortstop. . . . No, sorry. Frankie Crosetti was shortstop for the Yankees. It was Lou Chiozza for the Giants, I think, until that awful collision with what's his name in front of third base, when he broke his leg."

"My god," Dickie said, "how do you know all this?"

"Oh, I went all the time. Friday was Ladies' Day and you could get in for a quarter for the federal tax. Did you ever know Delmore Schwartz? He was an even more devoted Giant fan than me. No matter how early I got to the Polo Grounds, he would always be there ahead of me in Section 33. Marvelous man. Fine poet. Just terribly glandular. We had that in common also." Sophie sighed. "Actually, I wasn't too surprised when years later . . . not that I saw much of him after I moved to San Diego. And of course, there was no decent ball team out there. I finally caught up with Delmore again just before the end."

"I gather from the novel that you didn't care too much for San Diego."

"Ah, well." Sophie laughed. "It's all water under the bridge now, isn't it? And of course it was wartime. Luckily, my husband was 4F and worked in the Navy Yard. Still, the children and I—"

"You have others besides the daughter in Chevy Chase?"

"Oh, yes, indeed. Five altogether. Three girls and two boys. My youngest daughter is fifteen."

"My god, how did you ever get any work done?"

"Well, actually, when the children started to come along—"

"I can imagine."

"No," Sophie said, staring at him for a moment, "no, you can't imagine—" and laughed to offset the sudden veiny red moisture in her eyes.

"I'm sorry," Dickie said.

"My goodness," Sophie said, collecting herself, "what is there to be sorry about? It wasn't anybody's fault, just circumstances, circumstances beyond our control, as they used to say on the radio. I mean, can you imagine, the manuscript you have now I used to work on at two o'clock in the morning, after I'd finally finished the ironing. Isn't that funny? Though I must admit that when Irving had his heart attack and couldn't go to work any longer. . . ." She took a deep breath and laid a hesitant hand on Dickie's sleeve. "Richard, I have a terrible confession to make. I haven't read *Joseph Andrews* yet."

"That's okay," Dickie said.

"No, really, it was so kind of you to suggest the parallel, so heartening. I mean there are some writers one feels *instinctively* close to, whereas others. . . . Take Joyce. Frankly, I never have felt very close to him, have you?"

"Well, yes, kind of."

"Ah," Sophie said, "so did Delmore. Delmore regarded him as practically his spiritual father. Out of respect for his opinion, I used to keep *Ulysses* under the counter all the time when I worked at the Five and Ten and try repeatedly to—"

"The famous job at Woolworth's," Dickie said, and smilingly quoted, ". . . the tinselly, tinsmithy hawking of wares. . . ."

"Oh, well, it wasn't *so* bad," Sophie said, blushing with pleasure, "especially after Irving's mother came to live with us and help with the children until I came home to cook dinner. A tight squeeze, of course, with the eight of us in a four-room apartment, especially when all of the children came down with the measles simultaneously. . . ." She gave an even thinner, tinnier laugh. "Not that even that was so bad, really. It was only the ironing that made me feel desperate. Isn't that funny? There always seemed to be a permanent pile of it, waiting to weigh me down. Literally. I used to wake up with this heavy, heavy weight on my shoulders."

"I know," Dickie said. "It's so surprisingly painful."

"Ah," Sophie said gratefully. "Then you caught that too."

134

"Caught it?" Dickie said. "No, it was only that this morning. . . . Oh."

"Irving used to laugh when I stopped in the middle to fix his midnight snack. He used to say, 'Soph, you look like a Picasso of the blue period all bent over like that.' . . . It *was* the blue period, wasn't it?"

"I think so," Dickie said, unwillingly remembering Felicity's own private Picasso.

"She's ironing, but is it ruffles?" Sophie said.

"I'm not sure of the details."

"Of course these days it's all permanent press and paper, anyway, isn't it?" Sophie said with an edge of bitterness. "So what difference does it make? But with me it was always ruffles . . . though maybe I'm wrong. I'm sure you know more about current children's styles than I do. You have the air of a parent *très, très au courant.*"

"Well, not that all au courant," Dickie said. "We just have this one little girl who—"

"Just the one? But I'm sure your wife irons beautifully all the same, whereas I, alas—"

"We—Sandra has a maid."

"Very sensible," Sophie said, nodding. "And very pretty too, I'm sure."

"My wife?" Dickie said, quickly clearing his head of the unwelcome vision of Orvietta and the platinum-blond dynel curls. "Yes, I suppose you'd call her pretty."

"Good. It's a very serious matter for a woman, being attractive. One must never take it lightly. Not that I consider *myself* a great beauty these days, of course"--there was a little giggle and a pause, which by the time Dickie opened his mouth Sophie had managed to bridge by herself—"but during the time I was telling you about, I always felt myself to be extremely ugly, interestingly enough. Extremely. Which is a very bad state of mind for a young woman to fall into. You must make sure your wife never falls into it. I can even remember crying over my ugliness as I struggled with those ubiquitous ruffles. Although often I would just fall asleep over them, too heartsick, too sorely laden even to weep. Head on the board. Arms hanging. Always remembering to unplug the iron, of course."

"Of course."

"Have you ever been to the San Diego zoo?" Sophie said. "Fascinating place, you must take your little girl there if you're ever in the area. . . . Well, once I spent my entire day off staring at the monkeys in their cages, wondering where exactly, since we all had opposable thumbs, lay the intellectual superiority of Sophie Katz."

"And where was it?"

"No place. I wasn't even better at predicting consequences because six weeks later I was pregnant again."

"Oh, christ," Dickie said.

"*Au contraire*," Sophie said. "It was my *release*. My *salvation*. It got me my Guggenheim—I'd already decided to apply when I was in the maternity ward, you see."

"I see," Dickie said.

"And then, incredibly, six months later I got it. They sent me this absolutely astonishing booklet of winners that read like a medical directory: Dr. This, Dr. That—all professors. And right in between them, plain 'Mrs. Sophie Katz, for creative writing in fiction.' It couldn't be more specific unfortunately, because there were only these few lines of my novel to go on—your novel now, dear Richard—and my little ounce of courage born of desperation. I had wildly asked them for enough money for a year in Italy, and they actually offered it to me. It took me weeks to believe it. I remember that last Sunday. We were all standing around the baby's crib, Irving, his mother, the other four children and I, discussing the baby's new diaper rash. I had started to smear fish oil ointment on the tiny ass when I suddenly *knew* that the moment had come to sink or swim. I seized it. I left them all behind, Richard, and for one glorious year I *swam!*"

"And I'll bet they didn't suffer at all," Dickie said.

"Irving and his mother?"

"Actually, I was thinking more of the children."

"Yes," Sophie said, "well, there *was* some slight problem about that," and gave her thin little laugh. "In fact, they were all taken away from me. *Fantastico,* no? Irving and his mother had been quite busy in court, it seemed. I had what you might call a small nervous breakdown. Nothing serious. *Piccolo.* It was almost an *adventure.* Then I went to live in New Mexico for a while with some very dear friends, and then I thought, no! Sophie must return to her native habitat. And so here I am, ready for anything. Fit as a fiddle and ready for love!"

Up ahead, the SEAT BELT sign lit up again. Dickie looked at his watch. They would be landing in about twenty minutes and, allowing for weekend traffic, he would be home by about four thirty. In time to look over his mail, relax, maybe take Becky and Sandra out to the new Szechuan restaurant on Broadway.

"I've bored you," Sophie Katz said.

"On the contrary. Whatever happened to Irving, by the way? He didn't die of another heart attack or anything foolish like that, did he?"

"Irving?" This time Sophie really laughed. "Irving's a very rich man. He made a killing in real estate and then remarried. A very nice girl I'm told, very young. The children all adore her."

"Do you see them now?"

"The big ones? Oh, yes, at least once or twice a year. It's worked out beautifully. They tell me the baby is doing very well too, not, I suppose, that you ought to call a fifteen-year-old a baby." Sophie giggled. "Oh, it's all so silly, these modern courts, this modern psychiatry. It seems I'm not allowed to see the baby at all. Which I suppose is actually all for the best. I'm sure that one day she'll. . . ."

Sophie giggled once more, and then grew still. She looked out the window without any expression at all, as if after all the

137

long years of concealment, she no longer had a private face, only that silly, unconvincing imitation of joy. The plane continued its downward lurch, breaking through cloud after cloud until only a few wisps remained, and through the porthole a relief map of New York appeared at a tilt. Dickie began to think of the complications of sharing a taxi, and particularly of the moment when, since she lived in the Village, he would be getting out first and pressing money on her to continue downtown. He knew that she would refuse, that she would insist on pressing the money back, that some peculiar point of pride would keep her from letting him pay for the ride though she would surely understand that he could charge it to expenses if he wanted to, which he didn't, that she would make an issue of what every other female in New York would accept quietly and without comment, and that all the while she fussed and insisted and giggled and said, "Oh, no," the meter would still be running. Impossible woman. So absurd, so excruciatingly homely. The jet engine changed its tune to a higher whine. The NO SMOKING sign lit up.

"I'm taking a cab," Dickie said. "Can I give you a lift?"

"But how kind!" Sophie Katz said delightedly. "Won't it be taking you out of your way? I know. You must come up and see my tiny pied-à-terre. I'll make you some divine espresso in my little terra-cotta cups."

Dickie opened his mouth and shut it, sighing. She was making an issue of it, all right. He looked at his watch again and, oh what the hell. The two of them descended in absorbed silence.

"I'm definitely going to shift the seduction scene west of page 160," Sophie Katz said happily, cuddling up closer.

A *party?* The voices from inside came at him sharply and incongruously, even before he had succeeded in undoing all the locks on the front door. Sandra was always talking about

138

"having a few people in for drinks." But why today, on no notice at all, and why *this* motley crew? "I expected you back earlier," Sandra said, coming into the hall to relieve him of his attaché case and kissing him on the cheek as if he were a guest.

Like a guest, Dickie said, "I got stuck," and looked through the living room archway at Sandra's "few people," who stood about ill-assorted and ill at ease, most of them clearly about to leave anyway: Vaughn Cranshaw, Violette de Laniere, Ruby Cohen Mandel minus Eli, Umberto Robertini minus Gladys, Leah and Morty Schwartz. "They called from some off-Broadway matinee," Sandra murmured, misunderstanding his look, "and I couldn't—" "No, of course not," Dickie said, resenting Sandra's usual implication that she had to ferret in her relatives behind his back. Actually, if it were a question of sneaking people in, that elegant iceberg Violette de Laniere would have been more like it. But then, even after all these years, he had never quite understood Sandra's attitude toward Leah—not that he had either the energy or the desire to puzzle it out now—which was both too familiar and too remote, as if, instead of sisters they were two concentric circles touching painfully at their perimeters. Of course, on the other hand, as Sandra kept reminding him, he was an only child, and therefore not really qualified to judge. Taking him by the elbow, Sandra steered him toward the tag ends of the group, like a bridegroom or a trophy, a George Auerbach in the grip of his Vicky. He looked at Sandra again, wondering what had really brought all this on. No, it was absolutely unlike her to give anything resembling a party without consulting him endlessly, calling him at the office about who, what, when, reminding him to bring home ice, making endless lists for Zabar's. Also, although she was flushed and excited, and even wearing a pair of new wide rather unflattering white pants that were evidently meant to be hostess pajamas, it wasn't her true party excitement. She seemed nervous and depressed. Orvietta lumbered by, making her sullen rounds with a depleted tray of hors d'oeuvres and a safety pin holding together the

139

soiled front of her black uniform, and completely ignoring the corner where poor Leah was flirting desperately with Vaughn Cranshaw, all screwed up like a tense bird, as if it were still somehow her social duty to catch a husband, no matter what the circumstances. He thought unhappily of the time he and Sandra had led Vaughn into the kitchen and introduced him to Orvietta, hoping maybe she would like them better, and how it turned out the next day that Orvietta hadn't even noticed Vaughn was black. (Correction: in those days, Negro.)

"But aren't you generalizing, Vaughn?" Leah said excitedly, wriggling in her kelly green dress.

"If you don't generalize, you gossip," Vaughn said, taking a sip of his martini and reaching for the mantelpiece with his elbow. Nearby, Leah's actual husband, Morty, was saying to Umberto Robertini in front of the wall of books, that personally he had always felt that with a good rose there was never any need to worry about white or red. Umberto gave a troubled nod, as if he had stumbled on another great mystery of language, and Sandra let go of Dickie's arm.

"We were afraid you'd gotten arrested," Violette de Laniere said to him, giving Sandra a quick grande dame peck on her way out.

"No, I couldn't."

"I couldn't have either. I have this absolute terror of incarceration. Was there much violence?"

"Not on the shuttle," Dickie said.

Violette's exquisite jaw twitched with an exquisitely bitter smile. "Were there many blacks?"

"Only Percy," Dickie said, politely letting Sandra's cherished Mater Dolorosa out the door, and wondering why Violette didn't just give all her money to a convent for highborn ladies and be done with it. He wondered what the next cause would be. She seemed to have entirely missed Bangladesh. Seeing him return to the living room, Vaughn abandoned Leah to Ruby Cohen Mandel.

"I understand you were in Washington," Vaughn said.

140

"Yes, I—just came back."

"And I suppose our culture hero was there too, giving another one of his stirring performances?"

"Oh, well, it's all a matter of personal style, isn't it?" Dickie laughed, somehow wishing for the sake of Vaughn's elbow that the fireplace, which Sandra had restored to the natural brick, also worked.

"I don't think style is a word he'd understand anymore," Vaughn said.

"No?"

"You know, Dick, I could have played that game too. Believe me, it's harder not to these days. But I've always thought it was more important to cling to my own little vision of reality. You know, by now I think I've probably met every level of citizen in this country from the President on down—" On *"down"*? Dickie thought. "And square as it may sound, I'll tell you it *still* says something about America when the son of a fieldhand and a laundress. . . ." Vaughn paused with lowered head, like a minister who had just delivered himself of an invocation, and absently dusted off his rosette from the Institute of Arts and Letters. It was the line that always got him the most applause on the university circuit, or used to. Why the hell didn't he quit traveling around from college to college, desperately trying to be the ultimate black man of distinction, and get back to that second novel of his, which was already almost ten years overdue? Ironically, in the days before their break, Hershel said that he had seen maybe a thousand pages of new manuscript piled up in Vaughn's ultra-modern study next to his huge IBM electric, and that the tragedy was, it was terrific.

"I say it still says something about this country when—"

". . . Listen, I'll bet you don't know how to induce vomiting when all else fails," Morty was saying cheerfully to Umberto over by the bookcases. "Am I right?" Umberto nodded. "Well, first you put one finger down your throat and the other up your rectum. And if that doesn't work—reverse them!"

141

"Morty," Leah turned aside to say.

"What's the matter? This guy's okay. He's not afraid to call a spade a spade."

"My brother-in-law," Dickie said.

"We've met," Vaughn said, explaining he was sorry but he really had to run and meet Bill Styron for dinner. Sandra in the hostess pajamas made a great show of running up to hug and kiss him good-bye. But where was Becky? Usually she would be in the middle of everything in a little organdy party dress, circulating a bowl of peanuts. A furious Orvietta came up to inform him that a Mrs. Spots was wanted on the telephone and how was *she* supposed to know who that was? Dickie went and tapped Leah on the shoulder, interrupting Ruby Cohen Mandel who was saying how she and Eli always went to Miami Beach in the summertime.

"The summertime—? Oh, look, my gorgeous brother-in-law!" Leah cried, giving him a long sexy hug. There was an old-fashioned smell to her that piqued his memory, hovered around the edges of his mind, made him think of Sophie Katz's pitifully small and cluttered room in the Village, and the huge lumpy daybed with the green batik spread, and the bookcase that threatened to topple over on it at any minute, and Sophie smiling gratefully for small favors. He wondered why he should be so sure that Leah, and Morty too, would have both *recognized* Sophie even if they didn't understand her.

"You're wanted on the phone, Leah," Dickie said affectionately and, having assured Ruby that a small ad could be far more effective than a large one, joined Sandra in rescuing Umberto, who was now desperately reciting Dante, always his signal that he wanted to leave but didn't know how.

"L'amor che move il sole e l'altre stelle. . . ."

"He speaks a very fine Italian," Morty Schwartz said.

"He *is* Italian," Sandra said.

"Okay, where's Leah?" Morty asked, looking around as

Umberto beat it with many "ciao's" all around. "We have to get the hell out of here too."

"Janice wanted her on the phone," Dickie said.

"Janice?" Sandra said, startled.

"Itsy," Morty said, winking at Dickie. "Listen, your wife tells me you've been to a convention, kid."

"It was not a convention," Sandra said. "It was a peace protest by a group of very distinguished people in the arts."

"Yeah? I'll bet he still learned a few things they never taught him at Harvard."

"What does Harvard have to do with it?" Sandra said, linking her arm through Dickie's. "Why must you always keep bringing up Harvard? I told you. It was—"

Dickie excused himself to take Ruby Mandel to the door, expressing regret that Eli hadn't been able to make it. Which holiday was it this time? Just Shabbes? Oh, yes, of course. And please tell Eli he was terribly excited about *Jews of the New Country*. When he came back, Morty was still hooked on the subject of Harvard, which seemed to fascinate him endlessly—during the Kennedy era both the Schwartzes had been almost beside themselves with enthusiasm and excitement, sure that Dickie was about to be called onto a yacht at any moment. Though it was a peculiarly double-edged sword, like their idea that he didn't look Jewish, and, on the one hand, made them treat him with elaborate respect, a high priest (rabbi?) of esoteric mysteries, to be asked about sales in hushed voices and, on the other, some dumb shmuck who couldn't possibly know which end was up.

"I mean Harvard, Shmarvard," Morty said. "He still lives in an ivy tower, doesn't he?"

"But how can you *say* that?"

"Say what?"

Sandra hesitated.

"That I live in an ivory tower," Dickie said, laughing to offset his fleeting consciousness that a real Harvard gentleman

143

such as Morty took him for would never have made the small correction.

"Because you do," Morty said, smiling with annoyance. They all looked around, seeking the corroboration of the other guests, but except for Orvietta who was banging ashtrays into a silent butler and taking furious swipes at the furniture with a cocktail napkin, the three of them were alone in the living room. "I mean, let's face it. An excellent education is one thing. We all kill ourselves trying to give our kids excellent educations. But what does it teach you about real life?"

"Oh, Morty," Sandra said. "What do you think real life is? Living on a dead-end street in a dead-end suburb where everybody's the same age with the same income and the same number of children?"

"She doesn't understand," Morty said, smiling.

"I mean, for god sakes, Morty, look at our friends. Look at the different lives they lead, their freedom to do as they please."

"But actually, aren't you really talking about sex?" Leah said, coming back with her pocketbook and pulling on a pair of white gloves with an important air.

"Was Hersh there, by the way?" Sandra said to Dickie.

"I'll tell you about it later."

"She expects him to spill the beans." Morty laughed.

"She's talking about Hershel Meyers," Leah said, smoothing her fingers and then looking up to give Dickie a bright cultural smile. "He happens to be a very close personal friend of theirs."

"Oh, is that so?" Morty said, pursing his lips and tilting his head at a respectful angle, as he had when Umberto was reciting Dante.

"He even hit Sandra at a party recently."

"Is that *so?*" Morty said.

"—though of course he was only kidding."

"Of course."

144

Dickie looked at Sandra, who began to gather up some empty glasses.

"It was an accident. I explained that."

"Listen," Morty said, "how about joining us for dinner? We were thinking of going to that very fine French place you introduced us to last time."

"Oh, Morty, we can't," Leah said. "Mama's sick again. Itsy said the hotel called and wants her out of there."

Morty gave a good-natured shrug. "Okay. Come on. I'll see if I can get her a bed."

"You're putting her in the hospital?" Sandra said.

"Why, do you think you can get Blue Cross to pick up her hotel bill?"

"But you know she's not really sick. You know it's only a bid for attention."

"Listen," Morty said, "with that heart and that girth a woman like that could pop off any minute. . . . Come on, Leah, let's go."

Dickie and Sandra followed them out to the foyer, handing Morty his summer hat from the hall table, and Leah a white sweater with gold buttons.

"You ought to come over soon," Morty said to Dickie. "We have a new Cézanne watercolor that's a beaut. Did San tell you? We swapped our Chagall landscape for it."

"No, kidding. You have a Cézanne? I didn't even know you had a Chagall."

"You mean you never saw it? With the pink cow predominating?"

"No, I don't think so."

"When the hell were you out at our house last?" Morty said. "What is it with these girls that they can't get together?"

"Do you have to do it right away?" Sandra said. "Put her in the hospital?"

"You want her to have a real heart attack?" Morty said, laughing. "She's in enough pain already."

"But look," Dickie said, "you shouldn't have to do it all. Let us help you this time."

". . . yes, let us," Sandra said.

Leah and Morty looked at each other and smiled.

"You just came back from a convention, kid," Morty said to Dickie, winking, "your wife needs you," and started toward the door.

"Call me," Sandra said to Leah.

"Oh, and listen," Morty added, gesturing at Dickie with his hat, "this is one Cézanne you have to see."

When the telephone rang, Sandra ran to answer it. But it was only Leah ("San? . . . Lee. . . ." In her excitement she sounded like a Chinese laundryman), assuring her that Mama was resting comfortably and wanting to know when San was coming out to see her. Sandra promised tomorrow afternoon at the latest, said yes Vaughn *was* very distinguished, a perfect example of what *could* be accomplished, and then, having assured herself that Becky wasn't really feverish, though she whimpered and twisted fretfully in the dark bedroom, and feeling sicker and sicker herself with disappointment, went into the bathroom for a good cry. It was funny that so much of her emotional life seemed to be played out in bathrooms. Was it because they were always private with lock and key, or could there be some deeper, more atavistic reason? The real joke was that this time she didn't even really know what she was crying about, only that it had something to do with Dickie being home, but nothing to do with Dickie, the end of a piece of time in which nothing had happened, though god knew what she had wanted to happen. No, that wasn't true either. She knew very well what she had wanted to happen. Adam, calling on some pretext or other—again not true, she'd given him the pretext this morning—Adam saying he would have called anyway, that he had to call, Adam saying somehow, sotto voce, in code, lemon juice, invisible ink, that he loved her.

Sitting on the edge of the tub, she leaned her head against the white enamel sink, which ought to have been cool and soothing but in fact was gritty with Orvietta's leftover cleanser, and then stood up, turning on both faucets full blast, less to bathe her eyes, than to drown out the noise of her emotions. She wondered what poor Adam would say if he saw her now, blowing her nose with toilet paper. Though maybe he wouldn't mind. Maybe he was depressed too, waiting for her to get in touch again. The thought, though utterly unconvincing was peculiarly satisfying. Because, after all, wasn't Adam entitled to be cautious, nay suspicious, considering all those times he had said yes, and she no, no, no? Why should he believe she truly meant business this time? If only she could convince him. If only. . . . She sat down again and closed her eyes. . . . Oh, Adam, please call, please write, please touch me again . . . and saw the suite in the Plaza, now on a rainy day. Would they have met outside by the fountain? No, it was under construction, and furthermore, surrounded by hippies selling foodstuffs and glass flowers. Inside then. At the marble reception counter, surrounded by gilt and plaster, Old World elegance. Should they register as Mr. and Mrs. Adam Brill or use false names? She would leave it up to Adam. Anyway, there would be no embarrassment, no motel twinges of cheap shame. Adam would excuse himself and, unknown to her, duck into the hotel florist shop to order a dozen of those blood-red roses. Then up in the caged elevator, smiling at each other behind the bellman's head. What about luggage? Vuitton? No, too status seeking, and only brown printed plastic after all. Adam would be carrying something, an English briefcase, maybe black morocco. Then inside the suite. Then Adam reaching for her back zipper. . . . But what was she wearing? Not pants, though in some ways they were easier. Not these stupid flapping things that she had seen from Dickie's eyes were a terrible mistake, though they weren't "new hostess pajamas?", but the same ones she had worn at Umberto's party. . . . A new dress. A lilac silk that even

147

seemed to smell of lilacs, and underneath, the lovely garment, yes garment, not girdle or slip, that she had bought at the lingerie department of Lord & Taylor yesterday with just this possibility in mind. And, oh, yes, first the massage at Elizabeth Arden to be perfumed and smooth as silk all over, from elbows to heels. Then Adam would undress her: "How *does* this lovely thing come off, darling?" The last time she had just stripped herself quickly and then, for some reason, wrapped right up again in Adam's beach towel. The towel was damp and sandy, which hadn't mattered then. But now.... Oh, Adam. Backed onto the bed, the hotel sheets newly changed and cool. Adam kissing her all over. And then—oh, thank you, darling—Adam inside her, filling her up.... Actually, he was smaller than Dickie, though smoother and more pointed. She remembered thinking that the last time, she remembered not wanting to think that, not because it was embarrassing, an invidious comparison, but so totally extraneous, a trifling curiosity.... Adam inside her, filling her up. Oh, let's lie still for a moment, two pink cleaving spheres of a peach. And then on the rocking bed ... oh, Adam, I love you so. I love you naked, I love you clothed. I love your dark round head that my hand is cupping. I also love your face better when you're wearing those black-rimmed medical service eyeglasses, can't you make love with them on? I'll close my eyes. There, it's all right now, your skin so close, your body bestowing itself on me. And then I—Adam, Adam, Adam. Do we come together? We didn't the last time. It doesn't matter, that's only clinical. And this is so pink and sex and wild. And, oh god, I want you always.

Then afterwards the kiss, the little husbandly kiss like an anniversary present that, oddly, Dickie never bestowed. Then lying together, side by side, sweetly sweaty and sticky, holding hands, friends. Was this the best part, this loving part of love? It was hard to say. They would turn and murmur to each other a little, smile, look up at the baroque ceiling, not really talk. A knock on the outside door. The two of them look at each other

148

and laugh. Adam tiptoes out naked—he has no clothes, no bathrobe. Dear ass, she watches it leave, hears Adam say something through the door about putting whatever it was in the drawing room. . . . But why have they taken a suite? It's so terribly extravagant, so terribly out of character with Adam. Can they charge it to Gaskell Press? Never mind. It's necessary to the dream. . . . Adam comes back into the bedroom and locks the door behind him. A few safe minutes later, they peek out together. There on the coffee table are Adam's roses. Oh, Adam, my darling. Laughing at the flowers, at their nakedness, they embrace again, and then, oh god, Adam, will I never have enough of you? When you want me like this, I'm so insanely happy.

A shower together? A bath, and then dressed. Must they get dressed so soon? Yes, they have no robes, and anyway bathrobes aren't quite the thing for the drawing room of their lovely suite. Yes, they're back in the drawing room, she on the sofa in her lilac silk, he standing in his striped English shirt, hitching around the knot of his dear dark tie. They're off the active list. They're elegant beautiful lovers once more. Cocktails and tiny white tea sandwiches with their crusts cut off have materialized on the low table beside the roses. They sip and bite daintily. How is the suite furnished? Tastefully. Was that an untasteful word? Pale gold and gray walls. Pastel aquatints of Paris. But it's the window they turn their heads toward, with its billowing sheer white curtains, and the view of Bergdorf's and the fountain and the dark wet greenery of the park. There's a sweet drenched smell of early autumn. The fountain is gray and glistening. It's raining. She reaches out a hand to Adam. . . .

Yes, he would call, he would come, he would get in touch. She stood up and wiped off her cheeks with the back of her hand. It was just a matter of patience. It would all work out. She took a deep breath that hooked itself into a guilty sigh. Guilty toward whom? Leah, whom she had left holding the bag with their mother? (She couldn't help remembering that

that one time they had gone to La Rochefoucauld with the Schwartzes, Barry had said comfortably to Adolphe, "Whadya got in the way of soda?") Becky, who might indeed be coming down with a cold, but could have picked it up just as easily at school from one of her friends? Dickie, who had so oddly volunteered their services? No, it had nothing to do with any of them, though the thought of Dickie suddenly made her feel very affectionate toward him, very kindly. Where was he anyway? How long had she left him? She opened the bathroom door and with her shoulders squared, smiling, walked back down the hall as if she were once again about to face the noise of a party.

Dickie was lying on the sofa, obviously feeling bad. He had an arm slung across his forehead, an old mannerism that Becky used to imitate comically as a baby but that she had not associated with Dickie for years, a terribly tired kind of gesture, as if the very thought of thinking exhausted him, obscured the nearer distance. There was a low fat tumbler half-filled with amber Scotch on the marble cocktail table beside him, and he had also changed into a pair of chino pants and an old blue jersey shirt. All very unusual. Dickie never drank at night, and certainly never tried to save his clothes. She made him move over and sat on the edge next to him, touching the beginnings of a blond stubble on his chin—cute handsome young Dickie, but a little spoiled maybe, a touch gâté, a tiny, tiny bit frayed around the edges?—and then put a hand on his thigh. But it was hot, and the two of them turned from each other fretfully.

"You didn't tell me about Hersh," Sandra said.

"There was nothing to tell."

"But I'll bet he was there making a huge ass of himself, anyway. Am I right? Oh, why the hell can't he contain himself, learn a little human restraint like the rest of us? If only—" She caught herself. No, she wasn't going to pull a Vicky Auerbach

150

and engage in some silly, titillated speculation about Hershel's means and motives.

"And still," Sandra said, looking away, half-smiling, half-sad, "what an 'if only' proposition so much of our life is anyway, isn't it? I mean, all of us going around saying, 'if only, if only,' while meanwhile our actual lives, the very *texture* of our lives, passes us by—" She paused again, having meant to be deep, as ladies were in Chekhov, for example, on hot summer nights, lifting their hair from sticky necks, sighing with Russian despair, and realized even before Dickie actually did sigh that she probably sounded more like Hershel's clothing manufacturer. But why *was* it so hard lately to talk to Dickie, tell him what was really in her heart? Sometimes she almost envied Stella and Freddie those incessant, silly quarrels of theirs.

"Did he mention the book?"

"It's in my attaché case."

"He *gave* it to you? What's it like?"

"See for yourself," Dickie said, taking down his arm and reaching for the Scotch.

"Oh, Richard *that* bad?"

"Why did you call me that?"

"Call you what? Richard? It's your name."

"You never call me that."

"Of course I do. It's a joke."

But Dickie wasn't in the mood for jokes either. She had never seen him quite so weary, so discouraged. Shrugging, patting him on the leg again, she stood up and let him be, and walked over to the window. Down below, the night traffic on the West Side Highway was misty and mysterious, the automobile lights moving by with the distant swishing sound of the sea. It reminded her of nights at Cape Cod, of nights driving back from Westchester with her young head on some date's shoulder.

"Must you publish it?" Sandra said. "Yes, I guess you must. He lives so much on vainglory, the disappointment would kill

151

him. Still, is any one writer so important? Should any one writer be so important even to himself—?" and this time, even before Dickie had a chance to ask if she was kidding, sounded to her own ears like Stella Fruchtman. Why not just give up now and go to bed? It had been a lousy party, a stupid impulse, a totally depressing evening. Why not quit now and complain to Starkstein next time about it being not so easy to act independently. Tangentially, she couldn't help wondering what Stella had finally done with the stole. If she knew Stella, the baby was probably crawling around with it, wiping the floor with it by now. Ironic that Leah, so much maligned in her imagination, had come wearing a simple white sweater, even if it did have gold blazer buttons.

"You didn't mind about the Schwartzes?"

"Of course not."

"She loved Ruby, naturally. They talked about the downfall of the Catskills and also X's. She also thought Vaughn was very distinguished." Dickie wasn't interested. "Did I tell you it turns out they've known the Fingerwalds for years? Herb and Morty were in medical school together. Isn't that incredible?"

"Why incredible?"

"Well, I can't think of any other friends we have in common, can you?"

Dickie shrugged.

"Leah also says our dear quaint Muriel used to be a very hot number in the old days. She says she practically patrolled the hospital corridor waiting to go down on every off-duty intern who passed by."

"Leah said 'go down on'?" Dickie said.

"No," Sandra said after a moment. "Shit," yes, all the time, an occasional "fuck." "Go down on," no. It was an interesting nuance and clever of Dickie to catch it, with that subtle literary feel of his that made him such a good editor. Still, it was faintly disturbing to have Dickie understand Leah even in this one small particular better than she did herself.

"—she's so ridiculous, though, my sister. I mean either she

152

pays absolutely no attention to what you tell her or else she totally overreacts. Like that silly business about Hershel socking me—"

Sandra started to laugh. Alone. *Hershel, Hershel, Hershel.* Why the hell did everything always have to come back to that man? And wasn't Dickie overdoing it about the book? So it was lousy, so what? There were other fish in the sea. Other things that mattered. She looked down at what, when they had first moved in, was supposed to be a charming flowered Victorian side chair and picked a few threads from its thinning arm.

"Dickie, I invited Adam," Sandra said.

"Adam?"

"I called his hotel. I left a message. Nobody ever called back."

"They've probably left town already."

She waited for him to ask about the lunch, though she knew that being Dickie he would probably never ask. And what would she tell him if he did? The truth, alas, maybe deleting a few paragraphs.

"Oh, *Richard*," Sandra said impulsively, sitting down beside his legs again. "Dickie. . . . Don't you ever feel that we really don't do as well by each other as we should?"

"What are you talking about?" Dickie said, less suspicious than annoyed.

"Oh, I don't mean divorce, or anything like that. I only meant—don't you ever feel that together we only *help* each other miss the boat?"

"Divorce?" Dickie said. "Sandy, don't be whimsical. I don't think you realize quite what goes on in the world. The kind of loneliness and grief and despair people wallow in. I don't think you realize about all the furnished rooms and the dinners alone and the joy when the phone rings even if it's only a wrong number. And the kind of desperation that makes a woman—"

"What are you getting so excited about?" Sandra said.

153

"But why come up with such an idea tonight? Why must you think that way?"

"Dickie, I only—"

"You're my wife," Dickie said, grabbing her by the shoulders. "Why don't you be my *wife?*" He pulled her down to him. It was all so peculiar. Dickie was crying.

FIVE✦✦✦✦✦✦✦✦✦✦✦✦✦✦✦✦✦✦✦✦✦✦✦✦✦✦✦✦

S he opened her eyes slowly, warmed by the white June sun before she saw it, and smiling, simpering almost, like Scarlett O'Hara, turned her face to a big white empty dent in the next pillow. Dickie? Where was *Dickie?* Over in the big armchair by the window, drinking coffee and looking through the Sunday *Times* in his bathrobe. The *Magazine* section. The *Book Review,* which he had seen in the office on Tuesday, lay at his feet with the rest of the paper. He looked up, smiled pleasantly, and then went on reading. A seagull flew by behind him, swooping low between the New Jersey shore and the Food City supermarket on Broadway, catching the sun on its pale gold underbelly as the sun had also caught on the top of Dickie's bent blond head. Seeing him, so engrossed, so patient, so shiny, it was impossible to believe that this was the same man who had gone to sleep last night pressing his damp face against her breast. (Dickie always quietly sucked on her at such moments, an even more incongruous thought just now than Vicky Auerbach saying to herself when she saw George up on the lecture platform: "I *sleep* with that man.") This morning the black mood had gone as completely and mysteriously as it had come, so that for a moment she had a strange feeling that instead of husband and wife they had been, no, not lovers either, two *friends* making love in the night. Had Dickie ever actually made love with a friend, some nice Harvard boy he had never told her about? (She wasn't talking about Janice Brill, though they had gone to college at the same time, and she had long had suspicions in that direction.) Cliffies, Harvard men. The idea curiously excited her and, like the Sunday paper scattered on the A & S Persian rug, somehow reminded her of those long-lost lovely Sunday mornings in the apartment on Brooklyn Heights when she and Dickie were first married, and there was no Becky, just the two of them. She remembered the light streaming in from the high studio windows, throwing velvet shadows as in a Dutch painting, and the portable phonograph playing Mozart, and the bookcases, and the coffee cups abandoned on the low cut-down marble table, and she and Dickie still in their slacks and sweaters making love on the floor, laughing, pulling down the long sofa pillow to be more comfortable. And then later, maybe Hershel would come over and they would all three take a walk along the esplanade, all three full of sweet yearning as the seagulls swooped and dipped over a harbor turned from sparkling pink to purple, sometimes going to a movie to forget the Sunday night sadness that was beginning to creep over them. Then they would come back for supper, with Dickie making salad in the big wooden bowl with the silver pedestal and silver-handled servers that had been a wedding present from the Gaskells. Except that once, Aunt Rose from the *other* part of Brooklyn had dropped in, uninvited and unannounced, and remarked casually, "My Irving also makes the salad," and killed something right then and there. Though why blame Aunt Rose, when it was Hershel who had really killed it, marrying that fat cow Winifred whom nobody could

158

even talk to, who read *Mademoiselle* for pleasure—or was that Dottie?

The phone rang and her heart leaped as she imagined for one foolish moment it might be Adam, and sank as she realized it was probably Leah. But, in fact, it was Vaughn Cranshaw, an extremely agitated Vaughn to judge from the metallic squeaks and squawks coming from the receiver that Dickie held a bit away from his ear, and then Dickie's voice professionally calm and soothing, sounding so undoubtedly the way Morty did with his cancer patients. None of it was unusual. Vaughn was always calling to complain about something, justify his own little vision of reality.

". . . What? Yes, of course I see your point. Yes, of course I agree that that picture of him and Percy arm in arm on page one won't help anybody. But why let yourself be so annoyed by—? I mean outraged. Yes, of course I appreciate your outrage. The depth of your concern. . . . Yes, I know it's not a matter of personal pique. Well, sure, I agree it's better to cling to. . . ."

She threw aside the covers and went to look for Becky, whom she found sitting cross-legged in a corner of the living room sofa, chewing on a bagel and leafing through the White Sale supplement from B. Altman. Becky had gotten dressed by herself in a pair of navy blue shorts from last year's day camp, and a T-shirt whose red stripes ran without the slightest bump or ripple around Becky's little chest. "Are you okay?" Sandra said, coming back from the kitchen with a cup of coffee to look her over again. "I'm *fine*, Mama," Becky said, ducking away from Sandra's outstretched hand, but a bit bleary-eyed and glazed over nevertheless. The living room looked lousy too, New Year's Eve the day after, with a missed glass here and there, a crumpled cocktail napkin under the chair, peanuts in the ashtray. Sandra went to take a shower and get dressed, finding it hard to believe as she put on a pair of jeans and a shirt that only yesterday she had dreamed of massages at Elizabeth Arden's and lilac silk. Damn it, it was incredible that in this day and age when it was how do you do and in the sack for everyone, men, women, college kids, dogs, she should have to labor *vainly* at lunch to be seduced and then look at Becky and feel like Medea. I'm tired of being Jewish, she thought, even though it seems to be coming back into style.

"Are you taking her to the park?" Dickie said, looking up again from his chair as she sat on the bed putting on her sneakers.

"Why not? Why shouldn't I?"

"I don't know. She looks kind of coldy to me."

"Dickie, please. Let me decide such things, okay?"

"Well, do you want me to take her so you can see your mother earlier?"

"Dickie, I said it was okay. Okay?"

Becky stuck her head in the doorway, looked from one to the other of them, and went to get her ball and jump rope.

"What did he want this time?" Sandra said, looking at the phone.

"The usual."

"And yet, I really do feel sorry for him," Sandra said. "After all, it's not so long ago that we used to have to call La Rochefoucauld ahead of time to make sure it was all right to bring him. . . . And who the hell does Hershel think *he* is, cheering on the lower classes? Lancelot Hale?"

Becky came back, and she took the ball and rope from her, partly out of old habit, partly to keep Dickie from repeating his offer about the park. The fact was that she never really liked to see Dickie and Becky go off together anywhere, the Museum of Natural History, the zoo, a movie, anyplace. Not because Dickie wasn't always willing or that she was jealous, but because Dickie always looked so oddly *young* when they did. As in that snapshot of him in a V-necked pullover and open shirt holding Becky as a baby, that her mother always kept in her pocketbook. There was an embarrassed fuzzy look

160

to Dickie in that photograph that it irritated her even to think of. Whereas, Freddie Fruchtman, for example, who turned up in the park practically every Sunday pushing the baby carriage with one hand and hauling Danny along with the other, always seemed perfectly in character as a father. Stella had said something about their all coming over for brunch this morning, inviting herself as usual without waiting to be asked, and she hoped Stella had forgotten about it. They would only come late, and the baby would crawl around with a wet diaper hanging out of its pants and bite the legs of the furniture, and Stella would sit there gorgeously insouciant and imagine she had accomplished miracles by having brought six bagels.

She asked Dickie if she could have the *Magazine* section and he hesitated and said sure. Then he got up and politely escorted them to the door in his bathrobe, as if they were a pair of his authors being given his Harvard man's bum's rush. Why had Dickie's courtesy begun to annoy her so when in the old days it was the quality in him she most cherished, the antidote to the poisonous Jewish domestic hysteria of the Bronx? (Why *did* people assume Jews were warm when they were only heated? Like poor platinum-blond Marilyn Monroe deludedly smiling between Arthur Miller's parents.) And what did she want Dickie to be, that miserable boy who had sucked on her breast all night? Would *that* have made her happy, like a good Jewish mother? In fact, she hated the word "breast," too. It was so goddamn unsexy and utilitarian, so much the word of a Jewish mother's *boy*. She sent Becky to ring for the elevator.

"Dickie," she said, making sure Becky was racing down the hall. "Listen—what really happened in Washington?"

"What are you talking about?" Dickie said, surprisedly looking down at the hand that clutched at his arm.

"Truly, darling, you can tell me. I won't be angry. I promise you."

"Nothing happened in Washington," Dickie said with a

161

laugh. "I told you that last night." She felt instinctively that it was true. And yet, and yet. Becky called out that the elevator had come. . . .

Across the street, Riverside Park was filling up fast. Young husbands hurried home past the stone wall, carrying grocery bags spilling over with things for brunch. Other young husbands were hurrying back out of the same tall apartment buildings leading little children by the hand down the steep path to the playground, pushing baby carriages, strollers, jogging after tots on tricycles. Sandra followed them down with Becky and the jump rope and ball, and took a seat on a splintery bench near a big boulder. A couple of young men next to her were handing out red plastic fire trucks and pails and shovels, and she opened the *Magazine* section and leaned back, keeping an eye on Becky, who had already started to climb in and out among the dirt-filled rocks, and listening with half a mind to the distant swish of highway along the river, feeling more like a father than a mother. A couple of elderly Jewish ladies, left over from before the neighborhood went bad, walked by carrying broken-off branches of cherry trees. Their purloined piece of the good earth. If the Puerto Rican kids committed such vandalism, they'd scream blue murder.

"Mama, can I have some ice cream?" Becky said.

"What about your cold?"

"I don't *have* a cold," Becky said, again irritably squirming away from the hand extended toward her forehead, exactly as Sandra had squirmed away from her mother's hand on hers. How explain to Becky that though it was the same gesture, it was an altogether different experience? She gave Becky a quarter and watched her run off to the yellow ice cream wagon at the entrance to the playground. Then she opened the *Magazine* section again, in the company of the several young fathers who were now also looking into their copies of the Sunday *Times*. (On Saturdays, the divorced and intellectual ones read *Hindsight*.) It was all the usual boring stuff, an article by Bruce Bamberg, "Nothing New About Vietnam," an attack on students by that loathsome ex-Communist philosopher Samuel Slicke who all during the McCarthy period had attacked teachers. A new "comic" exposé of the New York literary mafia by somebody named Garry Blang whom she had never heard of, and who taught some unnamed subject at Pomona Polytech but seemed to have the inside dope on all the familiar little black and white postage stamp faces: Ralph Gorella, Gertrude Dienst, Angelica Ford, Lancelot Hale, William Kohlrobi, Vaughn Cranshaw—and Richard Baxter. The picture of Dickie was in the follow-up on an inside page. Serious. Distinct against a wall of books (maybe the one in Ed Gaskell's office). Nothing like that fuzzy fellow in her mother's cherry straw pocketbook. How come Dickie hadn't even mentioned the article, even when she asked him for the section? How could even Dickie be so blasé about what was probably thrilling Leah and her neighbors out of their pants in Great Neck at this very moment? She turned to the back page and looked at a full-color carpet ad. There was a picture of a young couple seated on a piece of carved green broadloom, he very handsome with longish brown hair and granny glasses, she less good-looking, with cropped brown hair and no eyeglasses. Both of them were wearing pants and sweaters, smiling, and holding coffee cups. Pure Bloomingdale's. But what about the studio apartment in Brooklyn Heights? Had that also been only a cliché? Even the Sunday mornings? She closed her eyes, though the park remained present in its dust and the river smell and the hoot of a Circle Line excursion boat on the water.

It was on a Sunday morning that she had first met Dickie also, the year after she graduated from Barnard, when every day was blank and plain, the color of wheat. They had met at her girlfriend Connie's apartment. Whatever had happened to Connie? Why did such girlfriends always figure in your life and then vanish? At the time, though, Connie was working for a publisher and had decided to give an Easter brunch, an idea which everybody thought terribly chic and also somehow very

163

literary. They were all standing around drinking Bloody Marys and eating deviled eggs and imagining they sounded like Salinger. She dreaded going back home, where she was temporarily reinstalled in her old room while her mother shuffled around in carpet slippers and looked in every once in a while to shake her head and cry over the continued lack of a husband. None of the jobs tried so far had panned out: assistant to the director of a settlement house on the Lower East Side, secretary to Rabbi Glickman, who was a friend of her father's, executive trainee at Macy's. She had written several stories with *The New Yorker* in mind and was by then selling books at Doubleday's, at night, to save herself for some mysterious daytime occupation. Then, blond smiling Dickie appeared and took her over to Gaskell Press, where suddenly the whole world opened up. Literally. She had a distinct impression meeting Ed Gaskell that a gold curtain was rising behind him as in an MGM movie. They were married in the rabbi's study—Dickie looked silly in his yarmulkah—and on the same day sailed to Europe for their honeymoon. They stood on the deck of the *France*—it had had to be a French boat—and as the skyscrapers of Manhattan slid slowly past she could hardly believe it, she had dreamed so long of this particular moment, seen it in so many movies. The Statue of Liberty eased into place before them. Gateway to the Western World. *Home free,* she remembered thinking, *home free.*

"Where's Becky?"

Becky? She opened her eyes. "Oh, Daniel—I'm sorry, darling, I didn't realize you were there."

He regarded her gravely, dressed up in his cowboy suit and hat, twirling a pretzel. Stella was a pacifist.

"Becky's getting ice cream. Do you want to go find her?"

"Okay."

"Maybe you'd better ask your father first."

"You mean my mother," Daniel said. The two of them

164

turned toward the steep path which Stella was striding down like an actress making a first act entrance, face lifted toward the sun, the mane of streaky blond hair tossed back.

"*Darling,*" Stella said, after Daniel waved to show her where they were. "How marvelous to find you here."

"I'm practically always here on Sundays," Sandra said, accepting Stella's cordial French handshake.

"Really? You like it that much?" Stella said, looking around interestedly. It was somehow not surprising that while the rest of the mothers, herself included, were dressed as day laborers in their jeans and shirts, Stella had managed to get herself up for a garden party in a pinkish gray chiffon dress straight out of the thirties with a low V-neck and floppy flower, and also pale gray pumps with crystal ornaments.

"Can he have some ice cream?" Sandra said of Daniel, who was looking at her steadily.

"Of *course* he can," Stella said and beamed as, after a moment, Sandra reached into her bag and gave Daniel a quarter. The two of them watched him set off toward the entrance to the playground where the man had parked his yellow wagon, and Sandra reminded herself that such things as small change and the right time had always been Stella's weak points, and that, after all, the night of the famous filet mignon dinner at La Rochefoucauld when Stella dumped her purse upside down on the tablecloth, she had been spending her last penny literally.

"What a splintery bench," Stella said, running an exploratory finger over its surface. "Come, darling, let's sit over there, on the grass."

What grass? "They won't be able to find us," Sandra said, getting up anyway with Becky's jump rope and ball, and tucking the *Magazine* section under her arm. She thought about saying something about the article on the literary mafia and Dickie's picture and was embarrassed that it had even occurred to her.

"Of course they'll find us," Stella said, laughing. She

stopped at the foot of a scruffy hillock near where a stand of city cherry trees hung their heads, having bloomed so briefly the pinkness and the beauty were all forgotten after the first week of searing heat. Through their worn-out and drooping branches she could see Becky's dusty boulder which was being so raced down, mounted, and clambered on, it looked like the site of an Indian massacre. The children came in all shapes and sizes: tiny Orthodox Jews with skullcaps and earlocks, ragged Puerto Ricans in torn T-shirts, tall scary black adolescents, the nice obedient bourgeois neat ones, little boys and girls together, a few from Becky's and Daniel's class, not that Stella would have known the difference. There was also the local crazy lady in white beret and long muffler and Nixon-Lodge button, yelling at everybody and looking sad because she clearly wasn't sure any longer she was crazy, and also a derelict stretched out on a bench under a stained newspaper. But Stella proceeded with her own private pique-nique sur l'herbe and, spreading out a paisley shawl, gracefully sank down on it with her skirt settling around her like a silken parachute and beckoned Sandra with a smile to join her.

"Where's Freddie?" Sandra said, looking down. "Still sick?"

"Freddie? No, darling, why do you ask?"

"There was some talk of your all coming over this morning."

"Oh, yes, that's right. I forgot. How's Dickie?"

"Depressed."

"About what, darling?"

"Hershel Meyers."

"Terrible man," Stella agreed. "So gross."

"That's not the point," Sandra said, finally sitting down too. "It's his book."

"You've seen it?" Stella said, suddenly very interested, as if Sandra were talking about having met a new celebrity.

"Seen it is the word. I don't think anybody can read the damn thing." She wondered why she hadn't mentioned to

166

Dickie that she had taken it out of his attaché case and leafed through it during the night, when she got up to put on a nightgown and check on Becky. Maybe because it was such a mess, an even worse mess than she had expected. Not a novel at all, just page after page of infantile pornography, adolescent political satire, page after incoherent page of masturbating Presidents, Berrigan brothers ejaculating simultaneously on gallows, sodomy, rape, lesbian Cabinet wives, endless descriptions of sphincters, genitalia. Burroughs could do it. Mailer sometimes. But Hersh? Impossible. So then why had a strange happiness seized her when she put it back in Dickie's attaché case, a strange feeling of justification, almost exultation, that it was so lousy? She certainly hadn't wished such a literary disaster on Dickie or the Gaskell Press.

"I don't know," Sandra said. "It's really impossible to describe. Just a kind of mass of self-indulgent obscenity."

"Asshole, asshole, cunt, cunt." Stella sighed, nodding agreement. "There's so little art in anything anymore."

She plucked at a few blades of grass struggling up near the edge of her paisley shawl and tried to weave them in among its fringes.

"—how good it will be to get away for the summer."

"Oh will it," Sandra said, putting down Becky's jump rope whose red handles she had been unconsciously tying and retying. "Not that we'll be gone for the summer, just a few weeks."

"Still I imagine the Cape will be beautiful."

"Oh, yes."

"I saw a charming ad for a house in Truro this morning," Stella said. "Maybe I ought to look into it."

"I thought you were going to Europe."

"Did I say that?" Stella laughed. "Well, you know me. I can never make any plans until the last minute. And why not the Cape?"

"Sure, why not?" Sandra said, looking around for Daniel and Becky who were nowhere to be seen. She didn't have a moment's doubt that vague as she was, if Stella fixed her mind on it, whatever house she rented would be some kind of artistic treasure. Stella just had that kind of luck without even trying. Not for her the pleading long distance calls to lady real estate agents, not for her the struggles with tight-lipped, tight-assed quaint New England spinsters like Miss Cash of the Salt Box Inn who each year grudgingly and reluctantly let her and Dickie rent two mildewed bedrooms with lumpy antique mattresses for the last two weeks of July and the first week of August at a price that should have bought the entire coast of Massachusetts. No, not for Stella. Stella just one Sunday in late June happened to glance at a charming want ad in the real estate section and there it was, a cabin originally designed no doubt by Marcel Breuer. But when she looked at the matter closely, considered it dispassionately, what the hell was so swinging about Stella's life and so square about everybody else's? Because, as she was prepared to explain to Dickie last night in case he wanted to know why she hadn't invited the Fruchtmans, if you broke Stella's life into its components, weren't they just the same as everybody else's? The big cavernous West Side apartment, the endless question of where to spend the summer this time, the same small children. . . . Where were Becky and Daniel, anyway? They should have been back from buying the ice cream long ago. A couple of other kids from their class were playing not far away at the water fountain, stamping their feet in the muddy water at its base. But Becky and Daniel weren't there, or climbing on the boulder either, or playing baseball in the big dusty patch of ground at its base.

"Will Freddie be able to get away for the whole summer?" Sandra said, craning in the opposite direction.

"I really couldn't say, darling."

"What do you mean you couldn't say?" Sandra asked, laughing a little irritably.

Stella patted down her plait of grass and fringes, smoothing them one last time with her lovely long artist's fingers, and then watched as a gust of wind blew it all apart in a whirl of twigs and leaves and dried-up branches.

"I sent him away last night," Stella said, giving her a wary smile.

"You sent him *away*?"

"He's in a hotel."

"He's in a *hotel*?"

"He picked the Algonquin," Stella said. "It was his own choice."

"Freddie's at the *Algonquin*?" Sandra said, suddenly realizing that she was repeating everything Stella told her.

"No, not actually. Because there turned out to be this mix-up about reservations, and he had to sit in the lobby for about two hours before they finally told him there wasn't any room. He called me three times to complain about the draft. Isn't that typical?"

"Oh, Stella, he picked the Algonquin. That's so sad."

"Of course it's sad. But what could I do?"

"I don't know. I mean, I suppose you had to take some kind of firm stand, but still—"

"Firm stand? I'm a jellyfish when it comes to Freddie. You know that."

"Yes, but still—"

"Sweetie, I don't think you realize what it's been like. I mean these unbelievable rages all the time, the attacks, the scenes, morning, noon, and night. It's gotten so when I wake up I lie there thinking, why wake up at all? Why not die and get it over with? There's even this little voice that keeps saying, 'Die, Stella, die. What does a stupid bitch like you have to get up for?' "

She looked at Sandra intensely and questioningly with her beautiful mascaraed blue eyes.

"Oh, well," Stella said, with a laugh that sounded like a thin twist of silver wire. "At least I've finally come to grips with the reality of the situation. I mean either I turn my face to the wall, once and for all, or else—"

"Or else what?" Sandra said.

"Well, it's obvious, darling, isn't it?"

"Stella, you're not thinking of divorce," Sandra said.

"I'm not?" Stella said, with a maddening fait accompli smile.

"Stella, don't be ridiculous."

"Why ridiculous? Didn't you say a couple of weeks ago—"

"I say a lot of things," Sandra said. "You don't have to take everything at face value. I mean I'm hardly denying that Freddie has his faults as a husband—what man doesn't?—and that he's pretty rough on you sometimes, but—"

Stella's smile grew blander.

"But you can't take a marriage of ten years and just—"

"Twelve," Stella said, curving her ruby lips more and more sweetly as she gazed off into the distance. "Twelve years. Would you mind, darling, if we changed the subject?"

"I'm sorry," Sandra said.

"No, darling, don't be sorry," Stella said, turning and patting Sandra's hand consolingly—as Leah had in the car. "Never be sorry for anything. There's so much to appreciate in the world. So much beauty. Such *fantastic* things. Look at our children."

Thank god. Where were they? But of course, typically, Stella had made an elaborate aesthetic case for what didn't exist, what had probably never existed. Never mind that though. Where were Becky and Daniel in actuality? What were they doing all this time? Worse, what was being done to *them?* Then, as if in answer to her silent pleading, two dear familiar sweet little heads poked around the corner of the boulder, one in a cowboy hat, and then Daniel and Becky stepped into the full sunshine. They started down the steep path, almost jogging in the occasional filigreed shade of the wispy cherry trees, the little girl almost a head taller than the little cowboy. A dead branch lying across their tracks stopped them for a minute, and they squatted to examine it before Becky finally decided to take it along and went on, trailing it

170

behind her. A park keeper told them something, and they looked up intently and nodded. Oh, Stella was right. These were their golden days. They would always remember them. Except that when Sandra turned to tell her so, Stella was far away again, training that lovely self-infatuated smile on some other exquisite invisible point in the distance.

"He was waiting outside our building at six o'clock this morning," Stella said. "Can you imagine? The doorman rang on the intercom to tell me. The nightman, actually, it was so early. I told him to make Freddie go away, I told him to tell Freddie it was unlawful to loiter. But he was there when we finally came out before, sitting on top of the fire hydrant, eating a knish and watching for us."

"How terrible."

"I know," Stella said. "That gummy potato filling."

"I meant the waiting, the silence."

"You know, you're absolutely right," Stella said, as if Sandra had just said something enormously clever. "Because, in fact, he never said a single word. He just got up and started to follow us down the street. I told Daniel to peek and he did. He said, 'Daddy's eating a knish and crying at the same time.' Then Daniel began to cry. Isn't that odd? I mean, I never mind when Freddie cries. It only bothers me when he doesn't *say* anything."

Oh, Stella. It was impossible to figure out when Stella was being brave and when she was being totally idiotic. Nevertheless, the woman was going to have a much rougher time than she expected, keeping house for two little children, one an actual baby, chauffering back and forth from the beach to the supermarket to the house day after day, going to parties alone, coming home alone, *giving* parties alone. What was it Dickie had said about being grateful for even a wrong number? Not that, in a literal sense, Stella would be as alone as all that, since of course what with the two children there would also be a maid or a mother's helper of some sort. And the driving wouldn't be that much of a burden either because,

171

coming from California, Stella had had a license since she was sixteen. (Somehow, like the long legs and the sheer panty hose with the sanitary napkin showing through, there was something disturbing about that too, it was so conventional and so free.) Also, being Stella, she was quite used to entertaining and had given so many dinner parties for Freddie's business associates (again like Leah) it almost didn't matter whether Freddie was there or not. She'd be free in many other ways too. Free to eat and sleep and drink whenever she wanted. Free to lie on her deck in the woods, watching the sunlight filter murkily through pine trees, private and green and silent, like sunlight under water. Because that was how the Cape could be. Other country places, Connecticut, Vermont, the Berkshires, could make you homesick and nostalgic for where you'd never even been and wouldn't belong anyway. But on the long white ocean beaches of Cape Cod, you could swim naked, lie naked, dry off in the sun, slithery, warm, waiting. . . . Waiting for what? Maybe Stella's sudden decision to separate had nothing to do with Freddie at all and their long years of notorious incompatability. Maybe she just had a new lover. The Nazi, for example. What had ever happened to him? It was a question she was suddenly dying to ask Stella and knew she never would. Not that they weren't close enough friends. Of course they were. In some ways, she was far more intimate with Stella than with her own sister, Leah. And there were many women she felt far more distant from that she could have asked anything. It was just that for all her effusions, her darlings, her wonderfuls, Stella was humanly speaking so utterly remote. Even the most startling private confidences from Stella, and there had been some very startling ones, somehow became impersonal. Which again, like the teen-age driving license and the legs, was so very un-Jewish, so *Californian*. And wouldn't it also be typical of Stella to acquire a new lover as she acquired summer rentals, easily, gracefully, absentmindedly falling off her log, while everybody else. . . .

172

"I wonder who'll turn up there this summer," Sandra said.

"Turn up where, darling?"

"The Cape, for christ's sake. What the hell were we talking about?" Sandra said and, ignoring Stella's hurt, mystified look, stood up abruptly, wondering out loud where those kids had gone to, though Becky was about two feet away, digging up a tree root with a popsicle stick. Okay, so she wasn't particularly fond of herself at that moment. Nevertheless, Stella could really be impossible sometimes. It was like being tuned in to a radio that faded out in tunnels, it was like writing on water. "Are you and Stella friends or enemies?" Dickie loved to ask, laughing as men did at women in pairs. Friends, friends!

"Is something wrong, darling?" Stella asked, all sweet sympathy as always.

Her mother wasn't in the bed. Near the door, a smiling lady who looked very much like Mrs. Zimmerman from the Hotel Waldbaum, lay cranked up high, a mound of hospital gown and coarse white sheet. But the bed by the window was empty. Then she saw her mother eating her lunch in the aluminum chair, very short and white, an elderly child backed up by several large pillows. A tray cut across her chest. There was not much on it. A baked potato, a piece of haddock sprinkled with paprika, two halves of an apricot swimming in yellow juice in a coarse saucer, a couple of metal dish covers. Nevertheless, her mother was eating industriously, her wrist bent at a high angle as it worked fork to mouth. She was wearing a baby blue print housecoat with a lace-edged Peter Pan collar, a present no doubt from Leah, who had said she would visit that morning.

Sandra tiptoed in, carrying the white paper cone of flowers she had bought in the hospital florist shop downstairs. "Hi, Mama," she said, extending the rolled-up *Magazine* section

173

by mistake, and then reversing hands. She bent down to give her mother a quick kiss on the cheek.

"*Sorele*," Mrs. Wolfe said, looking up with a smile.

The smile took Sandra aback. She had expected reproaches, demands about Becky.

"How do you feel, Mama? You look fine."

"I look fine?"

"I'll bet you're not even sick at all," Sandra said in a bright voice, a hideous parody of Leah. "Not if you're sitting up and eating that nice lunch."

"Nice lunch?"

"Well, sure it is. There's that lovely baked potato—"

"They're not supposed to give me potatoes."

"—and the apricots, and that nice piece of haddock—"

Closing her eyes, Mrs. Wolfe put the napkin against her mouth.

"What's the matter, Mama, are you sick? No, I mean honestly, does something hurt you?"

"My head is dizzy."

"Maybe you should go back to bed," Sandra said.

"No, it's all right."

Sandra smiled toward the bed near the door inviting the sympathy—for whom, herself or her mother?—of the latest Mrs. Zimmerman, who smiled back and nodded with cheerful understanding.

"Mother had a terrible time last night."

"Oh, really?"

"How do you feel now, Mrs. Wolfe? Do you want me to ring for the nurse?"

"It's all right," Mrs. Wolfe said, closing her eyes and opening them again. "And Becky?" she said in a weak voice.

"Becky's fine. You know Becky." No, she doesn't, Sandra thought, in spite of all the cavorting in the kiddie pool, she knows nothing about Becky. "I took her to the park this morning. That's why I'm late."

"You'll take her to the country also?"

"The country? . . . You mean the Cape? Of course I'll take her. What else should I do with her?" It was an odd-feeling question, as if her mother had touched on a nerve.

"I'd like to go too sometimes," Mrs. Wolfe said, looking up at Sandra over the still-extended cone of flowers. "I'd also like to see that place."

"No, you wouldn't," Sandra said. "Not really. There's nothing to see. Just a bunch of people sitting around on the beach, talking nonsense. You'd be very bored. . . . Here, you like tulips, don't you? These are tulips."

Her mother looked at her for one more moment and turned away. It had been one of their rare instances of perfect understanding.

"She has a wonderful daughter, Becky," Mrs. Wolfe said to Mrs. Zimmerman.

"Becky? That's an unusual name for a child."

"I don't know how long these tulips will last," Sandra said.

"You know how it is with modern children. They're always busy with something. School."

"Actually, they look awfully top heavy already," Sandra said. "Maybe I'd better have them put in some ice water."

"Ring for the nurse, darling," Mrs. Zimmerman said. "The button is there by mother's bed."

"Oh, it's all right," Sandra said. "Why bother her when there are so many sick people who—?"

"I'm also sick."

"I'll be back in a minute," Sandra said.

It was the height of the visiting hour. All the length of the corridor doors stood open so that each room was a little tableau vivant of hovering relatives, rented TV sets, gifts, flowers, bright bursts of laughter. The doorway of one room was dark and silent. A man sat quietly inside with his hands on his knees, staring incuriously ahead, waiting. . . . I have no gift for hospitals, Sandra thought, whereas people like Leah, even if she weren't married to a doctor, would always know what to make of them.

175

"I'm awfully sorry to bother you," Sandra said to a nurse who was sitting near the elevators in a well of charts, telephones, and pharmaceuticals, "but I thought I might just have a little ice water for these. They're tulips, and, well, you know how tulips are. They're so excitable, too much heat and they immediately collapse." She laughed, wondering why, having abandoned her dreadful travesty of Leah, she was now chattering away like an unwanted guest at a cocktail party. "I suppose I should have stuck to gladioli."

"Which room?" the nurse said, holding out a hand and continuing to make notations with the other.

"814. Mrs. Wolfe. Though if you'd just tell me where to get the water, I'd be glad to—"

"Oh, are you Mrs. Wolfe's daughter?" the nurse said, looking up, a redhead with no eyebrows and a skeletal smile. "Why, I knew your Dad. I knew him very well. He was the hit of the floor. The funniest terminal CA we ever had. Always good for a joke. When we lost him, we were all very, very—"

"Yes," Sandra said. Was this the one who had so efficiently packed the black shoes into the suitcase? Lost weekend. It didn't bear thinking about.

"Of course your Mom's adorable too," the nurse said quickly. "A real doll."

"Really?"

"Oh, yes, we're all crazy about her."

"Really?"

"Here, let me take those. You go on back and finish your visit."

Relinquishing the flowers, Sandra walked back down the corridor even more slowly and reluctantly than she had come up it. The man inside the one dark doorway was still staring incuriously at the wall opposite him. There was a hospital smell of fecal matter mingled with talcum powder. Back inside 814, her mother still sat in front of the window bisected by her tray, her little feet in their pale blue terry-cloth slippers crossed at a height of several inches above the floor. In the bed

176

near the door Mrs. Zimmerman gave her a smile full of plastic dentures from her great cranked-up height.

"I gave the flowers to the nurse, Mama," Sandra said. "She'll bring them back as soon as she's able."

"So come, sit down already."

"Mother was waiting for you all morning," Mrs. Zimmerman said cheerfully. "You should hear that woman talk about you. All morning long that woman talked about nothing but my Sandra this, my Sandra that, my Sandra has such a husband, such an education, such a brilliant baby. I'm telling you, you have a very devoted mother."

"I'm sure she talked about Leah too," Sandra said. "Leah's my sister."

"Oh, Leah, I know very well already. She's in and out all day long."

"She lives close by," Sandra said.

Mrs. Wolfe had closed her eyes, and looked even whiter than before, a gentle translucent baby, though whether from spiritual or physical causes it was hard to say.

"Oh, my goodness!" the nurse said, making a nurse's starched and bustling entrance. "What are you doing out of bed, you naughty girl?"

"She was eating her lunch," Sandra said.

"She shouldn't be sitting up, with her medication," the nurse said, smiling and shaking her head as she deposited the vase of iced clinking tulips on top of the white metal bedside cabinet that concealed the bedpan.

"I didn't eat anything. I have no appetite," Mrs. Wolfe said, raising an armpit so that the nurse could hoist her back into bed.

"Oh, Mama," Sandra said, laughing. "We all saw you a minute ago."

"What's the matter, Mama?" the nurse said. "Still no bowel movement?"

Mrs. Wolfe shook her head and clambered up on the bed with the help of the nurse, remaining perched there on the

177

edge with her feet dangling above the footstool while the nurse helped her off with the baby blue housecoat. Beneath it, the matching blue nightgown was sleeveless and smocked, like a child's nightgown, except that after a flatness her mother's breasts loomed out unexpectedly. Mrs. Wolfe began to sway, and the nurse carefully laid her on her side. There was a big old country vaccination mark on her fat exposed arm.

"There you go," the nurse said, going out for a minute and returning with a green plastic squeeze bottle. "Maybe you have a little impaction. Let's see what this will do."

"What is it?"

"A disposable enema," the nurse said.

"That's an enema?" Mrs. Wolfe murmured, raising her faint eyebrows with interest.

"Over and out," the nurse said, deftly lifting the sheet, inserting a nozzle. "Plastic, self-contained, hygienic. Use it once, throw it away."

"It's not too expensive?"

"Why, how many do you plan to take?" Sandra said.

Over her shoulder, her mother looked at her balefully. So, from the other bed, did Mrs. Zimmerman.

"Okay," the nurse said, finishing up and shifting in a bedpan. "Let's see what you make of that."

Outside, voices and footsteps echoed and re-echoed in the corridor, but the nurse, who had stepped back and folded her arms, glancing once at her watch, did not refer to the fact that visiting hours were over.

". . . Nice day," she said.

"Yes," Sandra said, turning her head quickly toward the window. She thought of Stella sitting on the patchy grass, a figure in an Impressionist painting. She hadn't mentioned the separation to Dickie, superstitiously fearing that if she did it might turn into a divorce. Damn Stella with those long legs and coming from California.

"I beg your pardon?" she said to the nurse.

"I said I'm glad you finally got here. She's been talking about nothing else all day."

"I already told her that," Mrs. Zimmerman said. "You don't mind if I look at your paper?"

"No, of course not," Sandra said. She handed it to the nurse, who handed it on. "I came as fast as I could. I live in Manhattan."

"Oh, sure." The nurse laughed. "But you know how mothers are." She bent down and peered under the sheet to investigate the contents of the bedpan—"Come on, Mama, do your job"—then straightened up again. "Beautiful flowers."

"She likes tulips," Sandra said. "But maybe I should have gotten something more useful, like solid cologne or something."

"Your sister brought her the lovely nightgown and duster set."

"Yes, I thought so."

"There's very little resemblance, is there?" the nurse said.

"Between my sister and me? No, I guess not. We lead very different lives. She's the good one."

"Oh, come on. I'm sure Mom loves you both the same."

"My daughter in Denver is begging me to come live with them on account of my asthma," Mrs. Zimmerman said, smiling. "But I don't know—"

"... I don't believe in coming to children. ..."
They looked at the bed near the window, then turned away again.

"Another daughter is married to a professor. He teaches in NYU. Two Guggenheims they gave him already."

"Two? That's a lot."

"... this one's husband went to Harvard. ..."

"He's in physics, my son-in-law. One of the biggest low temperature men."

"Is that so? Isn't that interesting."

179

From the window bed came a series of sharp grunts and gaseous emissions.

"Oh, good!" Mrs. Zimmerman cried. "She's been waiting for that for a long time!"

Unfolding her arms, the nurse stepped forward, lifted the sheet, and nodded with satisfaction. "Okay, sexy, you're a good girl," she said, wiping up efficiently, adding an extra amiable pinch on a briefly exposed buttock. "Now, I'm going to let your daughter stay a few minutes longer. Okay, cute stuff?"

Mrs. Wolfe, now on her back, smiled weakly. The nurse winked and carried out the bedpan like a trophy.

"Oy, Sorele. . . ."

"Listen, maybe I ought to leave you now, Mama. Maybe you ought to get some sleep."

"No, stay, stay," her mother said, shaking her head. ". . . So how is Becky?"

"I told you already. Fine."

"She's in school?"

"It's Sunday. She's home with Dickie. Anyway, they don't allow children in the hospital."

"I know. I know. He's all right too, your husband?"

"Yes, he's fine. He's been working very hard, though. He'd love to come actually, but you won't be here very long."

Mrs. Wolfe closed her eyes and nodded wearily, as to some idiot child whom there was no point explaining things to. Sandra sat down beside the bed just for a minute, and in the deep hospital silence, felt the sun warming the back of her neck, a reminder that outside it was still daylight, and June. Then she made as if to look out the window, but at the movement, slight as it was, her mother opened her eyes quietly and closed them, and she turned again and remained still. Tiny warm weather noises drifted up from the street: a distant squish of car tires, the tinkling bell of an ice cream wagon, the sharp cries of children in sunshine. Inside it was deep quiet and the toilet smell of talcum powder. The

180

tulips on the bedpan cabinet were yellow and waiting. Her mother dozed and grunted, chasing a dream behind the busy white crepe of her eyelids. Her little babyish mouth was sunken, indicating the lost treasure of her dentures. How can she love all this? Sandra wondered, reaching down for her pocketbook and preparing to slip quietly from the chair. Why is it the only thing that makes her happy?

"*Sorele?*"

Oh, god. "Yes, Mama?"

"You're going home already?"

"I have to. Becky's waiting."

"I must go to the toilet."

A mental flash of silver bedpans, followed by the quick relief of remembering that the nurse had carried off the one from 814. Anyway, her mother had already grasped Sandra's arm for support and was trying to heave herself into a sitting position. In the other bed, Mrs. Zimmerman appeared to have fallen fast asleep, one hand over the *Magazine* section. Sandra bent down, fumbling for the terry-cloth slippers to put on the wide veiny feet, fighting a sudden wave of nausea. She helped her mother climb down, first to the footstool, then to the floor, and the two of them hobbled to the bathroom, a reluctant Aeneas linked to an Anchises with flat feet. Should she follow her mother inside? No, it surely wasn't necessary. Better just to leave the door ajar and stand guard beside it.

"Mother's all right?" Mrs. Zimmerman said, stirring in the nearby bed.

"She just had to go to the bathroom."

"That's the way it is with enemas. Sometimes there's a second round. . . . Mother says your husband is a publisher?"

"An editor, yes," Sandra said, wondering if she had imagined those faint calls from inside the bathroom, like the cheeping of a bird.

"My daughter, the physicist's wife, happens also to be a writer. She's presently working on a play. With two children it's not easy, but every afternoon as soon as the sitter comes, she goes right out of the house. She's collaborating with a friend, also a former English major."

"Excuse me," Sandra said.

She flung open the bathroom door, hearing a thin high whine. In the corner her mother lay huddled on the tile floor, her head with its little gray curls resting against the toilet seat, her legs sprawled in opposite directions. A thin thread of vomit dangled from her mouth.

"Mama!"

She took a step inside, returned her mother's look of mute terror, and raced outside into the corridor. The redheaded nurse was pushing a little tea cart filled with tiny fluted paper cups for pills, thermometers sticking out of glasses with blue solution.

"Oh, please," Sandra pleaded. "Oh, please come right away."

The nurse parked her cart and proceeded briskly into 814. "Why, you poor little thing," she said, solicitously poking her head into the bathroom. To Sandra, she murmured: "You should have rung for a bedpan."

The fat little huddled mass that was Mrs. Wolfe stared up at them from her corner, vomiting harder. Was she expected to clean it up, Sandra wondered wildly, since it was her mother, or—? But the nurse had already stepped inside and with her back turned to Sandra stooped and soothed, patted and wiped, until Mrs. Wolfe was ready to be brought lurching back to bed.

"The medication made her dizzy," Mrs. Zimmerman explained as the nurse helped Mrs. Wolfe off with the terry-cloth slippers and heavily lowered her onto the pillows. "She should only evacuate on a bedpan."

The nurse nodded and stepped back to survey her work. "Okay now, kewpie doll? We'll get an orderly to clean up and everything will be fine." Smiling at Sandra, and then putting a finger across her lips, she pulled a curtain alongside the bed and tiptoed out. Where the interested face of Mrs. Zimmer-

182

man had been; there was a coarse white cloth. Her mother looked pale and drained against the pillow.

". . . *Sorele* . . . ?" She moved her lips soundlessly. *"Sorele,"* she finally managed again in a voice below a whisper. "Stay. I'm afraid to be alone."

"It's okay, Mama."

"Stay?"

Her mother's hand moved on the sheet and caught her wrist. The street noises were muted. On the other side of the curtain there was a loud clatter of mop and pail, and then nothing.

SIX ·······································

It had been raining on and off all week, and now in a sudden crepuscular streak of sunshine, Amelia Cash sat doing her accounts in the parlor alcove of the Salt Box Inn, bony-chested, thin-lipped, a New England antique among the other New England antiques that cluttered up the place, the kind of junk that people like Vicky Auerbach adored and considered the absolute ultimate in Americana: painted black rockers with pillows tied to their seats, knobby gate-legged tables, crocheted doilies, antimacassars, round glass paperweights imprisoning splayed red flowers, damp and dead fireplaces, aging magazines, swaybacked horsehair settees, all of it mixed up with notices of art gallery exhibits, announcements of square dances in the village parking lot open to the public, for a price. Even the accounts were suitably listed in a worn black ledger, and as she passed through the parlor with Dickie, there was no doubt in Sandra's mind that Miss Cash was padding them mercilessly, just like all the other local merchants, the hardware store man, the gourmet butcher and gourmet baker,

187

the newsdealer with his overpriced kites and candy bars and copies of the New York *Times,* Dame Alden of the Candle Shoppe: NO DOGS ALLOWED. SMOKING PROHIBITED. DO NOT TOUCH THESE OBJECTS. CHILDREN MUST BE HELD BY THE HAND. All of which, for some Yankee reason, made them more scrupulous and upright than the Jews they were overcharging.

No, it was exactly the kind of expensive discomfort that her mother would never have understood, much less appreciated, Sandra told herself not for the first time and wondered why she kept telling herself so not for the first time. Maybe it was just the presence of all those damn German refugees with whom she and Dickie had increasingly to vie for reservations, the refugees were so obviously impressed to meet with an arrogance that finally matched their own. Several of them sat in the lobby, smugly dressed and already waiting for dinner, the double-chinned child analyst who had solemnly pronounced Becky intelligent, Erika Hauptmann who with a hoarse barking laugh was informing some frightened young fairy about the meaning of violence in America. There. Erika Hauptmann. A perfect case in point. Gaskell Press's expert on Auschwitz, increasingly their expert on sadism in general. In a camp an undoubted candidate for kapo. Yet here, welcome everywhere, featured on the cover of the *New York Review.* Dickie, whose Jewish loyalties were tepid, to say the least, *admired* her. Whereas Lena Wolfe, waddling around in her Gertz's silk print, buttonholing the Yekkes to complain about her selfish daughters, informing Miss Cash of her gall bladder trouble, cracking lobster at the Sunday buffet. . . . No, it had been bad enough the time that Leah and Morty had come to visit after dropping Itsy off in camp, both dressed in their motel outfits, Leah in aquamarine pedal pushers, Morty in the plaid Bermuda shorts and golfing polo shirt, four arms laden with crayons, paint sets, board games, records for Becky. They had also brought along a tape recorder into which they had inserted a cassette of Khatchatourian's *Sabre Dance* and then sat out on the lawn listening with their eyes closed. Afterwards, she and Dickie had taken them to Provincetown to a fish restaurant dripping with fishnets and multicolored candles in wine bottles, where the Schwartzes had insisted on grabbing the check, and in return she and Dickie had pointed out Norman Mailer in a corner. Leah had spoken about the visit often. Maybe she would call her tonight, tell her about Stella's party, who was there, say Vaughn Cranshaw had asked after her.

Miss Cash stood up, wearing the long calico skirt in which she would stalk about the maple dining room at dinnertime, keeping a sharp eye on the free mints and young waitresses. She acknowledged Dickie's polite good evening with a grudging nod, making her mouth into a little sphincter, and then Sandra followed Dickie out to the parking lot where the blue Hertz Ford was neatly aligned on the gravel alongside the other cars breathed on by the exhaust fumes coming out of the Salt Box kitchen. She had never told Dickie what had happened on that visit to the hospital. What would have been the point? She had gone to see her mother again, and it was okay. The Schwartzes had laughed about the possibility of postponing this vacation. Besides which, Wilma would never ever have made Dickie lose his cool, torture himself with lacking humanity, compassion. Even when his father died—long before they met, but Dickie had told her about it—and the undertaker had tried to sell Dickie his most expensive casket on the grounds that it would make his father "more comfortable," Dickie at nineteen and a Harvard sophomore had casually told the guy to go to hell. And what if she did tell Dickie about her recurrent guilt and self-loathing? He would only tell her to go see Dr. Starkstein. But she had seen Dr. Starkstein. He would tell her to go again. She buckled her seat belt and looked at Dickie sideways as he switched on the ignition. He was very sunburned, boyishly handsome, particularly in profile, and she told herself that they would surely make love that night. But when she put her hand on the inside of his thigh, Dickie gave her a preoccupied, almost silly smile,

189

and she remembered Becky in the dark clammy bedroom next door, very little, obviously much too inquisitive, tucked into damp sandy sheets by a thirteen-year-old girl from the village because Miss Cash wouldn't even allow them to ask an off-duty college waitress to babysit. Oh, why did every thought of Becky come with its own little pang of guilt these days, its aftertaste of rue, as if in Becky she had given her own little hostage to fortune? Dickie wouldn't understand about that either, and again he'd be right. If only she could be less inhibited about it all, more casual about family matters, less despairingly Jewish. Like Stella, for instance, who probably didn't even know if the children were walking in on her in the middle or not. Or Adam who had once let casually slip that he and Janice slept naked, a remark that had stunned her for a moment. Whereas she not only got up to put on her night-gown, in the middle of the night if necessary, but had also buckled herself into this seat belt first thing, leaving it loose enough not to make a mark on her white pants. Had there ever really been a time when cars meant romance, pleasure, passion, and a date driving her home from dinner and dancing in Westchester would find Sandra Wolfe blissfully nestled against his shoulder, even in her sleep in love with the dark country night? Now she was filled with a kind of pervasive dread, and the long empty Cape Cod highway loomed white and dangerous in the deepening dusk.

Dickie drove on, preoccupied and content in his rented car, past mile after mile of souvenir basket shops, art galleries, stands selling beach plum jelly. They were probably early. Stella had said to come early and swim, which was again so carelessly and typically Stella, as if, after she had got all dressed, she would want to get all undressed again. The party was more or less in honor of Freddie, who had flown up for the weekend. Why had she so stupidly imagined the Fruchtmans would never get together again this time, though she had seen them through countless such dramatic separations? Still, Sandra thought, I ought to be happy for her, glad that it worked out so well. And instead felt disappointed and depleted, as if she had been put to a foolish emotional expense for no reason, been made a spectator to still another one of Stella's exercises in self-dramatization. Dickie turned off the main highway onto a black bumpy country road, which dipped up and down, past a sandy cemetery, past half-hidden summer cottages flickering behind trees. On the far horizon, a skeletal radar tower appeared and then disappeared against a vacant blue ocean sky. At a tree full of wooden markers and arrows—"Epstein, Cooper, Aaron, Cruse, Auerbach" ("Some Indians," Leah said)—they turned off into denser woods, bucking on the low-slung country road. Sandra read out Stella's surprisingly clear directions from a piece of Salt Box Inn stationery. And then there was no longer any sign of the sea, only pine trees, mottled and greenish-brown like the pines in a Cézanne landscape. "Cézanne doesn't paint crooked pictures," Leah said before her voice went out for good. The light had gradually effaced itself. It was all dark, mysterious, beautiful, a self-contained natural world. Then, through a break in the trees, there was a sudden astonishing patch of silver daylight. A bumpier road led them to what looked like a shack at the edge of a lake, and a driveway already blocked by a couple of cars, a rented blue Plymouth, a low-slung red Jaguar with its top down. They sidled up the drive, ducking the lower pine branches, Sandra carrying her sandals. It really was a shack, a converted old Army hut, set down on a strip of sandy beach. There was a splintery wooden deck behind, facing the pond. The deck was bare and empty, flooded with late white sunshine. A basin of muddy water was set near the door, under a hook that held several damp bikinis. What had made her so sure Stella had stumbled on an architectural gem of a beach house this time? After all, was the big West Side apartment so terrific? She looked uncertainly at Dickie, who called out "Hello! Hello!" several times, and then pushed open a reluctant screen door.

Inside, Stella and Freddie sat against the wall on a long

orange foam-rubber slab, holding a few purple pillows against their stomachs and smiling tiredly at a naked sunburned couple who were cavorting in front of them. It was Hershel and Irma of course, and though Hershel wasn't quite naked since he wore a brown serape, it only made his bottom parts seem more exposed. They were doing bumps and grinds, singing "Let It Be," as their bare white backsides jiggled with every move. At the first rusty squeak of the door, Hershel turned around, laughing expectantly, ready for their shock, and when neither she nor Dickie registered any, gave them a smile so ugly it frightened her, and reminded her of the night he had cracked Irma's head open at that awful party. His hair was wild and irregular, as kinky as an Afro, and the granny glasses gave him two white holes for eyes, like Little Orphan Annie's.

"They came over early to swim too," Stella explained, scratching idly inside the collar of her pink silk shirt. She tugged at her pink silk slacks and recrossed her beautiful long legs, bouncing a foot in a thin gold sandal. She was perfectly calm, perfectly contained, but Sandra suddenly thought: She was in pain that day in the park, and I betrayed her.

"We didn't come early to swim," Sandra said. "We came to see you."

"Oh?" Stella said. "How nice. Freddie, darling, get them a drink."

"You get them a drink."

"I got Hershel and Irma theirs."

"Why not just show me the bar?" Dickie said, smiling.

"Want me to show you the ice too, lover?" Irma said, rubbing her bare shoulder and a dirty brown nipple up against Dickie's polite, unresponding arm in the seersucker sleeve. Hershel jiggled up and down again, still expecting an audience response, and looking like a Jewish chorus boy in *Hair*.

"It's really quite marvelous here, actually," Sandra said. "The view of that heavenly little pond. The little beach."

Stella smiled indifferently. Please, Stella, be hurt, be angry, just don't be indifferent. "Don't you like it?"

"Sweetie, I'm awfully tired of other people's dirt," Stella said.

"Yeah?" Freddie said. "You're not tired of your crappy art dealer friends' dirt. Or your painter friends' dirt. Only your family's. Why the hell is it harder for you to be a woman than for anybody else?"

"*Let it be. Let it be-ee,*" Hershel sang, and flopped into a black canvas sling chair on one side of the fireplace. Irma flopped into the matching chair on the other side. The two of them spread their legs wide. They were terrible to look at and for that reason not personally embarrassing.

"What are you staring at, honey?" Hershel said to Sandra, laughing.

Nothing. That was the problem, that was the point. But now she gave him a good long look just for the hell of it. His body flesh was much darker than his face would have indicated, and a good deal flabbier, much flabbier than Dickie's, though they both would be forty in a couple of years. Beneath the coarse brown serape, his belly folded in on itself several times, like a washboard, and in the dun-colored hair between his thighs, a soft little thumb curled and nestled off to one side. His outstretched legs were thin, too thin, and ended abruptly in a pair of leather sandals that buckled to one side like a pair of children's party shoes. Had there ever really been a time when she had been thrilled just to graze this man in passing? Had it really ever killed her every time he got married? Dirty Irma was even more unappetizing, another surprise when she considered Hershel's constant boring boasts about that gorgeous sexy body of hers, and that in the early days he used to call and tell what he and it had just done in bed together. It was another perfect example of Hershel's ultimate novelist's narcissism, his infinite capacity for falling in love with what he had made up himself, because even granted that a man could be bemused by that vaguely pretty snub-nosed face, the head

193

of India-ink curls, the rest of Irma was decidedly unlovely: dirty olive skin that would never look washed, long breasts, a sagging stomach with a long scar going the whole length of it. A caesarean scar maybe, though Irma looked as if she went around squatting and expelling babies in fields. In fact, what she resembled more than anything else was one of those Mexican women in Leo Lev's anthropology series on Latin America.

Smirking, Irma lifted a leg and slung it over the side of her chair. Sandra looked away quickly, pretending to be fascinated by what Dickie was telling Freddie about George Auerbach's wanting to renegotiate his contract for the third time. Damn it, why did Hershel always reduce the atmosphere to a shambles? And why, when he thought he was being so smart-alecky, did he always get it wrong anyway? The Beatles were old hat. So was going around naked. It had been years since taking off one's clothes had had a bohemian, almost transcendental meaning among Cape Cod intellectuals, as long past as that summer when Hersh was staying with them to finish his book, and they had taken him over to meet William Kohlrobi, who had courteously risen from his own pond stark naked and shaken hands with dripping fingers. Or the time that the three of them were walking along the ocean with Martha West, and Dickie was up ahead trying to lure her with talk of ads, possible sizes of first printings, and Miss West had suddenly shucked off her Victorian skirt and blouse and bounded into the waves, bow legs and broad buttocks exposed for all the world to see. "Oh, sweetheart," Hersh had said, as Dickie recoiled and Sandra felt slightly nauseated, "the sight of that broad's arse is going to come between me and that broad's prose forever." So why did he pretend that he didn't know what he damn well knew? Why act like a crazy kid, when as the evidence of the flesh so painfully proved, he was certainly a kid no longer?

"You know, Sasha, I've been thinking about you a lot lately," Hershel said, still slumped in the black sling chair.

194

"Really? That's nice," Sandra said, turning to Stella with a half-smile. Stella smiled back and continued to swing her foot with boredom.

"Ever since that day I socked you. It's an obsession."

"Oh, that," Sandra said.

"What do you mean, oh that?"

Over in the matching sling chair, Irma gave them each a smoldering look and unhooked her leg.

"It was just an accident," Sandra said.

"Oh? How can you be so sure? How do you even know if there *are* any real accidents? What if I meant something by it? What if deep down in my heart I really did want to murder, you, rape you, violate you? My god, Sasha, consider the implications. I mean, it's one thing to take a crack at that dirty olive-drab whore over there. But to violate my *Sasha!*" He smote his forehead, then covered his eyes, granny glasses and all.

"That's your head, not your heart," Sandra said. "And cut it out. It's not funny."

"Funny?"

She smiled placatingly in the general direction of Irma, who was glaring in her corner. What she had once told Leah was absolutely true. Victim of assault, head cracked and bleeding from a beer bottle notwithstanding, it was that captive ape over there who scared her to death, not Hershel. In fact, she was pretty seriously scared right now. What if Irma reacted violently to being called an olive-drab whore—though which would inflame her more, the adjective or the noun, supposing she knew the difference? What if she had already heard the talk about a blond University of Chicago freshman named Trixie?

"Sweetheart," Hershel said, "take a look at these. What do you see?"

"Your hands."

"My fists. Clenched. A double-barreled image of the black night of my soul. Who knows what else lurks down there?

195

Who knows if next time I'll even be able to control myself?"

"There won't be a next time."

"No, Sasha, hold yourself responsible. You've unleashed Hershel Meyers."

"Oh, shut up."

"Sasha, don't *say* that," Hershel said, springing to his feet. Behind the glasses, there were real tears in his eyes. "Not you, Sasha. You're my—"

"I'm not your anything," Sandra said, "and stop making an ass of yourself. And stop talking about violence. You're just a good Jewish Mama's boy at heart and you know it."

Over at the kitchen counter Dickie was giving her a strained smile. There was something strange, something sinister in the air. Hershel nodded a couple of times and then, with a final little sparring gesture, put his arm around Irma and took her off to the bedroom to get dressed.

"What's the matter with everybody?" Sandra said, with an uncomfortable laugh. "Where *was* everybody?"

"Hershel says he's going to insist on an advance of two hundred and fifty thousand bucks," Freddie said. "Didn't Dickie tell you?"

"A quarter of a million dollars! But nobody's thinking of giving it to him?"

"We're doing more than thinking," Freddie said with a laugh.

"But why? That book is awful."

"He says they can't afford not to," Stella said.

The people out on deck looked very clean in the late summer light, spruced up and natty, most of them laughing, their teeth startlingly white against bronze skin, eyes scored with surprising thin new lines. (Except for Vaughn Cranshaw in his ascot and navy blazer, who had turned lighter, a kind of smooth ashen gray. No, she simply wouldn't be able to tell Leah he had enjoyed meeting her.) Most of the guests stood about chatting in clusters, though a small group, including Gertrude Dienst, Angelica Ford, Ralph Gorella, was sufficiently self-confident to have sat down at a sort of cocktail table made up of the remains of an old wagon wheel, rough-hewn, gray, splintery, on whose spokes Stella had set out her summer hors d'oeuvres (as opposed to her winter ones of pâté, caviar, etc.): great hunks of cheese, salami, a wooden bowl of unshelled nuts, little tomatoes with their pips intact to dip in coarse salt (maybe even kosher salt, who knew? It was probably chic these days), sliced raw mushrooms, unhulled strawberries to dip in sugar. Hardly anybody ate very much of anything, just sometimes leaned over the table casually, in between drinks, during pauses in the conversation—except of course Gertrude Dienst's nephew who was stuffing his mouth steadily from all directions as usual, while Gertrude fondly and absently patted his long lank hair. Dreadful child. Once, brought uninvited (again as usual) to a cocktail party at Sandra's house, he had single-handedly devoured at least six dollars' worth of Nova Scotia salmon from Zabar's and about two dozen mixed canapes at ten dollars the dozen, and since then the sight of him had never failed to set up a cultural tug of war in her heart, tearing her emotionally between wanting the child to eat something, and fury that by the time he got through there wouldn't be anything left for the grown-ups. Still, if he was there making bored overlapping circles with his wet glass of ginger ale, and Danny was weaving in and out of the forest of grown-up legs, holding a pile of plastic glasses against his naked little pink chest, why had she left Becky behind, alone and forsaken, with that retarded village baby-sitter? Hershel and Irma had gone some time ago, out of pique, though they pretended to boredom, having marched around naked some more to no one's edification or amusement, and in fact practically unnoticed by anyone except Xavier Cruse and Vaughn Cranshaw, who had turned to each other with fastidious revulsion, though each for his own reasons. In fact Xavier was even more

197

concerned with local opinion, especially Yankee opinion, which sometimes spied on them through binoculars, than Leah was worried about her goyim. Obviously, it took a Lancelot Hale to call Amelia Cash a dried-up old cunt. "Come on, honey," Hershel had said finally, "let's go on to P-town where the action is." But there *was* no action in P-town, he had got it all wrong again. Was it just having been a poor boy from Chicago that made him so mistakenly amenable to every possible cultural suggestion and trend? The hippie nonsense with Irma? The real-estate holdings with pin-curled Dottie? ("Very *solid* real-estate holdings," Vicky Auerbach had pointed out.) The delicatessen suppers with fat Winifred out in Long Island City? Not that it mattered. She was probably the only person who realized he had left. But why hadn't Dickie mentioned that crazy advance? Why the strained smile that seemed to be telling her more than she wanted to know? And why had she so stupidly and haughtily cut Hershel off in midsentence? "Don't *say* that, Sasha, you're my—" *What? His what?* What *was* she to him?

There was more coming and going, the soft crunch of tires on sand, more guests climbing up on deck, some from other hidden houses in the woods, the women ducking, holding up long skirts and laughing. Many of them, to Sandra's surprise, she hardly knew at all. They were probably people from Stella's art world, maybe also some shrinks, general hangers-on. Freddie was tending bar behind a long board set on sawhorses, natty too in a French striped sailor shirt and bell-bottom jeans, no doubt a little import Stella had picked out for him at a boutique in Bloomingdale's. Freddie made her a martini, and she went to join Stella, who was sitting on the edge of the deck in her pink slacks and blouse, waving to new arrivals.

"Look, Stella," Sandra said, "I think I owe you an apology."

"What, darling?" Stella said, watching the sand sift through her fingers like sand in an hourglass.

"I said I owe you an apology."

198

"What a marvelous party!" Vicky Auerbach cried, bending over them in a much too elaborate caftan. "How divine not to know everyone for a change. Who's that gorgeous Thoreauvian type over there?"

"What Thoreauvian type?" Sandra said.

". . . *Paul!*" Stella said, rushing off. *"Paul Grasse!"*

The two of them, Sandra and Vicky, watched the embrace, Stella, the beautiful papillon, somehow unbruised by the tall burly man with thick hands.

"A collector," Vicky said.

"Oh?"

"From Cleveland. Of primitive African sculpture, mostly, I think, which I happen not to care for myself. Certainly not for our house here. How's the Inn?"

"Well, you know Miss Cash. Only too aptly named. Expensive, damp, and dank. Except in good weather, when it's not so bad."

"I can't imagine not having one's own house here," Vicky said, joining the group at the wagon wheel, which like a ride at a carnival had lost some members and acquired new ones, including the Fingerwalds. "It was so *sad* not to see Bunny at the beach today.". . . *"Tragic."* Daniel came trotting by, having been sent by Vicky to get more ice. Instead of the swaying pile of plastic tumblers, he now held a blue and white mottled styrofoam ice bucket against his skinny too-pink chest. His face was also too pink, and sweaty, his hair bleached a yellowish white by the sun. "Hi, sweetie!" Sandra said, too loudly (he backed away), and bent to give him a proprietary kiss on the cheek. Daniel raised the little arcs of his eyebrows with the faintest flicker of recognition. He was confused, poor baby. In the crush and noise, she was only another guest at the party. "Becky said to say hello!" she said, again too loudly and, as Daniel continued on his way, looked around socially embarrassed to have been snubbed by a child. More and more people were crowding up on deck—how easily Stella acquired people, without even trying, without even caring: more of the art crowd, more familiar faces from parties in New York: Violette de Laniere, Adam Brill ("Oh, hi. Is Janice here?"), summer friends with conveniently situated beach houses, Sylvia Mudlow and her blond curly-haired boyfriend, an extremely handsome, intellectual carpenter, two elderly Russian drunks rumored to be cousins of either Vladimir Nabokov or Czar Nicholas, she forgot which. They were dressed in every possible variety of costume, palazzo pants, bush jackets, navy blue blazers, caftans, neat little early Jackie Kennedy linen sundresses, tie-dyed jeans, nippled knit halters, high necked long-sleeved leotards for those who like Sylvia Mudlow had recently lost a breast to cancer, but of them all, the most amazing getup, bar none, was worn by the lady who had arrived with Mildred Auerbach, George's divorced wife, the social worker. "*That's* Sophie Katz?" Sandra asked Dickie, as the middle-aged apparition waltzed out on deck in a long green batik skirt, fringed piano shawl, gypsy beads, and two Japanese knitting needles with large knobs sticking out of her graying-yellow bun.

"Yoo-hoo, Richard!" she called gaily over several turned heads. "I'm going to shift the seduction scene west of page 141!"

"Good girl," Dickie said automatically.

There was a mild diversion through the trees. A wizened little fashionable architect climbed up on deck with his two notoriously vicious German shepherds that everybody was afraid of, though they were more afraid to admit it, and though the beasts wounded and bloodied innocent deer in the woods, sent little children screaming along the ocean beach. In the discreet backing away, only Vaughn Cranshaw stood his ground while the police dogs leaped and barked, then bounded off to terrorize someone else. Meanwhile, Sophie Katz, arm-in-arm with Mildred Auerbach, continued to make her way toward Dickie, blowing happy kisses here and there, even at one point stopping to throw her arms around a very surprised Freddie Fruchtman.

"Richard!" she cried, arriving finally and thrusting out both arms like an actress, then fixing him and also Sandra, when they had been introduced, with an admiring, glandular stare.

"You're the one who *irons* so beautifully!" Sophie Katz said, and looked around excitedly at the rest of the party as if she wanted to swallow it in one great happy gulp. She pointed, laughing, to Ralph Gorella who stood not far away, laying down the law to an as usual genially attentive Herb Fingerwald. Vicky Auerbach, flexed and tense with the imminent possibility of being called on to be intellectual, stood by, of the conversation but not yet in it. Mildred Auerbach looked around sourly for George.

"Do you know what that man said when I brought him my book?" Sophie cried merrily, pointing at Ralph. "He said, 'Who's in it, anybody I know?' Can you imagine? You'll protect me from that sort of thing, won't you, Richard?"

Over at the sawhorse bar, Stella and Freddie were telling each other to get the modish little architect a drink, though he had just poured himself a glass of club soda, all three of them ignoring poor Danny who had flattened himself against the screen door in case the dogs came back.

". . . *Adam,*" Sandra said.

"You were absolutely right," Adam said, acknowledging her with an abstracted nod, and smiling at Dickie ruefully. "I made three different appointments with him in San Francisco and he broke them all."

"Oh, well, it really doesn't matter," Dickie said. "William has most of what you need in that early essay."

"He won't mind?"

"No, no, he's very into the nineteenth century now. Will you and Janice be here with George and Vicky the entire weekend?"

"Janice had to stay in New York. Morgan's got a bad cold."

"But *you'll* be here?"

"Oh, yes."

"You're flogging a dead horse, doctor," Ralph Gorella said,

raising his gravel voice beyond the immediate audience of Herb Fingerwald and Vicky Auerbach to include several nodding bystanders. "The role of fiction as social comment is played out. Kaput."

"Oh, I agree," Herb Fingerwald said.

"Who the hell even *reads* novels anymore?"

"Nobody, that's exactly the point," Herb said, ostensibly smiling at Ralph but also addressing himself to the growing peripheral audience. "People *buy* them, but nobody reads them."

"Why should they?" Ralph laughed. "Even if some of these jokers could still write a decent sentence anymore, which they can't—what the hell could anybody learn from a novel these days?"

"Well, of course that depends on who and where," Herb said, still smiling. "I mean, obviously, adolescent girls, middle-aged women, particularly those in isolated social situations—suburbs and so on—are still going to look to fictional fantasies to sustain them—I'm not saying of a necessarily high order. Whereas—again obviously—your average male past puberty isn't seriously going to address himself to fiction in the wake of Vietnam, Hiroshima. What he wants is the quick answers of the TV commentator, the fact magazine, the *Times*."

Ralph's tired eyes traveled around the circle, stopping at Sophie Katz's eager overexposed bosom and continuing on to the thighs, caught in a fat V-cleft by the batik skirt.

"Some quick answers." Ralph laughed coarsely, echoed by the obedient and ever-widening circle of listeners. "The *Times* hasn't printed the truth in maybe thirty, forty years." Little Danny wandered through the forest of legs behind him, and Ralph, maybe mistaking him for one of the dogs, automatically kicked back his foot.

"Sure it's a false image," Herb said, even more ingratiatingly. (What made analysts so agreeable outside the office

202

and so disagreeable in it?) 'You and I know that. But out in the boondocks? In the hinterlands?"

"An ecologist," Ralph observed, laughing, to Sophie Katz, who laughed back. "Listen, boychick, I'll tell you something simple. There hasn't been a good novel written since maybe 1932. And I'll tell you why. Events outstrip them. Tell me what you think is a significant modern novel and I'll tell you it's a crock of shit."

"What about *Wait at the Circus*?" Vicky Auerbach called out, squaring her shoulders.

"Crock of shit," Ralph said, turning around to Daniel who was still crowding the back of his legs. "Listen, kid, shouldn't you be in bed by now?" Danny looked up at the sun.

"It's not like it was in the thirties," Ralph said. "We were a political generation. We were in tune with history, we were in touch. We *were* history. But who but a crazy shmuck would even have the chutzpah these days to take it on himself and say, here, I'll explain the world to you?"

"The necessary megalomania of the creative personality," Herb Fingerwald said. "That's exactly it. Hersh was suggesting recently in Washington that maybe I ought to do a piece for you along those lines."

"Who was suggesting?"

"Hersh. Hershel Meyers."

"So now he's commissioning pieces for *Hindsight*?"

"No," Herb said, laughing, "what he meant, very simply, was—"

"The guy's a total paranoid," Ralph said. "His first book I praise. The second I think stinks, and now he's out to do me dirt for life."

Vaughn Cranshaw and Xavier Cruse shook their heads at each other companionably. She hoped Vaughn would never hear some of Xavier's favorite dinner party jokes, particularly the ones about remedial Swahili.

"No, we can't leave it all to those who think life is one long

Swedish movie, can we?" Xavier said, going to get himself a drink. From the wagon wheel table, Gert Dienst stopped urging her nephew to eat and looked around.

"You know, I may be about to change my mind," Vaughn said to Dickie. "I'm deep in my book, but damn it, it seems to be a time for personal sacrifice."

"Sacrifice?" Dickie said.

Vaughn patted Dickie on the shoulder and started to move on after Xavier. "So what I mean is, if Gaskell Press still needs me—"

"Dickie, my god," Sandra said.

"Sandy, please."

"But that's all he *has*," Sophie Katz said, speaking up unexpectedly.

"That's all *who* has?" Ralph said. "What are you talking about, do you know?"

"I mean a writer like Hershel Meyers invests his whole self in his work, so how can he not feel enraged and obliterated if you reject it?"

"If you can't stand the heat, get out of the kitchen." Ralph laughed gratingly. "What's the matter, Soph, you don't think I bleed inside too when I'm criticized."

"But it's different for you."

"Why?"

"You're an editor."

"I'm also a critic."

"Okay, but a purely creative person—"

"You think Hersh Meyers is more creative than I am?"

"Of course."

"No, not necessarily," Herb Fingerwald said. "There are many, many different types of creative activities. Editing a magazine can certainly be creative. Being a good wife and mother can be creative. Even baking a coffee cake can be creative, given the proper circumstances."

"A child at play is also creative," Mildred Auerbach, the social worker, chimed in, and then she and Herb Fingerwald

204

smiled at Sophie sadly and indulgently, as if she were a child who had been caught not playing enough.

"She thinks any kind of a shitty novelist is more creative than I am," Ralph marveled to the group.

"That's not what I said exactly." Sophie laughed, cocking her head coyly, blushing a bit. "Though I suppose now that you think I've insulted you, you won't have any part of *my* novel."

"Wrong again, Soph!"

"Oh?" Sophie said, practically tittering in her excitement.

"I turned it down *before* you insulted me!" Ralph roared with laughter. "We sent it back to Dick weeks ago. Even the switchboard girl thought it stank."

"Oh?" Sophie said in a small voice, looking at Dickie.

"What are you trying to do in that thing, anyway?" Ralph said, frowning reflectively. "Make fun of the intellectuals?"

Over at the sawhorse bar, Adam picked up the styrofoam ice bucket and started to take it inside. Sandra looked down into her own drink, and followed him.

"Adam?"

There were actually more guests indoors than she had expected, people trying to escape the sun, the elderly putative cousins of Czar Nicholas—or was it Vladimir Nabokov?—sprawled side by side on the orange foam-rubber slab, staring with glazed eyes into a black and deadened fireplace, Vicky Auerbach judiciously weighing and unweighing the possible value of a piece of driftwood that Stella had exclaimed over earlier and then left lying on the kitchen counter in a wet mess of abandoned drinks and squeezed limes. Adam was standing behind the open refrigerator door, trying to jimmy a tray of ice cubes out of the freezer compartment. He was wearing a light blue sweater and chino pants, Dickie's Sunday outfit, and looked younger than she had ever seen him, thinner, somehow more American. Behind him, the sun suddenly flared orange before it went out, so that for a moment the people out on deck were black romantic silhouettes, like the figures on the covers of those love novels Aunt Rose used to read secretly when Sandra was little and hide away in a hall bookcase. Vicky Auerbach, having alternated several more times between greed and disdain, put down the piece of driftwood, shrugged and walked out through the sliding doors to the outside. Adam finally got a silver tray free of its icy shelf and held it under running water.

"Adam?" Sandra said at his elbow. "Do you love me?"

"Of course I love you," Adam said.

"No, really."

"Really."

"Now?"

"Always."

"You never called. You never even tried to get in touch."

"How could I have?" Adam said, smiling, finally wrenching the handle free and emptying the ice into the bucket. He turned off the faucet. It was all what she had seen Dickie do a thousand times, without even noticing, without even caring, but that now sent a pang through her heart, a pang for their lovely lost domesticity. Why wasn't it *their* kitchen, their stuck ice cube tray? No, crazy. The kind of thought that would have made Dr. Starkstein sigh and shake his head and light another cigarette, hike up his bill. She hated housekeeping. So did anybody with any sense. So did Adam probably, though he had a reputation for being something of a gourmet cook, which probably meant that he made a mess and let Janice clean up afterward. No, it was just the plainness of the gesture that had made her ache, made her lonesome, homesick for all the things they had never done together, never would. Taking walks, going to the movies, fixing themselves sandwiches, making love all night in the same bed, sleeping together without making love, turning to each other between the same sheets in the morning, smiling, squinting at each other with one eye, listening in while the other one made a phone call,

206

going down for milk. She tried to at least memorize Adam's dear serious face as he closed the refrigerator door, the way he picked up the ice bucket with his sunburned nail-bitten fingers.

"What's that on the other side of the lake?" Sandra said, loudly enough for the drunken Russian aristocrats to hear, not that it mattered.

"Where?" Adam said, and then shook his head and smiled again—at her tenacity? her childishness? She didn't care. He held open the back screen door and the two of them stepped outside. She felt suddenly cold, and shivered in the dense shade of the pine trees. A couple of strange kids were sitting on a log in sandy bathing suits and sweaters, dangling their feet, but the night was lowering quickly and she and Adam passed behind them unnoticed on the crunchy cranberry bogs. She reached behind her and took Adam's hand—oh, Adam, I'm actually holding your hand, your skin is so warm and real—leading him along the scrubby path deeper and deeper into the woods. But when they stopped, it was Adam who turned and took her in his arms and kissed her. Oh, my darling, my Adam. Delirious with joy and relief, she rested against him while Adam's bare hand reached under her blouse, moved up and down on her bare skin. The other hand was trying to undo her slacks.

"Open these lovely things for me, would you, darling?" Adam murmured into her mouth. "They seem to have no beginning and no end."

"No, Adam, not *here.*"

". . . Not here? . . ."

"They're all around us."

Adam laughed, futilely trying the slacks again, then pulling her blouse free up in front after he had hastily put away the medical service eyeglasses into his back pocket. She smoothed the straight black hair of his bent head. *Oh, baby, baby, baby. . . .* She had never nursed Becky.

"Adam, darling, I do love you so, believe me. But please,

not here. Not by chance. Please let's arrange it. I want it so much to be on purpose."

"This is on purpose."

"I meant—"

"Meant what, love? What, darling?" Adam murmured, never ceasing to stroke, caress, search her, with an extraordinary and rather impersonal expertise, come to think of it. "Tell me . . . what did you mean? . . . Hmm?"

"Oh, Adam, please, right now, just love me from a distance."

Adam dropped his hands and straightened up, expelling his breath and sighing like an exhausted swimmer. The night was dark and silvery, and Adam's face was discouraged and plump, like the man in the moon's. A straight black piece of hair hung over one ear. As he looked at her his face grew colder and it was all cold, the distant damp salt sound of the sea, the pine needles underfoot, the black wind-flicked boughs overhead. She leaned back against the rough bark of a pine tree and returned his stare, no longer aching with physical desire, far from it, but with a much deeper yearning. What was it? Then, awkwardly at first, like Becky learning to undress, she crossed her arms and pulled off her blouse and the brassiere which Adam had already unhooked, took off the rest, the white slacks, and let them all drop to the ground. She thought of doctors, camps, imagined she would put a hand here, there, try to shield herself, assumed she might cry, and then suddenly started to laugh.

". . . *darling, dearest,*" Adam murmured, enfolding her in his arms again and ignoring the laughter, back on his own wavelength. He gentled her to the ground. Oh, this was worth it. This was how you bought an ounce of love. She closed her eyes in the thick black night. Adam, her darling. He had called her his darling too. Her warm, hard, smooth-bodied darling.

"Adan ?"

"Yes, love?"

"Except for me, have you . . . ?"

208

"No, love, *shsh*. . . ."

"Neither have I. . . ." It was a lie. She hurried over it. "We're practically virgins. . . ."

"No, we're not. You mustn't think like that."

She tightened her arms around him. *Adam!* Oh, please, what is this like? *Adam?* What is it like making love with Adam? I've waited so long for this to happen again, desired it so much. What does it actually feel like? How can I fix it in my mind? The slithery burning feel of him inside. My arms around him, no space between. Skin against skin. The prickly pine needles beneath. Please, let me fix it in my mind forever.

"Sandra—?"

Adam kept on, but the voice in the distance suddenly made her lie still.

"Hey, where's Sandra? Somebody wants her on the phone."

There was a crashing around in some bushes nearby. My god, how close *were* they to the house? She grabbed up her clothes as, mercifully, whoever it was stumbled past them on the leafy path.

The lights inside were dazzling. She opened the screen door and smoothed down her hair. Everybody was inside now. There was a lot of noise and smoke, the chink of glasses, spiky cocktail voices rising and falling. The fireplace blazed and crackled. She noticed abstractedly that at the far end of the room near the wet and messy kitchen counter, Sophie Katz was hanging on Dickie's neck and crying in a hysterically coquettish voice, "You'll never desert me, will you, Richard? Swear you won't desert me, darling." Part of her drink spilled down the front of his seersucker jacket.

"I told him he'd have trouble with that one," Ralph Gorella's gruff voice remarked from behind her as Stella came out of the bedroom asking if anybody knew where Sandra had gone to because her sister was trying to reach her from New York.

"My sister?" Sandra said.

"Oh, there you are," Stella said. "The phone's in there, darling."

The bedroom was large and rough-hewn and chilly, like an artist's studio, with a low bed covered with a burlap spread. The black telephone receiver lay carelessly tossed near a cluster of many-colored pillows. Suddenly a pair of strong hairy arms seized her from behind. "How come you're so unfriendly lately?" Ralph Gorella said, pulling her away toward the wall, his hand moving up and down her smooth thigh, still in search of that erotically titillating bump of a garter. "You used to be such a nice friendly kid. So enthusiastic. . . . Hey, who the hell do you think you *are?*"

She wrenched herself away from him and picked up the telephone.

"Excuse me," Sandra said, putting her hand over the receiver. And then added, with a kind of polite apologetic party laugh: "Excuse me—but I think my mother just died."

SEVEN.........................

Sophie Katz came late and wearing black, as if she already knew the worst but wanted to put off hearing it. There was a hurried nervous conference with Adolphe at the door, and then Adolphe was smiling and smoothly pointing out Dickie over by the window, as if it amused him that not everyone knew that Richard Baxter always occupied the prime corner table of La Rochefoucauld. Dickie rose a bit, drink in hand, to make himself more visible, and wondered why there wasn't some easier way to be a gentleman-editor than this demi-crouch between a white tablecloth and a red velvet banquette. He sank down with relief when Sophie slid in next to him. They shook hands, Sophie first undoing some snarl with the handle of her pocketbook, and then as she opened her mouth to speak, Dickie smiled apologetically, said, "Excuse me," and held up a finger to signal Adolphe.

"What will you have?"

"It doesn't matter. Whatever you're drinking."

"A martini? Mine is five to one."

"Okay, fine."

"Beefeater's?"

"Anything. No, some coffee."

"Café pour Madame," Dickie said, wondering if he ought to have said "Mademoiselle." "Café filtre."

Adolphe clicked his fingers at the waiter, repeated the order, pointed to Dickie's drink, and presented them with two huge menus, printed inside in purple ink and decked with tassels. "What's today?" Dickie said. "Friday? They have a terrific bouillabaisse, if you care for that sort of thing."

"Anything," Sophie said, shaking her head impatiently, and looking even more sallow and lank-haired than usual on account of the black dress. Why the hell did she have to wear black, anyway? Sandra wasn't wearing black.

"Maybe you'd like to wait a while before we order," Dickie said.

"Yes, yes, I would."

The waiter nodded and backed off, returning with Dickie's second marini, which he started on immediately, and Sophie's café filtre for which she asked for some cream.

"Cream," Dickie said.

"You talked to Gaskell," Sophie said.

"Yes."

"And he hated it."

"Oh, now, I wouldn't say that," Dickie said. "Not at all. It was more a question of—" He paused, caught by the terrible anxiety in her protuberant eyes, and then looked at Sophie's coffee dripping weakly and uncertainly from the copper mechanism into the glass.

"Well, I'll tell you this," Dickie said, almost enthusiastically. "I made him use his veto. I said, 'Ed, look, if you turn this one down you're going to have to use that veto.'"

Sophie Katz made a sharp sucking noise, and hung her head like a cow that had suddenly had its throat slit. Dickie looked out across the room where all the people he had waved and smiled to from a comfortable distance on his way in—

214

Carol Curtis and client with Seymour Froude, a couple of girls from *McCall's,* and of course Herb and Muriel Finger-wald—were now watching and pretending not to watch him with a kind of nervous doubt. What did they think, that he was ending an affair with the woman, disappointing her in love? Had they never seen an editor and his author at lunch before—okay an author no longer his author—but an editor at a business lunch nevertheless? The irony in Sophie's case was that it would have been far easier to be ending an affair with her than having to turn her book down.

"Look," Dickie said gently, "I think you ought to have something to eat. Try the bouillabaisse. I'd have it myself, only I've developed this damn allergy to mussels lately, and I—" Sophie sighed, a deep shivery sigh, almost in layers, and he gave up and ordered for them both. No, not the foie à l'anglaise, he decided after a short consultation with Adolphe, though yes of course he knew that it was a spécialité of the maison and that they sautéed it very lightly in a bit of black butter. Actually, as he recalled it, Sandra was the one who loved liver and ordered it whenever she could. No, today, he had a yearning for something even simpler, perhaps just a small entrecôte done à point, with a petite salade on the side? Adolphe understood that he really meant à point? Adolphe did, looking at Sophie Katz uneasily. Couldn't she at least have started off with a glass of white wine?

"Did he give a reason?"

"Ed? No, he just didn't get it, that's all. He simply couldn't get what we were after. Don't take it personally. That's Ed all over. A nice guy, but many people don't understand him, because he's got this funny streak that—"

"Couldn't you have persuaded him?"

"There wouldn't have been any point," Dickie said. "Truly. There's no point in being published without enthusiasm. Believe me, it's the worst thing that can happen to an author."

Sophie looked at him sideways, and he wished that it hadn't occurred to him that maybe it was worse not to be published at all. "I know it's lousy," Dickie said, reaching out a hand to console her, and quickly changing his mind. "But it's not the end of the world. You'll see, some house with a lot more intelligence and imagination than Gaskell Press will—"

"You didn't just leave little slips of paper," Sophie said. "You wrote in the margins."

"I realize that," Dickie said.

"It was the original. I was the one who kept the Xerox."

"Look, I'd be happy to reimburse you out of my own pocket if that's what you—"

"You said it was only a technicality."

"It was."

"Some technicality," Sophie said, starting to smile sardonically and then, after a wry twist of her mouth, bursting into tears. Dickie looked around helplessly, first at Adolphe and then at the Fingerwalds, who were now staring with undisguised, horrified fascination. Where was all that analytic cool? That patient and genial understanding of any situation? Sophie blew her nose loudly into a man's handkerchief which she stuffed back into her pocketbook, and then in an absurd effort to conceal her crying put on a pair of big round black sunglasses that made her look like a huge insect.

"Even my butcher can back his claims," Sophie said.

"Oh, now wait a minute," Dickie said. "I believe I made it very clear from the beginning—" Then, not remembering exactly what he had made clear and because the food had arrived, he stopped talking and put an expectant and courteous hand on the cutlery at either side of his plate. Sophie obediently took a sip of her bouillabaisse, lit a cigarette, dropped the match into the saucer where the copper filter still dripped coffee, and reached for the cream. Cigarettes, bouillabaisse, café filtre with cream. In his corner by the frosted glass and the potted geraniums, Adolphe closed his eyes for a moment.

"If you *had* been my editor," Sophie whispered, staring down at her plate, quickly wiping away a tear that seeped out

216

from under the buglike dark glasses, "what revisions would you have suggested?"

"I suppose to eliminate Lester."

"And shift the seduction scene?"

"Yes," Dickie said.

"West of page 141?"

"Yes."

"Then cut out some of the bedroom scene?"

"Dandy idea," Dickie said.

"Peut-être que Madame n'est pas satisfaite?" Adolphe said, presenting himself at the table and smiling with some difficulty at Sophie's welter of plates and saucers. "Madame désire peut-être quelque chose d'autre?"

"You bet your ass, Madame désire quelque chose d'autre," Sophie said.

"Pardon?"

"Sophie, please—"

"You bet your ass, *Madame n'est pas satisfaite. Mais ce n'est pas ce plat ridicule et mauvais qui me gêne, ni votre chic si prétentieux dont je m'en fous. Non, ce qui me gêne, c'est ce moment terrible, c'est ma vie-même que je ne peux plus supporter!*"

The tears streaming down Sophie's ravaged face were somehow not as terrible as that dreadfully fluent torrent of French. Adolphe backed away as if from waves lapping at his feet. It was all a shambles.

"Oh, Dickie, Dickie," Sophie wept. "After this you'll go back to your office. But what do *I* do when the lunch is over?"

Dickie put down his fork. "Now, just wait a minute. That's not altogether fair. I mean, after all, Sophie, I do have a job and—" He caught himself before he added a wife and children. The woman was a menace.

"Good-bye, Dickie," Sophie murmured, twisting sideways to kiss him on the cheek. She slithered out from behind the table and headed for the door.

Dickie rose up, sat down, rubbed his cheek backhanded with his knuckles. There were bumping sounds of tables being walked into, glassware jiggling. The Fingerwalds, too late analytic, swiveled their heads the other way.

"Adolphe?" Dickie said, clicking his fingers and miserably pushing away the entrecôte. "Could you please bring me another martini?"

"Beefeater," Adolphe said, nodding. "Five to one."

The yahrzeit candle flickered on the mantelpiece under the Piranesi print, though why she had lit it, god alone knew. Maybe just because they had given it to her in the funeral parlor and she didn't know what else to do with the damn thing. The little button with the black slashed ribbon she had put away with the other one, the dearer one, in a little compartment of her jewelry box along with an old JFK campaign button, and a couple of Becky's baby teeth wrapped in shredded Kleenex. Souvenir of the funeral. But she could hardly, like Leah, pin the thing inside on her brassiere so that she could be in mourning for thirty days and still not show. "All the girls do it this way," Leah had explained apologetically in the funeral limousine going home, and Rabbi Glickman had looked on, nodding approvingly, both of them outdoing even Xavier Cruse in religious aplomb, since Xavier was extremely bothered by Masses in English. Still, she envied Leah as she must be at this moment, sitting shivah in Great Neck in great state, surounded by friends, fellow school-teachers, steamer baskets, mixed nuts, glazed fruits, in-laws, and other tributes to her bereaved condition. She herself had been almost entirely alone these past two days: her only visitor, Ruby Cohen Mandel, who had come in a little pants suit —Was that really right, though? A shivah call in an aquamarine polyester pants suit?—and also left the traditional offering on the foyer table. Again, not quite traditional, since unwrapped it had turned out to be a whole French brie and a box of

218

Jacobs' English cheese biscuits, though the name Jacobs was a little bit more like it. Her only mail, a flowered sympathy card from Orvietta, who was sonorously vacuuming down the hall; and also a gray note on gray Tiffany stationery from Felicity Gaskell. Oh, yes, and one telephone call, from Stella, who said that she and Freddie were off to Paris for a crazy week and that she would call again when everything blew over. No word from Hershel. Why did that hurt so?

She looked at her watch, and sat down. It was still only about three o'clock and Becky wouldn't be home from her day camp for another half-hour or so. As the sofa cushion rose up on either side of her it suddenly reminded her of the sofa cushion slowly rising in the old Bronx apartment when she was little and company came and sat stiffly in the middle. Then more and more of the living room began to look strangely like the Bronx too, full of doodads, knickknacks, silly stuff, as if after all these years of wandering through the chic of Bloomingdale's furniture and housewares, she had only arrived back at a latter-day version of the snake plants and the oilcloth shelving and the china domino ashtrays from the Five and Ten. No. Absurd. In fact, masochistic, another word Starkstein ought to have used but didn't. What she really ought to do was end this stupid atavistic shivah of her own, get up, do something, take a walk, have a nap, see a movie, make a stab at translating the new Charmais book on the end of cinema verité. But it all seemed so *inappropriate*. "Listen, darling," she had said when she kissed Dickie good-bye that morning, hoping stupidly that maybe he would decide to stay home with her, "I know it sounds ridiculous, but I really don't know what to *do* today." The answer she should have expected. But no, she was *not* going to see him. There was a human condition here that had to be met.

She stood up and walked around, clasping and unclasping her hands, like a child in suspense, and then looked back at the lonesome dent in the sofa, trying to remember her mother as she had really been, before the old nagging nuisance in the

219

hotel, before the wax Orthodox Jewish doll placidly awaiting burial in an anteroom of Riverside Memorial Chapel. Okay, granted she hadn't been the greatest, most psychologically acute mother in the world, in fact an insult to Rollo May and Rose N. Franzblau, granted she hadn't belonged to any societies so that when she died there was no question of a big Roxy-type funeral like Sandra's father's with other big men in the jewelry business and fellow officers of B'nai B'rith making long winded, self-satisfied speeches and eulogies. But she had lived and breathed, hadn't she? Even *tried* in her fashion? Tried to bring up Leah, okay in the Depression. Then afterwards, when Leah got married, let Sandra practically bulldoze her out of the Bronx to the social sanctity of Forest Hills, endured Sandra's false starts and stops at interior decorating until Sandra went off to Barnard and forgot the whole thing, not even noticing when the new apartment relapsed and the bric-a-brac crowded the top of the hated piano again, and the religious scenes depicted on black velvet reappeared on the walls, plus pictures entitled "A brievele der Mamen," plus menorahs with hidden music boxes, plus more and more of those snake plants and china domino ashtrays from the Five and Ten. But all she could think of was the other day's desolate scattering of a few aging aunts and uncles in a half-empty funeral chapel, the pious second cousins from Brooklyn, Aunt Rose, seventy if a day, and hennaed almost up to the gray roots. Leah's teachers' delegation in the back row. Up front, skinny Barry, glum Janice, wisecracking Morty, Leah in a stiff black veil attached to a bow, Dickie back in his wedding yarmulkah, Rabbi Glickman consulting his index card for people's Hebrew names, exhorting them that good women were more precious than rubies. She had a vague memory of dreadful rabbinical jokes all the way to the cemetery, and then she and Leah had stood by the open grave saying Kaddish in tandem like a pair of damn fools. Oh, Daddy, Sandra thought, looking over at the nice green mound with its aging engraved footstone, oh Daddy. On the way back, Rabbi Glickman had asked Dickie whether he ever published collections of sermons. She had come home to tear off the scarf hat and take a bewildered, weeping Becky in her arms. Then Dickie had led Becky away and made Sandra a martini.

Okay, but was it any better, spiritually speaking, when her *friends* died? Look at poor Leonard Lefferts, who had been buried from Campbell's after one long poetry reading, with quotations from Donne, Wallace Stevens, an early tribute from F. O. Matthiessen, whose student Leonard had once been. Or Donna Ziff carted off from a chiaroscuro chapel room at Park West after a tasteful musicale ("Park *West?*" Vicky Auerbach had asked later), not one word spoken, only a string trio sawing away, so that when the pallbearers wheeled off the casket they might very well have all been members of local 802. Or the political-type funeral of poor Yankel Gershon at Temple Rodeph Sholom, at which Ralph Gorella had stood in the pulpit, pointing an accusing finger and crying, "And then came Hungary! And I said to Yankel here, I warned him! . . ." Which wasn't even to mention the elegant memorial service for Hiram Hawes at the Morgan Library, for which the invitations had read 5-7. With us it's *always* a god-damn cocktail party, Sandra thought, and realized that in her heart she still imagined death would be as terrible and vivid as when her grandfather, Zayde, died and all the aunts and uncles had sat around the dining-room table in their stockinged-feet keening and caterwauling, and Uncle Louie, Aunt Rose's husband, had kept exclaiming, "Money is no objection! Money is no objection!" Leah had been so sweet with her then, Leah with her dates and her job and her night school. It was Leah who had hugged and kissed her, bathed her until she was pink, cut her toenails, washed her hair and combed it out with a fine steel comb. Leah who had put her to bed and explained about dying, that it was like going to sleep but never waking up. Such a silly thing to say to a child, but sweet really, in its way endearing. She thought of her mother

221

again, lying so very patiently in the anteroom of the Riverside Memorial chapel, in a cream-colored lace mantilla, pink-cheeked, plump and waxy, not sleeping, though looking curiously like herself, maybe because she was fat and had died so suddenly, but also strangely foreshortened like the body of Christ in that Mantegna crucifixion. The yahrzeit candle flickered under the Piranesi. . . . Okay. But it was so *quiet*. Where was everybody? Dickie, Becky, Hershel? Why wasn't there even a Puerto Rican kid yowling out in the street. . . ? *"Oy, Sorele,"* her mother used to say, smiling ironically when she hurt herself roller skating and came running upstairs with bruised and bleeding knees. "You'll cry like that when Mama's dead?"

When the bell rang she let Orvietta answer it—Orvietta at least was treating her with unusual if unnecessarily dark and gloomy respect—and ran back to her dent in the sofa to arrange herself, planning to offer the Jacobs cheese biscuits and the French brie, should the possibility arise. But it was Leah, of all people, Leah in a strawberry print shift, white mesh gloves, and high-heeled white sandals.

"I thought you were sitting shivah," Sandra said, too surprised to get up.

"Yeah, *shivah*," Leah said, with a sardonic smile, stripping off her gloves and stuffing them into her pocketbook. She stopped and looked around at several pictures, including the. Piranesi, leg muscles tense, as if she were anxious to spot a reproduction.

"But, Leah—" Sandra began, smiling, and let it drop. So even to Leah the traditional mores were wearing thin. But there was no point in pursuing it, asking more questions. She would only make Leah nervous, and besides, she was ridiculously glad to see her, curiously honored by the visit. Her heart lifted almost as it used to when she was little and watching Leah get dressed for a date, and Leah unexpectedly turned from the mirror to talk to her.

Leah jabbed a cigarette into her mouth and sat down on the red velvet settee, breathing out smoke like a small pinched dragon.

"Would you like a drink or something?" Sandra said. "It's almost late enough."

"What? No. Yes, sure, why not?"

"What would you like?"

"Anything. Rye and ginger ale."

"I'm not sure we have any rye," Sandra said, wondering if the children had finished the ginger ale. She thought of all the cartons of tonic and club soda in the pantry.

"Okay, make it a rum coke."

Rum? There was no rum either. She didn't even know anybody who drank rum except maybe Ruby Mandel when she and Eli went on those off-season Miami Beach vacations of theirs.

"Listen," Sandra said, "this friend of ours—Ed Gaskell, actually, the owner of the Press—I told you about him, didn't I? He's the one with the town house and the orchids on the roof? Well, anyway, he gave us this incredible Napoleon brandy for Christmas, and we were just waiting for a special occasion to crack it out. Not that I'm implying we have cause for rejoicing or celebration or anything of that sort, though I must say for a while there I felt as if I were in the middle of my own private Jewish holiday. It's only that—" She leaned forward and touched Leah's skinny stevedore arm. "Oh, god, Leah, I was feeling so lousy. I'm so ridiculously glad to *see* you."

"Anything you want to get rid of will be fine," Leah said courteously, tapping her foot.

In the kitchen, seeing Sandra take down the brandy bottle, Orvietta abruptly stuck two big snifters on a little tray. A misplaced kindness and embarrassing besides. How the hell was she supposed to bring the ridiculous things in to Leah?

223

But even today, she didn't have quite the courage to face those wary, unexpectedly hazel eyes. What did Orvietta want of her anyway? She hadn't been white that long. Then the doorbell rang, meaning Becky was back from day camp, and Orvietta went to answer it. By the time Sandra came into the living room, Becky was already installed on the settee beside her Aunt Leah, face turned to face, like a pair of silhouettes on one of her mother's old cameos. Leah had put on her gloves again and was holding Becky by both white mesh hands.

"My maid's idea of splendor," Sandra said, putting down the tray on top of a pile of magazines on the marble cocktail table.

Leah barely looked around. "If you go into the foyer, baby," she said, "you'll find a present on the hall table."

"I'd rather stay with you, Aunt Leah," Becky said.

"Would you, sweetheart? That's very sweet. Even if I tell you what it is? A Pete Seeger album?"

"Oh, boy, neat-o," Becky said, glancing at Sandra to confirm that she had said the right thing, and politely refraining from mentioning that Leah had given her a Pete Seeger album the last time. Poor Becky, she had been so painstakingly polite the last few days, even for Becky excessively kind. But Leah must be more distraught than she knew, to have repeated a present when she had never repeated a present before, even with all the dozens stashed away in the hostess closet.

"I would have brought you a book. But I know how many are available to you through your father."

"I love books," Becky said.

"I know you do, sweetheart," Leah said. "My third-graders should only love books the way you do." The stringy neck veins tautened up genteelly. "Not that they aren't very lovely children, too, in their own way. We must remember that all people are different and respect those differences, mustn't we?"

"You're not wearing black either," Becky said.

Leah looked down at her strawberries.

"Becky, I've explained several times that—" Sandra began.

"That's right, baby," Leah said. "It's not necessary. Jews don't believe in it. They don't see what good a black dress could possibly do for a person who's—passed away."

"What does do any good?"

"Now that's a big question for a little girl, isn't it?" Leah said, with a smile.

"Do Jews believe dead people go to heaven?"

"Oh, yes," Leah said. "Certainly. Absolutely."

"Is Grandma in heaven?"

"Yes," Leah said.

"Looking down on us?"

"I don't know," Leah said, with a sudden acid twist to her voice.

"Go play your record, Becky," Sandra said. "Orvietta will help you." Becky looked at her with open-mouthed astonishment at the idea of Orvietta helping anybody, and then slowly and much too obediently climbed down from the sofa. In the doorway, she turned around with a last gentle smile.

"What a doll," Leah said.

"She'll come back later," Sandra said. "Anyway, it's such fun to be alone for a change. Do you realize that we really only talk on the telephone?"

"I guess so," Leah said.

"You know it's funny, but when I was little I always used to wonder how brothers and sisters became aunts and uncles. I mean I couldn't believe that Aunt Rose and Mama and Uncle Max all lived in the same house once and were kids together, no matter how many times Mama cried about it. Didn't they look shockingly *old* at the funeral? Do you remember when Daddy wouldn't let Uncle Max in the house because he was such a hot Communist? And did you see Aunt Rose's pitiful henna job?"

Leah gave a small tight smile. She had touched on some Depression nerve again. Maybe it was Uncle Max who had argued against the extravagance of summer camp and violin

225

lessons, maybe even Aunt Rose, though it was unlikely their father would have listened to anybody from their mother's side of the family.

"I suppose I'm just taking a worm's eye view," Sandra said, laughing. "I guess I really wasn't old enough to know what was really happening." Leah's neck veins tautened. "Like that incredible Marjorie Morningstar wedding—do you remember it?—at the Twin Cantors, when one of Uncle Max's children was getting married and I didn't know whose side I was on, the bride's or the groom's. Dickie thinks it's an apocryphal story. But, honestly, every time I asked somebody, especially Aunt Rose, they'd slap me on the back and tell me I was a great kidder." More tight, smiling silence from Leah. "Did I tell you by the way that yesterday in the bathroom, Aunt Rose told me she used to have a crush on Daddy? Can you imagine? Her own sister lying in an open coffin in the next room, and she—" Leah closed her eyes. She had gone too far again. "But then death always does reduce people to fundamentals, doesn't it? Sex, money, food—everybody becomes practically straight out of Maupassant."

Not *de* Maupassant, Sandra thought, finally grinding to a halt, though Leah would hardly have had enough French to appreciate the nicety. In fact, Leah, grinding out her cigarette, draining what was left in the brandy snifter in one quick l'chayim gulp, didn't seem to be appreciating the niceties of much of anything.

"Listen, Lee," Sandra said, "this friend of mine, Ruby Cohen Mandel—the one you met at the party? The one who wrote *The Devastated Decimal?* She has this Orthodox husband who's also queer, by the way. Isn't that marvelous, to be queer in a yarmulkah? Anyway, she left me this gorgeous ripe brie, and—"

"She's the one with the clean fingernails?" Leah sighed.

"Yes," Sandra said, reaching for her own brandy. "Anyway, she left me this gorgeous ripe brie, which is in a state of absolute runny perfection. So I thought—" Leah had stood up,

226

and was starting to pace around and look at pictures again.

"Would you like another drink?" Sandra said.

"I have to go. I'm picking up Morty at the office. His car's in for a tune-up. I'm driving him out to the golf course."

"Morty's playing golf today?"

"Why not? Doesn't *his* health count?"

"Sure it does. Absolutely. I only meant—wouldn't he understand if you were a little late? We so rarely—and today—I mean we could eat lots of brie and get plastered. Or else we could even send down for delicatessen. I know, we'll call the men and—"

Leah was staring out the window.

"She made a will," Leah said. "She consulted some shyster lawyer at that shitty hotel and made a will."

"*Mama?* You're kidding."

Leah looked around grimly.

"But that's extraordinary. She was incapable of doing anything for herself, much less something like that. Anyway, what for? All she had was Daddy's insurance."

"The will . . . ," Leah said, in her most precise schoolteacher's enunciation, "pertained to her personal effects. She left you the diamond pin and me her Melmac dishes. Plus a ketchup dispenser shaped like a tomato."

"Oh, my god," Sandra said, about to laugh, and then remembering to step cautiously. ". . . Maybe she thought you really did prefer plastic."

"I do," Leah said. "That's not the point. It's worth a fortune."

"The diamond pin? Oh, no, not really. Don't you remember that I mentioned seeing one just like it in an antique store on Madison Avenue? Gumbiner's I think it was."

"No."

"Well, anyway, it's not worth more than a few hundred dollars at the most. We could have it appraised."

"*You* could have it appriased."

"Oh, come on, Leah," Sandra said, laughing. "Don't be

silly. You know perfectly well I have no intention of claiming the damn thing. Take it if you want it. I'd give it to you now if I had it here. .... Listen, are you sure Morty wouldn't maybe like to forget about the golf for one day and come over? I mean it. I'll call Dickie. I'll bet I can still catch him at the office. We'll make *him* buy the delicatessen. We'll all be together. Okay? It'll be a family reunion. The men will sit around in undershirts and we'll be straight out of Odets. Like *real* relatives."

"She had no right," Leah said.

"Who had no right?"

"*She* had no right."

"Mama?" Sandra said, smiling harder. "Look, technically she could have left everything to the Black Panthers if she wanted to, UNICEF, the Hundred Neediest Cases. What do *we* care? I *told* you. I thought you hated that pin, but if you like it, for god's sakes take it. Be my guest."

"I wouldn't touch that pin with a ten-foot pole," Leah said.

"Now, that's a pretty silly attitude, isn't it?" Sandra said, feeling her heart begin to race. "I mean, after all, I just said that I—"

"I moved her to the garden apartment," Leah said. "I wiped her ass. I examined her goddamn bloody stool in the toilet. When she passed out, I carried her in my arms like a baby. And then she does this to me."

"What the hell did you want her to do?" Sandra said. "Pay you back?"

"You and your Dickie put the idea into her head. You and your fancy friends."

"Are you out of your mind?"

"You think you're somebody," Leah said, with tears in her eyes, gripping the white plastic pocketbook against her stomach. "You think just because none of your friends are normal people and you only hang around with writers and celebrities that you're somebody. But let me tell you, in my book, you're nobody from nowhere. You don't know a god-

228

damn thing. You and that superior husband of yours, you're just a pair of lousy crooks, sneaks, *thieves!*"

The neck veins had begun to work frantically. Her eyes were wet, intense, shiny black beads.

"Leah, take it easy," Sandra said. "You're getting overwrought about nothing."

"Nothing!"

"So what if she did hurt your feelings inadvertently, what of it? Why introduce this kind of emotionality into a situation where it doesn't belong, that doesn't warrant it? None of this has any real meaning. It doesn't *matter.*"

"It matters," Leah said. "To me, it *matters.*"

"All right. But even so, why let it come between *us?* Look, Leah, don't be foolish. I'm offering you that goddamn pin as a gift, from me. Will you take it?"

"I told you. I wouldn't touch it with a ten-foot pole."

"Leah, please—"

"I wouldn't touch anything that belonged to her with a ten-foot pole," Leah said, lighting a cigarette and crushing it out again.

"I belonged to her," Sandra said, after a moment.

"I know it," Leah said.

Dickie came home looking very tired. Maybe it was the heat. Maybe that he had just been working too hard. Maybe it was the interrupted vacation that he had never complained about. Oh, *Dickie,* Sandra thought, suddenly wanting to tell him how much she loved him, how much she cared whether he was overworked and tired. But he had gone through the pointless mail and was giving her a wan, patient smile, and she decided not to burden him with any of it. Besides, for a minute, on account of that smile, he had almost looked like a Puerto Rican delivery boy waiting for a tip before he could beat it out the back door. All he needed was some grocery cartons and one of those little black fedoras perched on the top of his head. No, that was ridiculous, unfair. What Dickie really looked like suddenly, though she didn't want to think that either, was a commuter at the Biltmore bar, a little bit too sunburned, a little bit too amiable, a little bit more gray than blond at the glinting temples. What if Dickie stayed this way forever? What if time didn't change Dickie at all, only petrified him, like Lorraine and Tony Talcott who gave the same little chic impoverished East Side Christmas parties as they had in the twenties, a perpetual Scott and Zelda, only gray and wrinkled. Could it be true that aging *was* worse than dying? Then she looked again, and Dickie was settled in on the couch, handsome again in his wrinkled seersucker suit, tanned, his eyebrows bleached by the sun. And there wasn't anything wrong with him at all. Far from it.

"Leah was here," Sandra explained, as Dickie looked questioningly at the two snifters on top of the marble cocktail table.

"Drinking cognac?"

"She wanted a rum coke, but we didn't have any rum."

"I thought she'd be out in Great Neck surrounded by steamer baskets."

"I did too. It seems I was mistaken. Do you want a drink?"

"No, I drank too much at lunch," Dickie said. "There's nothing wrong between you, is there?"

"No, no, absolutely not. It was just one of those stupid misunderstandings." She went into the pantry to make herself a martini—somehow now that Dickie was home martinis were okay again—and couldn't decide whether to be glad or exasperated that for the first time Orvietta had finally remembered to fill the ice bucket. Then she came back and sat down next to Dickie, who looked at her nervously, worried as always by the very possibility of unhappiness. He carefully slid the latest copy of the *New York Review* out from under one of the snifters, and as Sandra entwined her arm through his, read from a stiff distance, begging her pardon every time he had to turn a page. The feel of his arm and shoulder bones

230

through the thin jacket was terribly sweet and masculine, terribly reassuring. What a dear lovely man Dickie actually was, Sandra thought, admitting to herself that much of Becky's gentleness came from him, and what a gift he had for putting things in their proper unagonized perspective. She wanted to say again, "Oh, Dickie, I love you, I've missed you so all day," except that this time it was that damn *New York Review* that inhibited her, with its black list of contributors, made her feel that it was a cocktail party to which she, not Dickie, was uninvited.

"It was all so silly, actually," Sandra said. "My mother left me her diamond pin and Leah was absolutely furious about it."

"How did she leave you her pin?" Dickie said.

"Oh, she consulted some shyster lawyer at that crazy hotel and made a will or something. It doesn't even bear thinking about."

"Well, I can understand why Leah would be sore," Dickie said. "It's probably worth a lot of money."

"No, it isn't," Sandra said. "I even saw one like it recently in Gumbiner's window. Anyway, why are you suddenly concerned with what things are worth? You never even know what anything costs."

Dickie opened his mouth, on the verge of answering, and changed his mind and loosened his tie instead. "I was just trying to see it from Leah's point of view, sweetie."

Sour-y, he ought to call me sour-y, Sandra thought, realizing how shrill she had probably sounded. She took a deep breath and leaned back against his shoulder, comforted again by the mere physical fact of him. Inwardly she was still trembling. The scene with Leah had upset her more than she realized. It had been like finding herself back in the foreign country of her childhood, with all its ugly screaming and invective—what she had thought this afternoon she was all finished with. Dickie was peace, Dickie was civility, Dickie was understanding. It was kind of him to try to see it from

Leah's point of view. She should try to see it from poor Leah's point of view also. After all, why cling to an outmoded relationship from an uncherished past? She had no need of a mother, Leah or any other substitute. It was just that lately she had let her life go slack, culturally speaking, allowed herself to live in a spiritual desert, no, an unweeded garden where any tenacious stray root could take hold.

"You know what?" Sandra said. "I've been thinking of going back to work again."

"It's a lousy job market these days," Dickie said.

"I know. But you still haven't found a replacement for Aaron Lasch. And Ed really likes women."

Dickie's hand went to the already loosened knot of his tie. "Do you think that's such a good idea?"

"Why not? Don't you want me?"

"Oh, of course, but—"

"I can't believe that anybody worries anymore about nepotism, do they? And with Becky older—"

"Other ladies in your position sometimes get pregnant again."

"Dickie, I'm serious."

"So am I," Dickie said, smiling.

She unhitched her arm and drank some more of her martini, though it was too strong and too sweaty-making for July, and Dickie put aside the *New York Review* and looked at her solicitously, as if she actually were pregnant. She settled back again, reminding herself once more how nice Dickie could be to people in trouble. Not even in trouble, just the strays, the weird ones. Sophie Katz. Norma. How nice had he actually been to Norma? Did he think of her as a Norma now too? *Stop it, stop it,* she told herself, *control yourself.* Dickie belonged to *her*, not some homely secretary, and the meaning of their married life, faute de mieux, willy-nilly, really did lie in that old Persian carpet from A & S.

"Oh, Dickie," she said dreamily, staring up at the ceiling and ignoring the cracks from the last lousy paint job. "Do you

232

still remember how it was when we both did work at Gaskell Press together and all summer days were endless?"

"You're upset," Dickie said.

"No, really. I think about it so much lately. Was it because we were so young that it all seemed infinite, like the view from the Brooklyn Bridge? God, how beautiful that pedestrian walk was before they renovated the damn thing. Even the subway wasn't so bad then, which is now such an inferno. Do you remember how we used to get off at Wall Street, so we could walk home across the bridge, and the sky was all around us? And how tiny our apartment was. Just that one studio room and the Pullman kitchen behind the screen and the little bathroom. Why wasn't there ever any trouble about space then, or time? How did we both fit into it? And dinner. There wasn't ever any fuss about dinner. And we always even had time to go to the movies."

With his free hand, Dickie covered his mouth to stifle a burp, one level of his still youthful chin flattening itself against the other. There was also the incipient bulge of his blue shirt above his belt line, all of which reminded her that Dickie's problem hadn't ever been dinner, but lunch. Who with today, she wondered.

"Just some author," Dickie said.

"Which one?"

"Sophie Katz. . . . Look, maybe you ought to wait a while before you speak to Ed. I think September might be a much better time to approach him. Though if you're really anxious about it, maybe you could ask Ralph if there's anything open at *Hindsight.*"

"No, thank you," Sandra said. "The memory of that ape and that poor woman out on Stella's deck will probably last me a lifetime." She took another sip of her martini, no longer caring that it was hot and strong. "Do you think you'll be able to find somebody else to take another piece of it?"

"At the moment," Dickie said ruefully, "I'm wondering if I can find someone else to take *all* of it."

"What are you talking about? You don't mean that after all this time Ed rejected it?"

"Of course he didn't reject it," Dickie said. "How could he reject it? But he'd do it without enthusiasm. And as you know, the worst thing for an author is to be published without enthusiasm."

"You mean you didn't even fight for it?"

"Of course I fought for it," Dickie said. "I even made Ed use his veto power, if you must know. But what's the point? Frankly, I more and more agree with him. Why should we take a chance on a novel that's been turned down by everybody and his uncle and won't sell more than four thousand copies anyway? We're overextended as it is on account of Hershel. How do you think Ed feels to have to put up that kind of money?"

"What about Umberto? His books don't even sell *one* thousand copies."

"For God's sakes, Sandy, there's tremendous prestige to those poems, as you perfectly well know. That's currency too."

Becky started to walk in with a baked brown ashtray she had made at day camp, smiled and said, "Hi, Daddy," and walked out again.

"So Hershel was right, wasn't he?" Sandra said, after a small silence. "He *is* a murderer."

"If you're talking about Sophie's suicidal tendencies," Dickie said, "personally I think they've been much exaggerated. Personally, I'd be extremely surprised if she ever actually tried anything."

"What difference does it make? He's killed all her hopes and aspirations, hasn't he? Because that's all Gaskell Press is interested in anymore, isn't it? The quick sale, the big splash. What happened to your 'quality list' Richard? Oh, god, and when I think of how young and in love the three of us once were."

"Look, Sandy," Dickie said, "let's get at least one thing

234

straight, okay? *We* were not in love, as you put it. You were. I hardly even knew the guy until you came along."

"That's ridiculous."

"I liked his first book and I got it accepted. I encouraged him to do a second. But he only started coming around when he met you."

"That's nonsense. Flattering, but nonsense."

"Look," Dickie said, "I'm not questioning the nature of the relationship between you two. And I'm certainly not trying to rehash old times. If he was attracted to you, okay. It's under-standable. After all, so was I."

"Was?"

"—but your sentimental version of it all has gotten a little bit out of hand."

"There's a difference between sentiment and sentimen-tality," Sandra said.

"Barnard English I."

"Does that have to come up?"

"Okay," Dickie said, "I'm sorry. Scratch that. But if you're so concerned with love and friendship, what about Hershel's hopes and aspirations? Don't they count too? Or do you propose that we abandon him?"

"He's the one who abandoned us. He sold out."

"Sold out to what? To whom?"

"I don't know," Sandra said. "It doesn't matter."

"And what makes you so sure this book is so terrible, anyway? Have you actually read it through? Have you seriously tried to understand what he's after?"

"I tried," Sandra said.

"Well, personally, I happen to think it's a very interesting experiment," Dickie said. "Very good of its kind. But even if you don't, what makes you so sure he won't write something better the next time? Have you stopped believing in his talent so completely? My god, Sandy, everything else aside, you talk about this man constantly, he's always on your mind, you've known him—"

"All my married life," Sandra said. "Which isn't the point."

"All right then," Dickie said, "if you want to talk about selling out, don't forget that *she* didn't have to entertain the idea of revision either. Nobody forced her, nobody guaranteed anything. There's a little serpent in Miss Katz's garden too."

"I don't believe that."

"You know, Sandy, for all your talk about the texture of reality," Dickie said, "you balk at reality. You're bad at real things."

Orvietta poked herself in at the doorway, wearing what looked like a pot on her head and carrying a pot in her hand. She announced that she was just about through for the day, and vanished. The two of them looked at the empty place where she had been until the noises of Orvietta marching down the hallway and slamming the front door had all been accomplished.

"What are you going to do now?" Sandra said.

"What can I do? Try to send her on to somebody else. Write her a note saying it's all my fault for leading her into a traplike situation."

"This business has affected your syntax too. A thing is either a trap or it isn't."

"Sandy, *I* didn't make the rules," Dickie said.

His half-smile froze.

"Oh, Sandy." Dickie sighed. "What did you think slapping me was going to accomplish?"

Becky was eating her TV dinner in the kitchen, propping up her copy of *Uncle Wiggily* against the napkin holder with a free hand. She had put on all by herself the little blue shorty nightgown with its ribbons and ruffles that was a present from Grandma via Aunt Leah, and also done up her hair in two dissimilar ponytails, one tied with a green elastic with a little gold knob, the other with a red ribbon.

236

"How about the soup?" Sandra said, sitting down with her for a minute and lifting the ponytail with the elastic out of the mashed potato compartment. She pulled the thick strap of the nightgown back onto Becky's peach shoulder. "There's soup in the little covered part."

"I know it," Becky said.

"You won't have time to watch TV if you don't finish soon."

"I'm not watching TV tonight," Becky said, forking up some turkey and turning a page.

"Why not?"

"I'd rather read. I love books."

"You happen to love TV too," Sandra said. "As we both know perfectly well."

"Well, it's nothing to get sore about." Becky laughed.

"I'm not sore," Sandra said. "I didn't say I was sore."

"Mama," Becky said, with sudden interest. "Aren't you ever going to wear black?"

"Oh, that's a great help," Sandra said, standing up. "Thanks."

"Why? What did I do?"

"Nothing. That's just the point. Nobody's doing anything. Including you, Becky."

Becky looked away quickly, but not before Sandra had seen the hurt blue eyes swimming with tears.

"I'm *sorry*," Sandra said, bending to kiss the top of Becky's sweaty head. "Forgive me, baby. I'm *sorry*." She wiped Becky's cheeks with a paper napkin. "You don't have to watch TV tonight. You can read. Okay?"

"Okay," Becky said, nodding dutifully, though her eyes kept straying to the open page of *Uncle Wiggily* and she kept having to wrench them back again. Sandra walked back down the hall and automatically looked into the living room where Dickie sat in an armchair with his legs crossed, going over some new manuscript with the same smug self-satisfied intensity as if he had never had one in his lap before. He would remain there immersed in it until he was called to dinner,

237

which tonight would be a tuna fish casserole that Orvietta had lumped together in honor of her bereavement, though Dickie would just as soon have made the dinner for both of them if she asked him to, or else taken her out to La Rochefoucauld if she had wanted that. He was marvelously agreeable about such things, marvelously agreeable about so many things. How had she contrived a life so civilized that no one, not even her husband, would question the fact of her wanting to dine in a fancy French expense-account restaurant two days after her mother's funeral? In the bedroom, which she wandered into almost by mistake, without particularly meaning to, she sat down dispiritedly on the edge of the bed and looked into the Victorian oval mirror above the bureau, seeing not herself but Dickie, poring over his manuscript in the lamplight, patient, fair, elegantly rumpled. Had she gone too far with him maybe this time, would she maybe this time lose him? She dismissed the sudden chill fear as contemptible. Still, could he have been right about those old days with Hershel? But they had never even touched, never even been alone together, never even kissed except for hello and good-bye, formal occasions, birthdays. Only once, yes it was at night, on a Circle Line boat ride, a publicity stunt for a novel called *Friend-Ship*, she and Hersh were leaning over the railing side by side, looking down into the black and white churning water, and the sky was a cobalt blue, and dark skyscrapers were silhouetted on the distant passing shore like the silhouetted skyline in the planetarium, only that once she had laughed and said, "Hey, the fifth wife around, let it be me." But it was a *joke*. And hadn't Hersh smiled at her with a tenderness curious in him and then stared back down into the water . . . ? Her own reflection reappeared in the mirror, pale and looking lousy in the brown banlon dress she had fished out of the closet. Becky was right. The brown was a cop-out, shades of Janice Brill, even worse than the little slashed black ribbon that she had stuck away in the jewelry box and that was supposed to stand for rent garments, sackcloth and ashes. ("Some rent gar-

238

ments," Leah said. "Some sackcloth and ashes.") What had she wanted from the poor child, anyway? Why had she made her cry, especially now, so near bedtime? It was awful to make a child cry before bedtime. But Becky forgave so easily, she was probably back in her room, studying the chart of the elements some more, practicing drawing noses. She tiptoed down the hall, and suddenly stopped smiling when Becky's room was black and empty.

"Becky?" Sandra called in an absurd panic. *"Becky!"*

"Here I am, Mama." The voice came from inside the bathroom where Becky was sitting on the toilet seat, forlorn and in semidarkness.

"Oh, for god's *sakes,*" Sandra said. "What's the matter with you tonight?"

"I understand why you yelled at me before," Becky said. "But why are you yelling at me now?"

"I am not yelling at you," Sandra said. "But you don't seem to realize—" She stopped while Becky reached behind her to flush and then sighed and pulled up the little shorty pants from around her ankles.

"I realize, Mama," Becky said. ". . . Accept me back?"

She held out her hand and Sandra took it, the same hand as her own, the same shape, the same everything, flesh of her flesh, only small and distinct. Then she helped Becky climb up on the hamper, anchoring her there with a hand around her waist, and the two of them watched the night take its permanent shape through the bathroom window: a still moon above a silver river, a tug chugging by with dark pink smoke, the diamond lights of some more new buildings on the black New Jersey coast. On the brick roof across the street, a tangle of television antennae made thin pencil lines across a lowering sky.

"Mama—*is* there a heaven, do you suppose?"

"I don't know. I hope. I suppose."

Then the two of them went on watching the night at their bathroom window, cheek against cheek, heart against heart.

239

EIGHT......................

L a Rochefoucauld was coming down. It was hard to believe, particularly since it wasn't even a singular fate but part of the doom of the whole corner, which was already a complicated façade of wrecker's scaffolding, a jungle of iron pipes, assorted doors, signs with the company's name and actual date of demolition—October 4th, less than a week away. Meanwhile, the proprietors were selling off the interior furnishings. Dickie had looked in on his way home from work one day and told her about it, the piles of bar glasses, cups, saucers, dinner plates, stacked-up chairs, ashtrays, red-checkered tablecloths. And Stella had already picked up a dozen tin escargot plates for practically nothing, and not remembered until she got home that snails disagreed with Freddie. But bargains or not, wasn't there something almost cannibalistic about its former customers rushing in to devour all those piles of familiar insides, something that almost suggested a concentration camp? Or if this were too much of an exaggeration—(Dickie was very interested in the uses of overstatement these days; there was some new twenty-two-year-old Irish girl novelist)—at least to her personally it was much too reminiscent of standing in the garden apartment in Great Neck, and also in the room in Waldbaum's annex, side by side with Leah, going through drawers and closets full of pink rayon underwear, stockings, odd garters, wide summer silk print dresses, magnifying reading glasses, dentures, a baby blue duster, neither of them speaking, just sorting out what would go to Hadassah, what to Aunt Rose, what should be thrown out. (*"Who shall live and who shall die, who shall go hungry, and who shall be beheaded."*) "Oh, *pussy*," Leah had said once, and then, listening to the silence, had turned away and dropped a half-used jar of Lady Esther cold cream into the wastebasket. A few days later a soft-spoken lawyer named Abel Ginsberg had called and said sister just wanted to be fair, but. . . .

Still, on the other hand, she could hardly let them tear down La Rochefoucauld without a last look of her own, either, could she? An envoi, a courtesy call, a final farewell to that scene of so many of the highlights of her life, none of which she could manage to remember at the moment, they were so past, and the fact of the scaffolding so present. Funnily, at this distance of a block away, it wasn't even ugly, just a kind of interesting fretwork against a pink stucco wall, beneath whose dark shadowed overhang people walked as in a Venetian street gallery. She stopped at the window of a fancy jewelry store, Harrold's, about whose status in the fashionable world Vicky Auerbach could no doubt inform her exactly, as she had once informed her about Gumbiner's. In front, there was a row of fancy eighteenth-century ormolu clocks all telling time more or less in unison, all more or less telling her that she didn't have to be at the Gaskell Press party for quite a while. It was marvelous to have been able to leave home so early, but Kitty didn't the least bit mind staying with Becky until the Barnard sitter arrived. It was the difference of course between the quiet British racial pride of the West Indian and the

244

smoldering hatred of the Southern black. Not a pretty distinction, but Dr. Alpert, Herb's new recommendation and a very far cry from the Olympian, oracular, and also (as she had suddenly realized) loathsome Dr. Starkstein, was very realistic and reassuring about needing to face such feelings in oneself. She lingered on in front of a few more windows, not so much window shopping as letting her fancy roam free. It was still warm, unseasonably so. Aside from the leaves turning gold on Park Avenue against a dark polluted sky, the only hint of fall was in these shop fronts with their velvets and plaids and furs, some already even suggesting the cold excitements of New York in the wintertime. Plays, skating with Becky in Rockefeller Center, coming in from a walk with icy pink cheeks. Stella loved the fun furs, which personally she didn't find at all amusing. Stella was also great on fancy belts, palazzo pants, though here again they parted company, because Sandra was suddenly very tired of pants. What she wanted was a dress, a pretty new dress, though what length, what style, she wasn't sure. It was only a minor dilemma, anyway, something to worry about at odd moments, like how could Ralph Gorella and Hershel Meyers possibly be starting a new magazine together? (She touched her jaw.) Besides, when she looked around there was Adam Brill across the street. She smiled excitedly and started to call out, but her voice caught in her throat—a frog, not emotion—and he didn't hear. Then a warehouse delivery truck came in between, and when it moved on, Adam was busily turned away, signaling for a cab. There was somebody with him, an elderly gray-haired man she'd never seen before. Maybe an English publisher. The two of them were talking together, laughing, and Sandra laughed too, until a taxi finally pulled up and they climbed into the back seat. Then, sobering, she watched them smile and chat as they sat caught in traffic until the taxi jerked forward at the change of the light and moved into the great stream of other honking taxis and trucks and buses, until they were all lost to view. She walked

245

on to the next window, where there was an interesting chic display of mink hats, gold costume jewelry, French silk scarves with signatures in their corners. Suddenly she realized that she was also admiring the reflection of Felicity Gaskell and her borzoi in the glass. How marvelous to be so rich you even had time to walk your dog before a party. True that it was all catered and prearranged. Nevertheless, the possibility was so fraught with wealth that Felicity's face, looming closer, seemed to absorb all the gold and mink into itself, like a trompe l'oeil painting in which features and objects blended and became interchangable.

"Lovely pin," Felicity remarked.

"I beg your pardon?"

"The pin that you're wearing on your blazer," Felicity said, tugging at her borzoi. "It's perfect on black velvet."

"Oh, this," Sandra said, looking down at herself as if she were already telling a lie. "It was my mother's."

Felicity nodded sympathetically. There was a strong implication of old money recognizing other old money.

"No, the point is that it was already an antique when my father bought it for her," Sandra said. "She was merely pursuing an interest that I—"

"Chic," Felicity said, allowing herself to be led adrift by the borzoi again. "Very chic. . . ."

Her voice faded so completely it was hard to remember really having heard it, as hard as to remember actually seeing Adam on that corner, though it had been so exactly what she once imagined it would be, crossing and recrossing the street hoping for a glimpse of him. Yet she felt no disappointment at all, no disillusioned "Oh, much too late," only a faint, pleasurable "How odd." In fact, she was glad it had happened, even almost proud that what she had so long imagined had finally occurred, as if she had willed it, though of course it *was* too late—much too late—and out of context. Would Adam be at the party? Pablo Spinoza, the Chilean novelist (not critic) was rumored to be a dwarf, so maybe she would finally

246

recognize the guest of honor for a change. Smiling, she walked under the maze of scaffolding and entered La Rochefoucauld, where she soon lost herself amid endless piles of chafing dishes, dinner plates, and glassware, until she finally bought Dickie a carafe for vin ordinaire—the kind he had loved to see on the little checkered bistro tables when they were on their honeymoon in Paris—and, for herself, a couple of kitchen towels with *La Rochefoucauld* printed in blue across them.